THE WEDDING PLANNER

Danielle Steel has been hailed as one of the world's most popular authors, with a billion copies of her novels sold. Her recent international bestsellers include *Upside Down*, *The Ball at Versailles* and *Second Act*. She is also the author of *His Bright Light*, the story of her son Nick Traina's life and death; *A Gift of Hope*, a memoir of her work with the homeless; and the children's books *Pretty Minnie in Paris* and *Pretty Minnie in Hollywood*. Danielle divides her time between Paris and her home in northern California.

By Danielle Steel

Upside Down • The Ball at Versailles • Second Act • Happiness • Palazzo
The Wedding Planner • Worthy Opponents • Without a Trace • The Whittiers
The High Notes • The Challenge • Suspects • Beautiful • High Stakes • Invisible
Flying Angels • The Butler • Complications • Nine Lives • Finding Ashley • The Affair
Neighbours • All That Glitters • Royal • Daddy's Girls • The Wedding Dress
The Numbers Game • Moral Compass • Spy • Child's Play • The Dark Side
Lost and Found • Blessing in Disguise • Silent Night • Turning Point • Beauchamp Hall
In His Father's Footsteps • The Good Fight • The Cast • Accidental Heroes
Fall from Grace • Past Perfect • Fairytale • The Right Time • The Duchess
Against All Odds • Dangerous Games • The Mistress • The Award • Rushing Waters
Magic • The Apartment • Property of a Noblewoman • Blue • Precious Gifts
Undercover • Country • Prodigal Son • Pegasus • A Perfect Life • Power Play
Winners • First Sight • Until the End of Time • The Sins of the Mother
Friends Forever • Betrayal • Hotel Vendôme • Happy Birthday • 44 Charles Street
Legacy • Family Ties • Big Girl • Southern Lights • Matters of the Heart
One Day at a Time • A Good Woman • Rogue • Honor Thyself • Amazing Grace
Bungalow 2 • Sisters • H.R.H. • Coming Out • The House • Toxic Bachelors
Miracle • Impossible • Echoes • Second Chance • Ransom • Safe Harbour
Johnny Angel • Dating Game • Answered Prayers • Sunset in St. Tropez
The Cottage • The Kiss • Leap of Faith • Lone Eagle • Journey
The House on Hope Street • The Wedding • Irresistible Forces • Granny Dan
Bittersweet • Mirror Image • The Klone and I • The Long Road Home • The Ghost
Special Delivery • The Ranch • Silent Honor • Malice • Five Days in Paris
Lightning • Wings • The Gift • Accident • Vanished • Mixed Blessings
Jewels • No Greater Love • Heartbeat • Message from Nam • Daddy • Star
Zoya • Kaleidoscope • Fine Things • Wanderlust • Secrets • Family Album
Full Circle • Changes • Thurston House • Crossings • Once in a Lifetime
A Perfect Stranger • Remembrance • Palomino • Love: *Poems* • The Ring
Loving • To Love Again • Summer's End • Season of Passion • The Promise
Now and Forever • Passion's Promise • Going Home

Nonfiction

Expect a Miracle
Pure Joy: *The Dogs We Love*
A Gift of Hope: *Helping the Homeless*
His Bright Light: *The Story of Nick Traina*

For Children

Pretty Minnie in Hollywood
Pretty Minnie in Paris

Danielle Steel

THE WEDDING PLANNER

PAN BOOKS

First published 2023 by Delacorte Press
an imprint of Random House
a division of Penguin Random House LLC, New York

First published in the UK 2023 by Macmillan

This paperback editon first published 2024 by Pan Books
an imprint of Pan Macmillan
The Smithson, 6 Briset Street, London EC1M 5NR
EU representative: Macmillan Publishers Ireland Limited, 1st Floor,
The Liffey Trust Centre, 117–126 Sheriff Street Upper,
Dublin 1, D01 YC43
Associated companies throughout the world
www.panmacmillan.com

ISBN 978-1-5290-2220-9

1 3 5 7 9 8 6 4 2

A CIP catalogue record for this book is available from the British Library.

Typeset in Charter ITC by Palimpsest Book Production Ltd, Falkirk, Stirlingshire
Printed and bound by CPI Group (UK) Ltd, Croydon, CR0 4YY

Visit www.panmacmillan.com to read more about all our books
and to buy them. You will also find features, author interviews and
news of any author events, and you can sign up for e-newsletters
so that you're always first to hear about our new releases.

To my very special, much loved children,
Beatie, Trevor, Todd, Nick, Samantha,
Victoria, Vanessa, Maxx, and Zara,

"Real life happens when you're making
other plans. . . . Life is a surprise"
sums up how life works.

May your surprises be good ones and
your real lives be blessed, fruitful,
happy, safe, and peaceful.

May your lives be filled with love and joy!
With all my heart and love,

                              Mom/d.s.

THE WEDDING PLANNER

Chapter 1

The alarm went off at five-thirty, as it did every morning. Faith Ferguson opened an eye, saw the time, turned off the alarm with a graceful hand, and a minute later, rolled out of bed, ready to start the rituals of her day. She was a consummately disciplined person. At forty-two, she had the body of a twenty-year-old. Ballet exercises in the morning six days a week kept her in shape. She got up, brushed her teeth, combed her shoulder-length blond hair, and wound it into a tight knot. She looked like a ballerina as she put on her black leotard and pink ballet shoes. She was wide-awake by the time she called her ballet teacher on her computer. They smiled and wished each other good morning, and started the same exercise routine she did every day. She had a highly disciplined life. Teacher and student did not converse as they went through the familiar exercises.

They finished their work together promptly at seven A.M., wished each other a good day, ended the connection, and Faith headed for the shower. It was a dark blustery January morning, and she had a busy day ahead. January was one of her busiest times of year. She was one of the most sought-after wedding planners in New York. People often came to her to plan their weddings right after the holidays.

She had appointments with three new clients this week, all referred by satisfied previous clients. Some had seen interviews she'd given or read her books. She had published three successful books. They were the bibles for anyone about to get married. Her first was a coffee-table book, full of photographs of the most beautiful weddings she'd done, and packed with helpful hints about how to achieve the same effects as in the photos. Except, of course, that couldn't be done, not without her help and expertise. The second book was a wedding planner, detailing how to keep everything on track in the months before a wedding. It was the gift everyone gave to a newly engaged woman. The third book was filled with background on all the traditions that related to weddings, the etiquette, the things you had to know to plan a wedding, from seating to formal titles, what was proper and what wasn't. Her book rivaled Amy Vanderbilt's and

Emily Post's. She had a definitive, friendly, accessible style, while being definite about what was correct etiquette and what wasn't. Another must-have for any bride.

Faith had never been married herself, although she had come close twice. She was young the first time, and it had been a devastating experience. She was a junior editor at *Vogue,* given a wide range of assignments, from beauty to parties covered by the magazine. Her upbringing in New York City in a genteel home with well brought up, aristocratic parents made her well suited to assisting the editors she worked for in covering socialites' parties and events, and even occasionally weddings. Her grandparents on both sides were of equally distinguished origins and blue blood.

On one of the shoots she'd been on, to photograph a very important young bride, she had met Patrick Brock, a handsome young photographer. She was twenty-five, Patrick was a year older, and they had hit it off immediately. They dated for almost a year before he proposed. Their engagement had been a whirlwind. Faith, her twin sister, Hope, and their mother, Marianne, had planned her wedding. They had bought a beautiful, delicately embroidered French lace dress at Bergdorf's bridal department. She felt like a fairy princess in it, and even more so when she tried on the veil, made of delicate French tulle that floated like a mist over her face. Everything was in order for the wedding at the

Metropolitan Club. Her parents had divorced when she was ten, and her father was coming from Europe with his German wife, a baroness, to attend the wedding and give her away. Her parents had remained on cordial terms. Her sister was going to be the maid of honor, and six friends from college at Georgetown in Washington, D.C., were bridesmaids. Hope was a very successful model then, had done shoots with Patrick, and liked him. Her parents and grandparents approved of the marriage. He came from a respectable family in Boston and had talent, and good manners. Faith was crazy about him.

Everything had gone according to plan until a week before the wedding when her fiancé showed up at the apartment she shared with her twin, and dissolved in tears in her arms as soon as he came through the door. It took him an hour to explain that he had had some earlier "forays" which he had thought were only experimental but turned out to be a lot more than that. He explained that he had just realized that he was gay, and had fallen in love with a Russian ballet dancer. There had been no sign of any doubts about Patrick's sexuality. He said he couldn't marry her. He loved her as a friend, but he had had the growing suspicion that he couldn't live up to what would be expected of him in marriage, and he needed to be free to explore the relationship with the Russian dancer, with whom he admitted he was deeply in love. His own family was shocked beyond belief when he told them, as was Faith's.

What happened afterward was a blur of tears, despair, and humiliation. Formal announcements were hastily printed and sent out, canceling the wedding. She had taken two weeks off from work to hide, and was still a shambles when she went back. Her twin, Hope, had nursed her as though after an accident or an illness. Faith was shattered by the shock.

She had never seen Patrick again. He had left New York and moved to London with the dancer. She had heard that their relationship was passionate but didn't last long, but he was sure of his sexuality by then. He had eventually come back to New York, and mercifully their paths had never crossed.

In one of the ironies of life, six months after the aborted wedding, she had been assigned to exclusively cover weddings for the magazine because she did it so well. It had taken her years to get over the blow of being nearly jilted at the altar. Her father couldn't understand why she was so upset. He told her it was a blessing to have found out before they married, rather than years later. Her mother and sister fully understood how traumatized she was, and how covering weddings for *Vogue* was like aversion therapy for her, or a form of inoculation. Something hardened in Faith as she went from wedding to wedding and wrote the descriptions in rhapsodic terms, after directing the photographer to get all the shots they wanted for the magazine. She felt numb for a year. Her mother had packed away the wedding dress. The whole experience was a sensitive subject for a long time.

It was nearly ten years later when she considered trying it again. William Tyler was a strong, interesting man, an architect. She admired his work. She had left the magazine and set up her business as a wedding planner by then. After covering dozens or hundreds of weddings for *Vogue,* it was what she knew best. She had learned her lessons well.

At first, William had seemed like the perfect partner. He was as disciplined and precise about his work as she was about hers. Then shadows began to creep in as he started to tell her what to do and what to wear, what to say, and what not to discuss. He lived in an apartment he had designed in Chelsea. She and Hope each had their own apartments by then. Faith was living in SoHo and Hope had moved uptown. William didn't like her friends and had none of his own. He told her precisely how he wanted their wedding to be and where. He had a strong aesthetic sense, and the only opinions he respected were his own.

After being engaged for two months, she felt as if she were suffocating, that he was trying to strip her of her identity and redesign her to his own specifications, like a building he was buying to remodel. She felt as though she had been gutted. He was constantly tearing her down. She returned the ring to him and fled. She was older and wiser, and wondered how she could have made such a grave mistake again. She felt free and light as soon as she got away from him.

She had no regrets this time about the failed engagement. He never understood what went wrong. He had controlled every move she made, and wanted to control her every thought. She recovered more quickly the second time, since she was the one who had left. The legacy William left was that she was convinced that marriage wasn't for her. Weddings were her job, even her career, but they were no longer her dream. She could create an exquisite wedding for anyone who came to her for help, but the thought of a wedding of her own filled her with dread. William had cured her of ever wanting to be a bride, forever.

Six months later, her twin sister, Hope, had announced that she was getting married, and all Faith could feel was pity for her. Hope had had a lively, liberated life as a model, and insisted that she had found her soulmate in Angus Stewart.

Hope and Faith looked nothing alike and had entirely different personalities. Faith was smaller and more delicate, blond with green eyes. Hope was nearly as tall as their father, with dark hair and brown eyes. She'd had fun for a dozen years in New York as a model. She met fascinating people, traveled all over the world, and was ready to give it all up for a man whose favorite pastimes were hiking and fishing, skiing and mountain climbing. Angus soon absconded to Connecticut with her sister. He was a writer, and they'd had three children in seven years. Hope claimed that she was blissfully happy, which was hard for Faith to imagine, in a rural suburban life, surrounded by noise, chaos, and mess. The children were adorable, but lively and uncontrollable, which Hope seemed to enjoy. They only behaved when their nanny was around. Hope could never quite seem to get them to sit still, which didn't bother her at all. They had three very boisterous boys, Seamus, six, Henry, three, and the baby, Oliver, who was a year old.

Faith and Hope had loved being twins as children, particularly since they looked so different and had such distinctive personalities. Hope was casual and more relaxed. Faith had always been wound more tightly, and wanted everything to be perfect. It suited her to live alone. The house she had bought in the city, from where she ran her business, was as impeccably chic and neat as Faith herself, and the weddings she planned. Nothing was ever out of place. She watched every detail. A Faith Ferguson wedding was flawless, just like Faith and the home she lived in. Hope was more helter-skelter. Her house was always chaotic, with shoes and magazines and books and sports equipment lying all over the place. Faith loved visiting her, but she was always happy to come back to the silent order and peace of her own home. Having three boys would have killed Faith. She loved her nephews, but she loved her twin sister more, more than anyone in the world. She wasn't sorry she hadn't had children. It was all part of a package she had decided wasn't for her. She helped others get there, but not herself.

After she showered and dressed, she made a cup of green tea and sat down to call her sister, as she did every morning before she started her day. It was the ritual in her life she loved most. She called her at eight o'clock, when her brother-in-law, Angus, of good Scottish stock, had just taken the two older boys to school, and the nanny had arrived to take the baby to get him dressed. She and Hope could have a peaceful chat about whatever came to mind, or whatever they were doing, or any interesting gossip they'd heard about old friends. Like Faith, Hope didn't look her age. She had a striking natural beauty devoid of artifice. Her long hair always looked as though she had forgotten to comb it. She rarely wore makeup, and she had an unconscious sexiness about her, as though she had just climbed out of bed. She usually wore jeans and riding boots or Wellingtons. She liked to ride every day at a nearby stable. She favored fisherman's sweaters and often wore her husband's parkas and jackets, which looked just right on her.

"What are you up to this week?" Hope asked, sipping a latte. It was her second one. Her son Seamus had spilled the first one at the breakfast table. It was just part of the morning landscape for them.

"I'm seeing three new clients," Faith reported to her. Hope was always happy for her success. After twelve years of modeling, she had been thrilled to leave the workforce and stay at home, especially since Angus did his writing in a cozy room over the garage that he had set up for himself. It was nice having him close at hand. She didn't miss the city at all, and Faith had to beg her to come to town to do some shopping and have lunch.

Hope hated to shop, and said she'd seen and tried on enough clothes to last a lifetime. She had felt that way when she was modeling too, although she looked fabulous on the runway when she walked in a fashion show. She had been one of the most sought-after models for most of her career, and now she just wanted to stay home and be a wife and mother. Faith would have been bored with that life, but Hope was happy and fulfilled. Angus was a great guy, and he was always happy to see Faith, and encouraged her to visit more often. But Faith kept busy in New York. The twins often talked to each other two or three times a day, just checking in, or reporting on something they'd done and seen. "All three were referrals," Faith said about her new clients. "It's always busy this time of year." Hope knew that too, and admired her sister for her talent, and the successful career she had built. The weddings she created for her clients were fabulous. Faith had done Hope's wedding too, with all the men in the wedding party in kilts in their family tartans.

The twins knew everything about each other's lives, and shared their most private thoughts, and always had. They were close to their mother, but even closer to each other. They had been best friends growing up, to the exclusion of other friends much of the time. There was something very deep and special about their relationship. They had loved each other when other girls their age, in their teens, were fighting with their sisters. But it was different as twins. They rarely argued as children, and never as adults. Their mother was a kind, sensible, intelligent woman who had accepted that the twins' relationship left little room for anyone else, even her.

"Have you talked to Mom lately?" Hope asked, and Faith sensed it as a gentle reproach.

"No, why, is something wrong? I talked to her a week ago. Did she complain or say I hadn't?"

"No, she knows you're busy. She doesn't want to bother you. I think she gets lonely at times." Their mother had

11

married three times, the first time to their father, Arthur Ferguson. It had lasted for twelve years. The girls were shocked when they got divorced. They had always seemed to get along so well, and were so polite to each other. The twins were ten when they divorced. Their father had never been a constant presence in their lives, even while their parents were married. He traveled a lot, and wasn't very interested in his wife or children.

Their father had married Beata, his second wife, fairly soon after the divorce. Their mother, Marianne, had taken longer to meet the love of her life, a brilliant, well-known playwright, who was said to be a genius, but was also depressive and alcoholic. The marriage had lasted for five rocky years. The twins were already in college by the time they married, and steered a wide berth around their erratic, volatile stepfather and felt sorry for their mother while she was married to him. He wasn't an evil person, but impossible to get along with. They weren't surprised when it ended in divorce. The third time she married an Italian count, who had seemed insignificant to the twins. They were living in their own apartment together by then and hardly knew him. He made no effort to get to know them, and left their mother after two years to find greener pastures and a richer wife, just as their father had done. Marianne was disappointed, but not amazed.

She lived on what she had inherited from her family and never worked. She didn't have a huge amount of money, but enough to live very comfortably. She took a few trips a year to visit friends, mostly in Palm Beach or Newport in the summer. She had a trust, which enabled her to send the girls to private schools in Manhattan when they were younger, and she rented a house in the Hamptons in the summer. They'd had everything they needed, without being ostentatious or living in great luxury. But Marianne was financially secure, without worries. She had just enough money to attract men who were after it, like the twins' father and the Italian count.

Marianne was proud of how successful Faith's business was, and of Hope's modeling career. They'd had an easy, happy life as children, with a devoted mother and a father who was seldom around. He'd had an insignificant banking job while he was married to their mother, and wanted a wife who didn't expect him to work and would support him. He had finally found it with Beata.

Their mother still lived in the apartment on Park Avenue where they'd grown up, and stayed after their father left. Marianne was sixty-seven now, and careful with the money she had. It was comforting to know that she had enough to live on, and could be independent, but there would be no big inheritance waiting for her daughters at the end of her life. They didn't expect it and had done well themselves, and had invested their earnings well and wisely. And Angus was successful as a writer, and had family money. It pained Hope at times knowing that their mother was alone. Faith always said she was better off than if she were married to a bad guy who'd spend her money or interfere with her life, which was what she felt for herself too. Hope reminded her that not everyone was as self-sufficient as she was, or preferred to be alone. Her mother preferred to have companionship but after three tries hadn't found the right man.

"Why would Mom want to marry now? She has everything she needs. A man would just screw it all up at this point. She's better off the way she is," Faith said matter-of-factly. They disagreed on that point. Hope always suspected that their mother would have preferred to have a man in her life rather than be alone, but she hadn't had anyone for a long time. She'd been devoted to her daughters when they were young. She had always amply made up for their father's rare appearances, visiting New York with Beata once or twice a year, to see friends. The girls had never liked visiting him in Germany in the summer. They always felt unwelcome and out of place. Beata was polite to them, but she wasn't a warm person, and had no children of her own. They had always understood that their father had married her lifestyle, which he enjoyed, and preferred it to working, but he wasn't madly in love with her. He played his role of devoted husband well, and they had been married for almost thirty years. It was an arrangement that seemed to work for them. He was a handsome, distinguished husband for Beata, and he traveled a lot on his own. His family had gone through their money when he was young. And the second time, he had married well. He hadn't worked since he'd married Beata. He was from an old New York social family. He'd been a good example of what neither of the twins wanted. Hope had married Angus for love and was happy. And Faith was perfectly happy unmarried, with occasional companionship, which never lasted long. She didn't want a husband telling her what to do, spending her money, or running her life.

The twins chatted for half an hour, and then Faith made her way to her office. Her desk was impeccably organized, as she left it every night. She'd had two big weddings to do right before the Christmas holidays, and then there was always a lull. No one seemed to get married in January. But they planned their summer weddings immediately after Christmas, and she knew that she'd be busy soon, particularly if she took on the three new clients she was scheduled to see this week. Faith could pick and choose which weddings she would do. She was the best in the city. Anything too splashy and too vulgar, or in seriously bad taste, she always gracefully declined, explaining to the client that her schedule was so overloaded that she couldn't do them justice. She had a feeling that the first client she would be seeing was planning a big affair. The client who had recommended them had spent nearly two million dollars on their daughter's wedding at their estate on Long Island the year before. It had been spectacular, with six hundred guests, and a very sizable fee for her. Weddings like that always brought in new clients. She'd already had two excellent referrals from them.

The one thing she hated was destination weddings. They were so hard to organize and do well, with local suppliers she didn't know, depending on the location. She avoided destination weddings whenever possible. She loved weddings in people's homes, if their homes were large enough. She'd done many at magnificent estates. She did simpler weddings too, if she liked the people, and the budget was workable. She loved making people's dreams come true. Weddings were all about fantasy, understanding what people wanted, and making magic happen for them.

She always loved the look on the groom's face when he first saw the bride and watched her come down the aisle, often with tears in his eyes. It was like watching a carpet roll out toward their future, with everything they hoped would happen. It was a very special day, and she loved being part of it. It was a dream she no longer had or wanted for herself, but she loved giving it away to others who still believed in the dream. No longer having that dream was a choice she had made, not a disappointment for her. Giving a successful wedding was also a question of imagination and logistics, and having the best suppliers in the world, who never let her down.

She heard Violet, her assistant, come in, while she was making herself another cup of tea. Faith didn't like having a lot of staff underfoot and was satisfied with a housekeeper, who came in daily, and one assistant in the office. She did the rest herself. She was sitting at her desk when Violet came into the room. She was a bright, smiling young woman who loved her job, and made every day better for Faith in some way. She was twenty-nine years old and had worked for Faith for three years. They worked well together, and Violet dealt beautifully with their brides, and handled their mothers with discretion and patience whenever things got tense, which happened often between mothers and daughters while planning their Big Day. The fathers rarely cared about the details, only the bills. But coming to Faith to do a wedding was never going to be an inexpensive event. They knew her reputation before they came to her. They were going to have an unforgettable wedding, at a serious price. And it would be well worth it.

Faith was wearing a simple black pantsuit with high heels for the meeting. She always dressed respectfully for her meetings with clients. It didn't matter who they were. Violet had worn a black skirt with a simple white cashmere sweater, and high heels as well. She could wear jeans when she worked on-site, but never in the office. She never disappointed Faith.

"What do we know about the Alberts?" she asked Faith as she took away her empty cup of tea, and Faith smiled.

"Not much. He's a big real estate developer. They were referred by the Ferdinands, so I have a feeling it's going to be a big event. We'll know in a few minutes." They were due in five minutes, and Faith expected clients to be prompt.

Half an hour later, they were still waiting for the Alberts. They hadn't called to say they'd be late, as Faith looked at her watch again. The doorbell rang forty minutes after the appointed time, and Violet went to let them in.

She ushered them into the living room on the main floor that Faith used to see clients during work hours. Faith gathered up several folders and a pad in a leather folio to make notes during the meeting. She walked in just as they sat down, and Violet left to hang up their coats. Mrs. Albert's was a bright red mink.

Faith could already guess the size and style of the wedding as soon as she saw them. Jack Albert, the father of the bride, was heavyset, wearing an expensive suit, with a large gold watch on his wrist. His wife, Miriam, was wearing a red

Chanel suit, a large diamond ring, and too much jewelry and perfume for so early in the day. In contrast, their daughter, presumably the bride, was wearing leggings, combat boots, and an ancient gray sweater with holes in it. She had a tattoo of a rose noticeable on her left wrist, and her blond hair was held in a tangled mass with a clip. She appeared not to care how she looked, and seemed uncomfortable. She was an attractive girl, and she didn't look particularly happy to be there with her parents. Faith guessed her to be in her late twenties, thirty at most, around her assistant's age. Jack made a point of saying that Annabelle didn't work. She'd gone to college but never got a job. He said she didn't need one. And Jeremy, the groom, worked in his father's business occasionally when he felt like it. Jack was generous with the information.

Faith handed a folder to each of them, with some sample photographs and ideas and her basic materials, so they could go home and get a feeling for the kind of weddings she did. The photographs showed a range of them, both city and country weddings, a few of the more famous ones for celebrities. She could see from looking at the Alberts that one of her missions would be to keep the wedding within the bounds of good taste. It was often one of her most important functions, as well as being a mediator between the bride and her parents if their visions differed. She wondered whose idea it had been to come to her. She suspected in this case it was the parents, not the bride. She knew she had guessed right when Jack Albert explained that their older daughter, Eloise, had eloped five years before. He said they weren't about to be cheated of a wedding again. They were clearly planning to make up for what they had missed.

"She was divorced in a year," he said, with a disapproving look, and Annabelle, the bride, rolled her eyes. She had heard it all before. The implication was that the failure of the marriage had been a certainty since her sister didn't have a big wedding to show their stamp of approval. He made an odd comment too about Annabelle's fiancé, that he had needed some "convincing to step up to the plate." Faith wondered what that meant. Money, a Ferrari, Jack's connections for a better job, or threats. Faith wondered if the groom was after money or just not ready to get married. In any case, they had apparently convinced him or they wouldn't be there.

Faith could already sense that they wanted a wedding to show off for their friends, and maybe even business associates. Jack Albert was a very successful real estate developer, and had built several skyscrapers in the city. They said that they wanted the wedding at their estate in East Hampton.

"They want seven hundred guests," Annabelle said with an angry look, and Faith smiled at the three of them, while Miriam Albert studied the art on the walls. Faith's home was simple, modern, and beautifully decorated. She had done it all herself, and the art was by well-known artists.

"Maybe we can compromise at three or four hundred. How does that sound to you?" she asked the bride, as though they were alone in the room, and Annabelle smiled for the first time.

"Better. I wanted a small wedding. That's why my sister eloped. She didn't want a circus, and neither do I."

"The wedding is going to be on July fourth." Miriam Albert spoke for the first time. "And we want fireworks." She didn't ask her daughter's approval. It was *her* decision. Annabelle didn't comment, but rolled her eyes again.

"Anything is possible." Faith smiled pleasantly. "We just don't want to draw the attention away from the happy couple by having too much going on," she said, and she could see Annabelle start to relax. Faith needed to win her trust by the time they planned the wedding. She was competent and calm and not unduly swayed by Annabelle's parents, which gained her the bride's faith.

"And we want a crystal tent with chandeliers," the mother of the bride went on. "And two bands."

"I'd like to do a site visit, if that's all right with you, and then I can make some suggestions. That's hard to do before I've seen where the wedding is going to be." Jack nodded at that, and Annabelle did too. It made sense. Aside from talented, Faith was practical and wanted everything to run smoothly, which her weddings always did. She was known for that too.

Faith jotted down a few notes about what they'd said, the fireworks, the tent, the chandeliers. She spent an hour getting a feel for what each of them wanted. Jack and Miriam clearly wanted show. Annabelle wanted something more meaningful, and not as overwhelming as they had in mind. It was Faith's job to blend the two and come up with a wedding that Annabelle would love, and would make her parents feel that they'd gotten their money's worth and all the bang for their buck she could provide.

"If we do the fireworks at the very end, it won't distract from the wedding, and will give the couple an exciting send-off into their new life," she suggested. She could see that they had their hearts set on it, and she had to find a way to make it palatable to Annabelle. "Have you looked for a dress yet?" Annabelle shook her head.

"We're thinking Dior couture," Miriam said, and Annabelle didn't comment. She clearly hadn't made up her mind yet about what she wanted. All she knew was what she didn't want, most of which was high on her parents' list of requirements. "With a long train and an embroidered veil," Miriam added. "We're going to Paris in three weeks to see the couture shows."

"And some other designers," Annabelle said, as Faith

wondered how many other tattoos she had. She had a feeling there were more, which might dictate what style dress she wore, unless she wanted to show them off, which some girls did.

"We have lots of work to do," Faith said, smiling. When they left, she gave them each a copy of each of her three books. They had set a date for Faith's site visit to their Long Island estate, and she invited them to call if they had any questions, and she was sure they would. Jack implied that money was no object, which was usually a sign of some serious bad taste to come. But she was ready for it and reining things in to keep the wedding tasteful, even if lavish, was what she did best. Her events were never vulgar. She wouldn't let them go overboard.

It was starting to snow when they left, and as she saw them to the door, she noticed a driver waiting in a Mercedes Maybach outside. She had guessed that it would be something like that, or a Rolls.

She could still smell Miriam's perfume lingering after they left.

"How was it?" Violet asked her when she walked back into her office, and Faith sighed with a smile.

"Interesting. They want lots of show, seven hundred guests and fireworks, on the Fourth of July. The bride wants something smaller. She's not going to win this one, but we can

23

try and tone it down a little. I'm going to see their estate next week. They're thinking Caesars Palace, I'm thinking Versailles," she said, and Violet laughed. She reached out for Faith's leather-bound notepad, and Faith immediately noticed a sparkle on her left hand.

"What's *that*? Something new?" Faith looked surprised, and Violet blushed.

"It just happened. Jordan proposed on New Year's Eve. But don't worry, we can't afford a honeymoon, I'll only take a week off." She looked instantly concerned, she didn't want to upset Faith.

"And when is this supposed to happen?" Faith asked her. "Hopefully not in high season, in June, July, or August."

"We're thinking about sometime in May. I know how busy it gets in June. I was going to ask you about it later today."

"That's perfect." Faith smiled, happy for her. It was still too chilly for most weddings in May in New York. "Do you have a location?"

"There's an Italian restaurant near my parents' that my dad thought would be okay."

"Let's see if we can come up with some other ideas he'd like and might be more your style. I'll give it some thought." Faith loved a challenge, and Violet smiled. She couldn't afford a Faith Ferguson wedding, but maybe Faith would have some good suggestions in their budget. She loved working for her.

She was someone Violet knew she could count on, and the job was fun and exciting. She had learned a lot from Faith. "Best wishes, Violet," she said properly, since it wasn't appropriate to "congratulate" the bride, which was in her book. "I hope you'll both be very happy." She had met the groom once and he seemed like a nice boy. He had trained as an accountant, and worked for a startup, and you never knew these days who would be successful one day. Some big success stories started small.

They'd been dating for over a year, and Faith made a note to herself to look up some locations for them, since she knew they had very little money to spend on a wedding, and maybe she could help, and even get discounts for Violet, at least on a dress.

After that, she sat at her desk making preliminary notes for the Albert wedding on the Fourth of July. There was a lot to think about, and it would be a big moneymaker for her, but it was Violet's wedding that made her smile and warmed her heart. She wasn't quite as hard-nosed and cynical as people thought. The kind of wedding Violet was going to have was what weddings were supposed to be about. Two people in love on a very special day, with their life together shining like a bright star ahead of them. With Faith walking ahead to lead the way and help her to have a wedding that would be a precious memory forever. Whether for a million-dollar wedding or for her assistant on a tight budget, Faith loved her job, and making magic for her brides, as long as she never had to be one of them.

Chapter 2

Faith met with the second couple after lunch. The groom had made the appointment. They were an attractive couple. Douglas Kirk was in his early forties, he was tall and athletic-looking with a decisive manner and a quick smile. He had dark hair, blue eyes, and chiseled features. And Phoebe Smith, the bride-to-be, was a very pretty blonde with a great figure, she was thirty-two. He was a very successful plastic surgeon, and he made a point of telling Faith that Phoebe worked for him, and was a surgical nurse. She had a gentle manner, and let Doug do all the talking when they first sat down. He also made it clear that he was paying for the wedding, which translated to his making it clear that he also wanted to call all the shots.

He wanted to hold the wedding at his club, which would cut some of the costs, Faith knew, and he had in mind around a hundred and fifty to two hundred guests, which was a good-sized wedding. He had grown up in Grosse Pointe, Michigan, and had gone to Harvard Medical School.

"And where are you from, Phoebe?" Faith asked her gently, trying to draw her out. Douglas hadn't let her get a word in edgewise for the first twenty minutes of the meeting.

"San Diego," she said with a smile. She didn't seem to mind Doug having center stage. As his employee, particularly in surgery, she was used to deferring to his wishes. He smiled at her frequently and patted her hand. "Doug has more definite ideas about the wedding," she explained. "I've only been in New York for a year, so I don't know a lot of people here. We started dating as soon as I arrived."

"I finally met the love of my life, the woman of my dreams," he confirmed.

One who let him do all the talking, Faith thought. She found Doug somewhat grating, but there was something so appealing about Phoebe that she wanted to help her find her voice and have the wedding she wanted, not just the one Doug had in mind. When Faith asked them about the number of attendants they were planning, Phoebe said she wanted her sister to be the maid of honor, but she didn't know if she could come. It was hard for her to leave their mother, who had multiple sclerosis and was bedridden now. So her mother wouldn't be able to attend, and she said that her father had passed away when she was in college. Her sister lived with their mother in San Diego, but they had both been supportive about her moving to New York, and were thrilled for her when she got the job with Doug. She was wearing a simple, very pretty engagement ring, and it was obvious that marrying Doug was going to be a big step up for her into a better life. Doug said that his medical partner was going to be his best man.

He had some magazine pages from *Town & Country* to show her the look he was envisioning. They wanted the wedding in June, and he had already reserved the date at his club. He was businesslike and well organized, and the wedding he wanted wasn't complicated. He mentioned his preferred florist, which was one of the best in New York, and Faith had worked with them many times before on weddings in the city. They weren't cheap, but they did a beautiful job. He wanted white orchids, which Phoebe said sounded beautiful to her.

"Have you thought about a dress?" Faith asked her. Doug answered for her, and said he thought that Oscar de la Renta or Carolina Herrera would be the right look for the wedding he was planning for them. Faith didn't disagree with him, but it made her uneasy that he was taking control of everything, and leaving little room for Phoebe to make any of the decisions, right down to the dress, and he wanted the wedding to be black tie.

He had no strong opinions about the religious ceremony, and Phoebe cautiously said that she'd like to be married in a church, and there was an Episcopal church near Doug's club. Doug made no comment either way.

"I'd be happy to look at dresses with you," Faith offered, since her mother and sister weren't around, "unless you want to go with a friend." She realized as she looked at her that Phoebe looked like a young Grace Kelly when she married Prince Rainier. She was going to be a beautiful bride.

Faith spent two hours with them. They were easy to work with since Doug had such clear ideas about what he wanted, but she felt uneasy after they left. She sat in her office, thinking back to the meeting, and she was frowning when Violet came in to ask how it had gone.

"They sure are a handsome couple," Violet stated the obvious, and Faith nodded.

"He's a little overwhelming. He makes all the decisions. He knows exactly what he wants. And he's paying for the wedding. She works for him, and I had a hard time drawing her out. She's willing to just let him do whatever he wants. He's incredibly controlling, and she just sits back and lets him run the show."

"I guess it works for them," Violet said philosophically. They'd seen every possible combination come through Faith's office just in the three years she'd worked for her. Some of the couples you thought would never make it turned out all right in the end. At least, both their names were still on the same Christmas card a few years later. "Does it seem to bother her that he makes all the decisions?" Violet asked.

"No, it doesn't. But it bothered me. Every time I asked her a question, he answered for her, and had already made up his mind." He reminded her of William, the fiancé she hadn't married.

"Maybe it's a relief for her not to have to deal with it. She just has to show up on the day, get dressed, and look beautiful. I wouldn't mind a little of that myself. Jordan is hopeless about helping me plan the wedding. He just says 'whatever you want,' and goes back to watching football or hockey on TV. Are they having a big wedding?"

"A hundred and fifty to two hundred, at his club." She mentioned the florist he wanted to use, and Violet nodded approval. They did beautiful work. "He wants orchids, chamber music during cocktails, a small dance band during dinner and after. She wants a church wedding, and he didn't comment. I'm not sure he agrees. It won't be hard to get everything in place. The chef at that club is good. They have the date in June, and the club is already booked. They really don't need me, but he wants everything to go perfectly. We need to get them a good photographer. So far, our big event of the summer, if they sign with us, is going to be the Albert wedding, which

31

has a thousand moving parts. This one will be easy, and it's three weeks before the Alberts', which is perfect. I offered to look at dresses with her. You can come with me. It'll give her a younger opinion than mine, although she'll look great in everything. I have to work up the estimate for him anyway, before we do anything, but it doesn't sound like it will be a problem." Most people who came to her for their wedding knew that they would be paying a premium for her name and her reputation. People with tight budgets did not expect to have Faith Ferguson do their wedding.

"I'd love to go with you," Violet said. "I have to start looking for my own dress too. I just want something very simple, and not too expensive. I don't need a fancy dress for a reception at a neighborhood restaurant," she said, looking only slightly disappointed. But they didn't want to wait a year to save for a bigger wedding. Four months was long enough, and she was happy about who she was marrying, which was the most important thing to her.

They were planning a morning wedding, because the restaurant was cheaper to reserve at lunchtime than dinner, which her father had pointed out to her. The restaurant was just big enough for a couple of musicians so they could dance. It was laughable compared to most of the weddings that Faith planned and Violet had worked on with her. But she lived in a whole different world. She didn't expect to have a big wedding, and she and Jordan would be living on a budget once they were married. They both made decent salaries, but life was expensive in New York. They lived in the unfashionable part of Brooklyn, and rents were climbing there too. They had a tiny apartment. Their long-term plan was to wait to have a baby until they were both thirty-five, six years from now. That gave them plenty of time to save and be doing better than they were now. They had a bright future ahead of them. They were both hardworking and intelligent, and loved each other.

Faith had a salad for dinner after Violet left that night, and she called Hope when she went back to her office after dinner, to work on the estimates for both prospective weddings, the Kirk-Smith wedding and the Alberts' extravaganza. The second one would take longer to prepare.

"How was your day?" Hope asked her. She could hear that Faith was tired. They were always in tune with each other's moods and how the day had gone.

"Pretty good. A little weird, but that happens in this business. The clients this morning were like a caricature of themselves, slightly reluctant bride, flashy nouveau riche parents who want to show off to six or seven hundred of their friends, including a fireworks display since the wedding is on July fourth. And then I saw a nurse and a doctor. He's so controlling it gave me chills, but she's so sweet, I really want to help her. She looks overwhelmed, and he runs right over her like a bus every time she opens her mouth. And Violet is getting married in May, and I want to see what I can do for her. The poor thing has no money for a decent wedding, and her father wants her to get married at a pizza parlor, or close to it."

"You should tell the nurse not to marry the guy," Hope said seriously, thinking of William too.

"I wanted to. He reminded me of William. She's a sweet girl from California with an invalid mother her sister takes care of. And she fell in love with her boss. I think he likes the fact that she's so meek and gives him no resistance."

"That's never a good move except in fairy tales, or romantic movies," Hope said, and Faith agreed with her, although she had seen it among her clients, and it had turned out well in many cases, with a kind of Prince Charming/ Dream Come True feeling to it. But in a case like Phoebe and Doug, she could easily imagine her being very unhappy once she was married to him, if she was never allowed an opinion of her own. The improvement in lifestyle didn't seem worth it.

Angus did well with his writing, and Hope had invested a lot of her modeling money, so they lived exactly the life they wanted and had more than enough to provide for their children and have a housekeeper and nanny. Doug and Phoebe would probably live well too. He had a booming practice, but he was also making all the decisions, which Faith had hated when she was engaged to her second fiancé. Hope and Angus were equal partners. Faith couldn't imagine living with a man who controlled her to the extent that Doug seemed to with Phoebe. She wondered if Phoebe was aware of it.

"A lot of times, women think that they do it because the controlling guy loves them. I don't see it that way myself," Hope said.

"Neither do I," Faith agreed with her. "I'm going to spend the rest of the week working on the estimates for both weddings. The lavish one is going to be out in the stratosphere, but I think the father of the bride doesn't care. The more expensive it is, the more he'll like it. And the wife is very showy too. She arrived at ten in the morning in a red mink coat." They both laughed at the picture Faith painted of them, but she didn't dislike them. They were a special breed she'd run into before, people who just had a huge amount of money, and not a lot of taste to go with it. And with what they wanted, it was easy to spend a million dollars on a wedding, or more. And even though she got a big fee out of it, she never encouraged her clients to waste money. She was very handsomely paid, but she earned it and wasn't greedy.

They chatted for a while, and then Faith went back to work, and Hope went to watch TV with her husband. They had a quiet domestic life, which suited them both, and when they wanted a touch of glamour, they came to spend a night in the city and go out for dinner. But they were so comfortable at home that they hadn't had a date night since before their last baby, who had just turned one a few weeks earlier. Hope had had her wild days as a model when she was young. She had married when she was ready to settle down, not before. She was thirty-five when she married Angus, and had their first baby a year later.

Faith's last new client meeting was on Friday, when she met the third couple, who had made the appointment with her before Christmas. They had been referred by a previous client, like the Alberts.

She dressed less formally to meet them since it was Friday. She was wearing a heavy black cashmere turtleneck sweater, black jeans, and high heels, it was a slight modification of her usual uniform. She had almost completed the estimates for the two other weddings the night before, and was in a good mood. She just needed to put the finishing touches on them, and a few final details. She was hoping to drive to Connecticut the next day to see Hope, Angus, and the kids, if the weather permitted.

The Wedding Planner

She missed her twin. She always did, and she liked seeing her for the day, and then coming home to her own peaceful home that night. Waking up to three small boys the next day was too much for her, although she did spend the weekend there occasionally. Angus was a good sport about how close they were. He had learned early in their marriage that the twins were basically inseparable, and couldn't live without each other. Fortunately, he came to love Faith almost like a sister of his own, and he included her in their plans whenever possible. She even went on vacations with them sometimes.

The third couple who came to see Faith arrived promptly on Friday afternoon. Their names were Morgan Phillips and Alex Bates, and she wasn't sure which was the bride and which the groom, due to their names. She walked into her living room where they were waiting for her and saw two strikingly handsome men, one with dark hair and the other with silver hair. Morgan looked slightly younger, in his mid-thirties, and Alex seemed prematurely gray. They were sexy and handsome in black sweaters and black jeans, and were on their way to their country house in the Hamptons for the weekend. She tried not to show her surprise that both were men. She had done weddings for same sex couples before, but it hadn't occurred to her this time. And after talking to them for half an hour, she was in love with both of them.

They both had a great sense of humor, and she had the instant sense that she had just made two new friends. Morgan was the designer of a very established brand of women's clothing, and Alex was the producer of a hit TV show and had had several big successes before this one.

They lived in Tribeca, and spent weekends in the Hamptons. A famous actor friend who was living in England for a year had suggested that they use his very chic townhouse for their wedding. They wanted to keep it just under a hundred guests, which the house could accommodate easily. It had a big garden. It was a double-sized house and they wanted an August wedding on a date that was meaningful to them.

They had been together for ten years, and had decided before Christmas to get married. They were planning to start a family, with the help of a surrogate they had chosen, and they wanted to be married before the baby came. They had spent the last year interviewing surrogates, and had finally decided on one, conveniently in New Jersey, where surrogacy was legal.

Faith liked them better than any of the other couples she'd seen that week. They had been to several weddings she'd done, and had always said that if they got married, they would call her. Both men were well educated, well spoken, had great jobs, and they seemed to get along well. She spent an hour talking to them, and loved their ideas for the wedding. Astonishingly, the house that was being loaned to them had a ballroom, which would be perfect, and could seat a hundred guests with enough room to dance, and a small band. It sounded ideal and Faith couldn't wait to see it. She wondered whose house it was and didn't want to ask. They preferred getting married in a private home to avoid the press and the curious, which made sense to Faith.

She genuinely liked both of them, which wasn't always the case with couples. Often she liked one or the other, like the plastic surgeon and his nurse. And she had yet to meet Annabelle Albert's fiancé, Jeremy, and after what her father had said about his needing "convincing" to marry her, she guessed that he was either a fortune hunter or too weak to stand up for himself, if they had forced him into the marriage. Morgan and Alex were charming, sophisticated, intelligent, funny, and would be a pleasure to work with. Morgan knew what flowers he wanted, Alex had a preferred caterer, who was one of the best in the city, though most people found him too expensive. And she was sympathetic when Morgan said his parents would be attending and fully supported the marriage, and Alex quietly said that his parents wouldn't be. His parents were ultra conservative, lived in Des Moines, had never met Morgan, and didn't wish to. He said that his family, including his two brothers, wouldn't be there. Morgan said that his family had been fully supportive since his teens, including his older brother, and were happy to embrace them both. They had loved Alex for the past ten years.

Faith loved the variety of the people she worked with, from the nouveau riche to the more distinguished, aristocratic clients, old, young, people with great taste or none at all, while she helped them to create the wedding of their dreams. She was able to create a fantasy each time. She had a real talent for it.

Their August wedding date worked well for them, when Alex's show would be on hiatus, and Morgan said everything in the fashion industry was closed in August and he had downtime before everything went crazy during Fashion Week in September. And the date worked well for Faith too. With Violet getting married in May, Douglas Kirk and Phoebe Smith in June, Annabelle Albert in July, and Alex and Morgan in August, it all spread out nicely and she could go on vacation herself at the end of August if she had time.

She loved being the magician who could pull a rabbit out of a hat, or the fairy godmother in "Cinderella," to make everyone's dream come true. And it was so much better than being married herself! She was looking forward to all three weddings of her new clients, if they approved the estimates and signed on with her. And she hoped she could encourage Phoebe, the nurse, to stand up for herself and express her opinions before it was over. Sometimes she was just a wedding planner, and sometimes she had to be a shrink too. And all she had to do to make Alex and Morgan happy was use the best florist and caterer in the city, have fabulous taste herself, and hire a great band and photographer. She could already tell they were going to be fun to work with. Both of them had demanding jobs, and didn't have time to work on the wedding themselves, and would leave it up to her. The three of them clicked immediately, and she showed them photographs of some of her favorite indoor city weddings. They liked the idea of having the ceremony in the garden under a canopy of flowers, and to protect them from the sun if it was hot that day. Then they could move into the air-conditioned house for champagne and cocktails. She loved all of their suggestions, and they loved hers. They had already decided to get married in white linen suits. They were going to Morgan's tailor in London to have them made. Morgan's older brother was going to be their best man, and his parents the witnesses for both of them.

They were excited talking about it, and Faith promised to work on the estimate that weekend, and email it to them at the beginning of the week.

They were planning to charter a yacht in the South of France for two weeks for their honeymoon, and then Morgan had to be back in New York for Fashion Week, and Alex would be back to work on his show by then. They had already put a great deal of thought into it. Of all three weddings for the clients she had met with that week, theirs sounded like the most beautiful and the most fun, and the closest to what her own dream would have been. The Albert wedding was going to be over the top, no matter how much she tried to put the brakes on. She just hoped it wouldn't be too extreme. And the plastic surgeon's wedding sounded a little too traditional and unimaginative to her, but it was what they wanted and she tried to stay within her clients' guidelines. But between the elegant townhouse with the ballroom and the garden and the topflight resources they wanted to use, and their whole attitude about it, Morgan and Alex's wedding sounded perfect to her. She could hardly wait to get started on it, if they approved her estimate. They already knew that a quality wedding like the one they wanted would be expensive and didn't mind. They both had high-paying jobs.

They mentioned wanting the ceremony to be very traditional, and to use classic, traditional vows that were the most meaningful to them.

"I have a whole binder of them. I collect them," she said, and promised to show it to them.

They hugged Faith before they left, and thanked her for her time and great ideas, and promised to be in touch as soon as they got her estimate.

It was not going to be the most expensive wedding she would do that summer, but she was sure it would be the most beautiful, and they seemed like the happiest, most well-balanced couple. Their relationship was solid, they had lived together for a long time and knew each other well. They had managed to survive the disapproval of Alex's family and had made their peace with it. They were getting married to celebrate a relationship which worked well, and not to fix one that didn't work, which she saw all too often, or to jump into something prematurely that wasn't fully cooked yet, which was the feeling she had with both Annabelle Albert and Doug and Phoebe. Alex and Morgan were equals and well suited to each other. You couldn't ask for more in a couple, whatever their sexual orientation was. It was totally irrelevant.

They wanted to send out Save the Dates as soon as possible, and she promised to send books of them as soon as the contract was signed.

All in all, it had been a good week, and Faith was pleased when Violet left on Friday night. She had done all the research Faith needed to finish the estimate for the Albert wedding over the weekend, and the one for Jack and Phoebe.

"Have a great weekend!" Violet called out as she left, and Faith wished her the same. It had been a very good week. And two more calls had come in from older couples who wanted to get married with small weddings in June. She had room in her schedule for them. Planning Doug and Phoebe's wedding wouldn't take up too much of her time, and she had plenty of time to work on the Albert extravaganza. She had busy months ahead, which was just how she liked it.

Chapter 3

As she promised she would, Faith drove out to Connecticut to see Hope and her family for the day on Saturday. They made lunch together, she played with the children, and had some quiet time with Hope when Angus disappeared to his studio over the garage to do some writing, while Seamus played quietly and Hope put Henry and the baby down for their naps.

Angus knew Faith and Hope liked to have time to chat alone sometimes, although they enjoyed his company. He had made delicious pasta carbonara for them for lunch. It always made Faith happy to see Hope. When she didn't, she felt as though a part of her was missing, and Hope felt that way too. There was definitely something different about being a twin. It was like being sisters with a special bond added.

When they had been children, they had their own language, which no one else understood. They were closer to each other than they'd been to any friend they'd ever had.

Faith told Hope about the clients she'd seen that week, and how much she had liked Alex and Morgan, and how beautiful she thought their wedding would be.

"The one on Long Island is going to be the biggest challenge, the one with the fireworks, so it doesn't turn into a circus." Annabelle wasn't wrong about that, and Faith could see why their oldest daughter had eloped, to avoid a wedding that size, where the bride and groom could get lost in the shuffle.

Faith felt happy and at peace when she left her twin and her family in the late afternoon and drove back to the city. She had had her fix for the week, and Hope promised to come to town and have lunch with her soon.

"Yeah, don't be so lazy," Faith said as she hugged her.

"Are you sure you don't want to spend the night?" Hope offered again before she left.

"I can't. I have work to do. I want to get those three estimates finished, so I can send them on Monday."

She worked on them that night when she got home, and all day Sunday, and at midnight on Sunday night, she finished the last one, for Alex and Morgan.

Doug and Phoebe's was the least expensive. His club had given him a good deal on the price. You could only do so much with flowers there. It wasn't cheap, but it wasn't extravagant either. She thought he'd be pleased with the price. They weren't having a rehearsal dinner, since he had said there were no out-of-town guests coming. Phoebe had no family who would be attending, so they had decided to skip the traditional rehearsal dinner.

Alex and Morgan's was going to be fairly costly, with a canopy that had to be custom-made for the garden, and the quantity and type of flowers they wanted. They were very specific and wanted to go all out with the floral decorations, and the caterer they wanted to use was expensive. They wanted to serve good wines and champagne. They weren't skimping on anything, and Faith knew they expected to pay for it. Given her experience and reputation, her fee didn't come as a surprise to her clients, with the flawless weddings she provided, each one designed especially according to their wishes. She made magic happen.

The big-ticket wedding, as expected, was the Alberts'. The estimate came in at just over a million dollars, with the caveat that there were still several unknown elements about the fireworks show. The tent was going to be shockingly expensive, with everything they wanted in it. They needed lights and electricity, air-conditioning on Long Island in July, the chandeliers that Miriam wanted to light it, a fabric liner for the tent, a specially built floor, and a generator to run it all.

Danielle Steel

Faith had taken everything into account, and guessed that the add-ons could easily come to another two hundred thousand dollars. She fully expected Jack Albert to call her and try to negotiate. It seemed like an enormous amount to spend on a wedding, although she had other clients who had spent that before. The only way she could cut down the price if he complained was to eliminate some of the things they'd said they wanted. She had given them a break on her commission, because the cost of the wedding was so high. For everything they wanted and the number of guests, it was actually a fair price, which still sounded shocking, even to her.

She sent all three estimates by email late Sunday night, read for a while, and then went to sleep, after she set her alarm for five-thirty as she always did, in order to do her ballet class by Skype at six A.M.

She felt fresh and rested when she woke up the next morning, got to her computer on time in her leotard, and called Hope when she was finished.

"Did you get your work done?" Hope asked her.

"Yes, I did."

"How much is the wedding on Long Island?"

"I estimated just over a million, with a warning that it could go up as high as a million two, because of the fireworks. I'm sure the father of the bride will complain. I don't blame him. But a wedding like that is insanely expensive. They want

48

everything but dancing bears and ballerinas on zebras. The kind of tent they want will cost a fortune."

"I can't imagine spending that for a wedding," Hope said, in awe of the numbers Faith had quoted. "But people do, I guess."

"Lucky for me," Faith said, and giggled. "I'd much rather do what I do than work for an insurance company. And I'd be starving if I still worked as a magazine editor. I don't know what I'd do if I didn't do weddings."

"You could marry for money," Hope suggested, and Faith laughed.

"In the long run, that comes at too high a price," she said. "Besides, I like my life as a spinster. I can do whatever I want, whenever I want. No one tells me what to do. When I see guys like the plastic surgeon, it makes me shudder. I could have been married to that, if I hadn't broken it off. I'd have killed him by now and I'd be in prison." Hope had to admit, and had said to Angus recently, that Faith was so independent and used to being on her own by now, that Hope wasn't sure that her twin could still adjust to living with a man. She liked her freedom and she never seemed to have regrets about being alone. She went on a date now and then when she met a man she liked, but after one or two dates, he got on her nerves and she moved on. Hope couldn't see that changing, and neither could Faith, and as long as she didn't mind being alone, maybe it didn't matter.

"Well, have a good day. I'll talk to you later," Hope said, and went to play with the baby before he took his first nap of the day. She liked her life too. It suited her perfectly, and Angus had turned out to be the perfect man for her. After seven years, she had no complaints about him. It warmed Faith's heart to know that her twin was happy.

Alex and Morgan's estimate was the first one to come back to her signed and scanned, with their thanks. She was sure they would be just as prompt with the deposit.

She got Doug's a few hours later, and Annabelle Albert called to make an appointment with her for the next morning, to go over some details without her mother interfering. Faith didn't have their signed estimate yet, but she was happy to meet with Annabelle anyway. She was surprised that she hadn't heard from Jack Albert, one way or another. She fully expected him to complain about the price.

She worked on the two small weddings she had accepted for June for the rest of the day. That night, she cruised the Internet, looking for small venues for Violet's wedding. She still hadn't come up with alternatives to the neighborhood pizza restaurant, which she just couldn't allow to happen. Violet deserved so much better than that, and she wanted her to have it.

* * *

On Tuesday morning, Annabelle Albert arrived promptly at nine-thirty, and Faith was surprised to see her father with her. She had made a point of saying she would come alone. Instead, Jack walked in right behind her.

"I won't stay long," he said as he sat down, and took an envelope out of his pocket. "I thought I'd deliver this to you in person," he said, handing her the envelope. "It's the signed contract, and check for the deposit." He was smiling, without a word about the amount of the check he had written. Faith was too startled to speak for an instant. She had expected some resistance.

"Thank you very much. I tried very hard to reduce some of the amounts. I'll continue to work on it, as we refine some of the elements of the wedding," she reassured him.

"If it's that expensive, it's bound to be fabulous," he said, looking pleased. "I give my girls whatever they want," he said proudly about Annabelle and her mother. "I want this to be the wedding of the century." She could tell he meant it. He might have had rough edges, but his heart was in the right place for his daughter. Violet came to offer them coffee then, and he declined, as Faith made a suggestion to Annabelle to keep her busy while she wrapped things up with her father. She wanted to thank him for his prompt payment.

"Why don't you look at the binder of tents I wanted to suggest?" she said to Annabelle. "Violet can show it to you."

51

Annabelle looked relieved to leave the room, and followed Violet back to her office, while Faith took the opportunity to thank Jack again. "Thank you very much for bringing the check so quickly. It's wonderful to do business with you. And I promise you an extraordinary wedding for your daughter."

He smiled, leaned forward in his chair, and lowered his voice. "Why don't we have dinner to talk about it?" he said, with a look in his eye she didn't like. "Just a quiet, intimate evening, the two of us. Annabelle doesn't need to know, or her mother."

Faith leaned back in her own chair instinctively. He was unattractive, and what he was proposing to her was repulsive. His intentions were clear.

"I don't think that's a good idea, but thank you for the invitation." She stood up with a chilly look.

"Maybe another time," he said hopefully. Maybe never, Faith thought.

She stood formally, as he picked up his coat to leave, and she kept her distance as she followed him to the front door. She wondered how many women he tried that with, and how often it worked. He was spending a fortune on his daughter's wedding, and making a pass at her. She thought he was disgusting, even more than she had thought at first. That was why he had brought the check himself, so he could ask her out to dinner. Even if he had been attractive, she wouldn't have done it, but the combination of inappropriate and repugnant was too much, no matter how big the check was. The door closed quietly behind him, and she went to find Annabelle in Violet's office. They were poring over the enormous binder of tents, and Annabelle had chosen the most expensive one, which didn't surprise Faith. She realized now that Annabelle was very spoiled, and to what degree. She was twenty-nine years old, and didn't work. She'd never had a job, and had made the comment herself at their last meeting, to which her father had responded that she didn't need one. Faith couldn't imagine a life of such indolence and self-indulgence. She wondered what Annabelle did all day. It had always been understood in their family that she and Hope were expected to work when they finished college, and they both had. She at *Vogue,* and Hope as a model. And Faith had started her own business six years later. Aside from the money she earned, she couldn't imagine life without it. She would have died of boredom without a job. It gave her life meaning and substance.

She had fully understood that everything in the Alberts' life was about money. The most expensive wedding, the most expensive tent. Jack Albert wanted to show everyone he knew how successful he was, and his daughter's million-dollar wedding was the perfect way for him to do it. It was more about him than about her.

Douglas Kirk had the same theory, on a smaller scale. He wanted to show off to the people he thought were important, professionally and personally. Faith hated to see people use weddings in that way. She was a purist and thought that they should be a sacred moment in a couple's life, to be cherished forever, and only shared with people who were important in a deeply personal way. Only Morgan and Alex seemed to be respecting that, and considered it a highly private occasion to be protected and safeguarded. Alex and Morgan wanted a chic, stylish, fun wedding, with high-quality providers, to share with their closest friends, which was why they'd come to Faith. They paid their deposit the day after Jack Albert. She had Doug Kirk's deposit in hand by the end of the week. She never had trouble collecting from her clients. They were desperate for the most beautiful wedding, and were willing to pay for it to ensure that they were a priority to her, so most people paid promptly. It was a great way to do business.

As she'd been scheduled to do, Faith drove to the Albert estate at the end of the week, which was a fascinating experience, but not a surprise.

Everything in their enormous forty-thousand-square-foot home was expensive, and all of it was flashy. It was easy to see that they had been willing prey for decorators and art and antique dealers. Some of the pieces were beautiful. There was an incredible Picasso from his Blue Period, a Degas, and a Monet. But none of it was related. There was no "story." It was just an amazing collection of fabulously expensive pieces that had no relationship to one another. Each was simply there because of its monetary value.

There was nothing you could fall in love with, no corner that was warm and cozy. The house looked like a château, but the periods and styles were eclectic, Italian with French with Danish with English, from different periods. Jack had bought it all as investments, and not from the heart. She realized she'd have to be careful he didn't do the same with the wedding. She wanted the wedding to have meaning, and to represent Annabelle and Jeremy, not just her father's bank account.

With all three estimates signed and deposits in hand, Faith started working in earnest on all three weddings, researching the best suppliers for whatever services she needed. Alex and Morgan wanted to rent the finest crystal, china, silver, and table linens. In the quantities they needed them, Miriam Albert wasn't as particular. And the club was providing what Doug and Phoebe needed, so they didn't have to deal with rentals.

Faith wanted to be particularly careful with the fireworks show, so they didn't get some risky group to do it and set their house on fire, or injure someone. Faith took out large insurance policies for every wedding and charged the clients.

She prepared binders of their various options for rentals, table linens, types of flower arrangements, lighting, tents when needed for each one. There was even a wide variety of luxurious-looking porta-potties, which the Alberts needed for the hundreds of guests on their back lawn. She had the binders delivered to her clients, a copy for the bride and one for her parents, and two for Alex and Morgan. She met with the two older couples, both of whom wanted lunchtime weddings, preferably in a garden setting for fifty of their family members and friends. One couple was in their eighties, the other in their seventies, and neither of them wanted a big formal wedding. The couple in their seventies were divorced, the one in their eighties were recently widowed, and happy to have found each other again online. They had gone to high school together. She had appropriate suggestions for what they had in mind too. Faith took pleasure in doing every wedding well, no matter how big or small. She wanted each one to be like a jewel.

Since they all had their dates, she sent them stationery books for the Save the Dates and the wedding invitations, so they could choose what they liked best and she could have it ordered. When she finished her tasks for her clients, she spent time on the Internet looking for a venue for Violet in May, and she was combing all the designers on Vogue.com to find a dress for her. She hadn't seen anything that looked like her so far. A simple slip dress didn't seem like enough and it might be a chilly day, and a big elaborate wedding gown didn't seem appropriate either, for a simple daytime wedding reception in a restaurant. She checked out all the young contemporary designers, and none of them looked good to her, or right either. It was beginning to feel like Mission Impossible to find a dress and a location for her assistant.

She spent Valentine's Day doing more research, since it was a day she didn't celebrate. She kept busy all day with projects related to the upcoming weddings. She was distracted, frowning and staring at options on the Internet for Violet, when her mother called her that night.

"Hi, Mom. What's up? Are you okay?" she asked, and she didn't expect her mother's answer.

"I'm getting married," Marianne said in a rush, as though she had just exhaled. She sounded nervous. She had no idea how her daughters would react to the unexpected announcement.

"You're kidding, right? Mom. It's Valentine's Day, not April Fool's."

"I know what day this is. I'm sixty-seven, not ninety-two. Jean-Pierre proposed this morning."

"How is that possible? I haven't had a date in centuries, and you're out there dating and getting married? How does that compute? It really doesn't for me. Who is he? You haven't said a word that you're dating."

"I wasn't dating. We met at a dinner party last year in Palm Beach. We had dinner a few times when we both got back to New York. He took me to the theater and the ballet. He doesn't have children, and he's French. We've been seeing each other off and on for seven months. It's a reasonable amount of time for people our age. We can't wait as long as you can."

"You never said anything. And now you're getting married, after seven months?" It sounded crazy to her.

"We thought we'd wait till next summer," she said, sounding embarrassed. "He proposed this morning at breakfast, so I thought I should tell you."

"Mom, you've been married three times. Why do you need to get married now?" Faith asked her bluntly.

"I'm tired of being alone," she said.

"Why can't you just live with him?" Faith urged her.

"I'd rather be married, and so would he. Your generation doesn't get married anymore. Mine does."

"Well, don't rush into anything," Faith said, feeling panicked.

"I want you and Hope to meet him."

"I hope so." Faith sounded ruffled and called her twin as soon as she hung up.

"I know," Hope said, with at least two of the children crying in the background. "I hope to hell he's a decent guy. I told her she should just live with him." Hope sounded distracted while she tried to comfort her kids and talk to Faith at the same time. It was the nanny's day off.

"I told her the same thing. We'd better meet this guy soon, before she runs off and marries him." Faith was worried.

"What is it with this family?" Hope sounded exasperated. "You never want to get married, and Mom never stops." They both laughed, and Hope promised to come to the city soon for dinner to meet him. "I guess she's lonely," Hope said, feeling sorry for her.

"She should take up a sport, join a gym, or get a dog," Faith said, unnerved by her mother's announcement. "I hope he's not some creep trying to take advantage of her. The last one wasn't much of a winner and didn't last. She doesn't need to go through that again. I don't understand this. And as for me, I know better, and I get my vicarious wedding fix every day. I don't need to get married. I wish she would just date him, and forget about getting married."

"Or live together," Hope said.

Faith was shocked for days and Hope talked about it ad nauseam with Angus, who was eager to meet the man, but didn't think it was a totally absurd idea.

"Your mother's still relatively young, and she has no one

to share her life with. You're busy with me and the kids, and we live out here. And Faith is busy too. Your mother needs someone to hang out with and talk to. Think about it. She's alone all the time." He was sympathetic toward his mother-in-law, which surprised his wife. Angus came from a big family, and he felt sorry for people who were alone, like Faith, which was why he included her whenever he could. But Marianne kept to herself, and didn't want to be a burden to her children. She respected both their independence and their privacy. And now she wanted to get married, which seemed insane to the twins.

Faith was so worried she could hardly concentrate on the weddings she was supposed to be focusing on. She took Annabelle to look at dresses. She hadn't seen anything she liked at the couture shows in Paris. And even Jack had balked at the idea of a four-hundred-thousand-dollar dress. They were already over the million-dollar line. That would push it closer to two.

They finally found a dress at Valentino that molded her figure. She had a Rubenesque, womanly shape. They were willing to remake it with a train. It was a beautiful white lace evening dress, with long sleeves and a high neck, and a cinched-in waist that just fit her. It was going to take two months to custom-make, which was well within their time-frame. And Miriam found an emerald green Oscar de la Renta satin ball gown. Things were moving along nicely, except for Marianne's announcement that she was getting married. And she said she wanted to do it in June. She didn't want a wedding this time, just a simple ceremony and a nice dinner with her family. She'd already had three weddings, and didn't want a fourth, and she said that Jean-Pierre didn't care about a wedding either. He had moved into the apartment with her, a week after they got engaged, which worried the twins too. He kept his old apartment but no longer stayed there. It all seemed so soon, particularly since they didn't know him. They were relieved that he didn't have children, but they found that suspicious too. Why didn't he?

Angus looked him up on the Internet, and found that he was a retired award-winning architect. He had been decorated with the Legion of Honor for hospitals he had built all over France, government buildings, and several impressive hotels. He was widowed, just as Marianne said. His wife had been a physician and professor at the Institut Curie for cancer, and had been dead for ten years. So, he was obviously lonely too. And he was seventy-seven years old, ten years older than their mother.

"He sounds like a respectable guy," Angus said to Hope in his defense.

"He's too old," Hope pointed out. "He'll get sick, and she'll have to take care of him." Angus didn't say that their mother could get sick too, and he might take care of her. Neither of them seemed to be concerned about it. The twins were highly suspicious of him.

Between worrying about her mother and seeing her clients, Faith still hadn't had time to meet Jean-Pierre. And she hadn't found a restaurant for Violet to use for her reception. She had even gone to several places herself, without saying anything to Violet. But none of them looked right to her. It was two weeks after her mother's startling announcement, when she finally saw a restaurant she liked, and took Violet to see it the next day. It was in Gramercy Park, and had a pretty garden, and they were willing to close the restaurant on a Saturday at lunchtime, which many other restaurants weren't. The food was French, it was about the right size, and it wasn't expensive. It was slightly more than the pizza parlor, but not much.

Violet thought it was perfect when she saw it, and the price was right. She couldn't believe that Faith had gone to the trouble of finding it for her. Her parents went to see it that weekend, and liked it too. It looked like a little country inn in France. They had dinner there to check it out, and the food was delicious. The owner's mother was the chef. It was country-style food, which Violet liked. The owners liked Violet and her family so much that they lowered the price.

So a deal was made and she had a place she loved for her wedding. Faith didn't tell her, but she arranged with one of the florists she used to decorate the restaurant with white flowers the morning of the wedding, and put little vases of lily of the valley on the tables. All Violet needed now was a dress. But they still had time. The wedding was still two months away, which wasn't long to find a dress, and she'd had no luck so far.

They finally settled on a date to meet Jean-Pierre for dinner in the city. Hope and Angus had agreed to come, and Faith was so nervous about it, she lay awake for most of the night before, and for the first time in five years, she slept through her ballet class on Skype. They were meeting on Friday night.

Faith decided to try to treat it like a special night rather than a disaster, and made a reservation at La Grenouille. Her mother was touched when she told her. Both twins agonized over what to wear, and finally agreed to wear black, which suited their mood about the marriage, but at least they'd all have a good meal.

Hope and Angus offered to pick Faith up on the way, but she decided to meet them there. She got into a cab that night, her blond hair tightly pulled back in a bun, wearing very little makeup, in a serious black dress and coat. When she caught a glimpse of herself in the mirror on her way out, she thought she looked like she was going to a funeral, which was how she felt. She hoped he wasn't some kind of smooth French gigolo, and her mother was being taken for a ride. But if so, they'd see it for themselves soon enough.

Chapter 4

When Faith got to the restaurant, Hope and Angus were already there. Angus was having a glass of wine, and Hope had ordered a martini, which told Faith how nervous her twin was too. She refrained from ordering a drink herself, afraid to get drunk and blur her powers of observation and judgment. She wanted to be fully alert to check out the man her mother wanted to marry on such short notice. Both girls looked stressed when their mother walked into the restaurant with a tall, well-dressed man in a dark blue suit, with a mane of snow-white hair. He had a youthful face, and he was saying something to their mother as they approached the table. The girls could see that their mother was nervous too. Faith had a knot in her stomach that felt like a fist, and Hope stared at them as they approached.

Marianne introduced Jean-Pierre Pasquier to her daughters and son-in-law, and he shook hands formally with the three of them and waited to sit down until Marianne had taken a chair facing her girls. It was hard to seem casual about it, knowing what their mother's plans were, and that unless they made a huge fuss about it, they were being faced with a fait accompli. Even if they objected, she might marry him anyway. It was unlike her to be impulsive, and they thought she must be madly in love with him, but she didn't act it. They ordered wine, and Jean-Pierre made a point of chatting with Marianne's daughters, and said how glad he was to meet them, and he realized what a shock it must have been to them to learn that their mother wanted to get married. He apologized for not meeting them sooner. He wasn't unctuous, he was warm and friendly, and took the bull by the horns by bringing up the subject right away. Angus was impressed by how direct he was, and didn't dodge the subject. Hope noticed in the slight haze from her martini that their mother looked happy and relaxed once Jean-Pierre started speaking to them. She and Jean-Pierre seemed to have a comfortable understanding, and he was interesting to talk to once they'd ordered dinner. He had lived in China and North Africa as a young man, and had studied architecture in Germany and Norway and at the Beaux-Arts in Paris, and he had interesting stories to tell. He spoke of his late wife with warmth and respect, and said that their one regret in their later years was not having had children. He said that he and his wife had been focused on their careers. She had been a dedicated researcher, and by the time they had second thoughts about not having children, it was too late, and they couldn't have them.

"It's a decision one makes, about family or career, and not always the right one. In our case, it wasn't. Your mother is very fortunate to have both of you," he said, smiling at the twins, "and you have three boys?" he asked Hope, she nodded and then pulled out her phone to show him photographs of them. "They're beautiful children," he said warmly. "They must keep you very busy."

He was easy to talk to as they enjoyed the meal, he had modern, open ideas, and with the help of two bottles of good wine, the conversation flowed, and he and Angus hit it off. By the end of the evening, Marianne looked relaxed. Everyone had behaved, and Marianne could see that they understood now why she had fallen in love with him. It wasn't a wild passion like she'd had with her second husband when she was younger. It was a comfortable, warm relationship. He was interesting and intelligent and kind, and obviously well brought up. The evening had been a test, and he had passed it without stumbling once.

No one mentioned their June wedding date, but the evening was a first step and allowed them to get to know him, and him to discover who her children were. He found Faith harder to talk to and more tense and anxious than Hope and Angus, and she spent most of the evening observing him, watching for some fatal flaw, or danger sign, but there were none. He was just a very nice older man who had led an interesting life, and was probably as lonely as their mother now. He had moved to New York when he retired after his wife died, for a change of scene, and he went back to Europe frequently. He still had an apartment in Paris, and a summer house in the South of France, in the mountains behind Nice. He didn't seem to be after money, and Angus had the feeling that he had more than Marianne did. He wanted to share the rest of his days with a loving companion after a decade alone as a widower. He felt ready to share his life now, and his memories of his late wife were gentle, peaceful ones. He no longer felt like he was betraying her by spending his remaining years with a new partner. He had been alone since he was widowed.

"I don't think either of us expected our friendship to become serious," he said over coffee at the end of the meal, after they'd all had soufflés for dessert. "You don't expect to fall in love at our age, and it's different than when you're younger. You build things then, your life expands, you're constantly adding people and places and children to your life. When you're older, you want to enjoy what you have and share it with someone. Our feelings for each other came as a surprise to us as well. We could stay as we are now, but it's nicer to have someone you can count on. We all need stability at every age . . . and love," he added, with a smile at Marianne. He was no gigolo and no lightweight. He had turned out to be a really lovely man, and as they left the restaurant, they all felt as though they had made a friend. Hope and Faith exchanged a look. They each felt the same way. Their mother was in good hands.

"I hope to see you again soon," he said politely, and then he and Marianne left in a cab. The girls had wanted to pay for dinner, but Jean-Pierre hadn't let them. He had discreetly arranged to put it on his credit card when he left the table for a few minutes, and they all thanked him for a wonderful dinner, and a lovely evening.

The girls stood on the sidewalk for a minute afterward with Angus. "So what do you think?" Faith asked Hope.

"I think he's terrific," Angus spoke up first. "And he's totally genuine. He comes across as serious and sincere, he's not a bullshitter. I think your mother got really lucky this time."

"I agree," Faith said, endorsing him, although she hadn't been chatty at dinner. She was too busy watching Jean-Pierre.

"I really like him," Hope added. "They could get married at our house, if they want to." Faith nodded. So they had a wedding in their future, and they could both see why their mother loved him, and they made a nice couple. He didn't look his age.

Hope called their mother the next day and made the offer, and Marianne was touched. Faith called her a few minutes later, to give their mother her blessing. "I'm happy for you, Mom."

"What did they say?" Jean-Pierre asked her, looking nervous as they shared breakfast, after she hung up.

"They loved you," she said with a happy smile. "Hope asked if we'd like to get married at their house in Connecticut."

"I'd like that very much," he said, and leaned over and kissed her. He didn't want to separate her from her children and their approval was important to him, because it was to Marianne. "I haven't been that nervous since I took my architectural exams. I was afraid I'd fail." He smiled ruefully, greatly relieved. He wouldn't have married her if they objected. She needed her children too.

"You didn't," she said, with everything she felt for him in her eyes.

"You have lovely children," he said. "I never thought I'd have children and grandchildren, and now I have a whole family." He smiled at her.

"You don't mind that I was married three times?" She was sorry that she'd done that now. Neither of her last two marriages had been worth the pain they'd caused her.

"What does it matter?" he said gently. "As long as we get it right in the end, and we both know we did. I think your children see that too." She nodded and knew that what he said was true. "In French, you say, '*L'amour n'a pas d'âge.*' Love has no age. It's right whenever you find it."

They went for a long walk in the park after breakfast. And now, they could be excited about their wedding. June couldn't come soon enough, and they were both sorry it was still three months away. They had much to look forward to.

Faith went to a fitting of Annabelle's wedding dress with her in early April. Miriam was at a spa for a week to get in shape for the wedding. Everything was on track so far and going smoothly. But when Annabelle tried the dress, it didn't fit at all the way the sample had. There was a two-inch gap at her waist, and they couldn't close the zipper. There was a wide gap between the long row of tiny buttons in the back, and they retook her measurements. She looked the same to Faith, but the tape measure didn't lie. She had gained three inches around her middle. Annabelle burst into tears as soon as the seamstress said it. There was barely enough fabric to make the adjustment, but they thought they could manage it, and when she said it, Annabelle just cried harder. It was the first time Faith had seen her so emotional. Violet had come with them and left the fitting room discreetly, not wanting to intrude on a difficult moment.

"It's fine, Annabelle, it happens all the time. You heard what she said, they can fix it. And the train falls from your shoulders, you won't even see the alterations." It was a spectacular dress, and Annabelle looked beautiful in it. The tiny, cinched-in waist was the only thing that looked different and didn't fit. Then the seamstress noticed that the bust was tight too. She measured that as well, and Annabelle had gained two inches at her bustline. The head seamstress stared at Annabelle with knowing eyes, and shook her head.

"And when is the wedding?" she asked.

"In July," she said in a hoarse whisper, and the seamstress shook her head again. Faith could only guess that she had been stress eating, and thought she should have gone to the spa with her mother, but was too tactful to say it.

"The dress won't fit you in July," the seamstress said, and Faith was furious with her for saying it. She was going to complain about her to the manager after the fitting.

"That's ridiculous, of course it will. It fit you two months ago when you picked it," she said to Annabelle. "You'll lose weight before the wedding. Brides always do. They usually have to take the dress in right before the wedding."

"I won't lose weight before the wedding," Annabelle said miserably, and Faith felt sorry for her. Her parents had slipped on their compromise, and the guest list was up to five hundred, with mostly their friends, which wasn't what Annabelle had wanted.

"You will lose weight, I promise," Faith said, handing her a tissue, and Annabelle looked at her mournfully and sat down in the dressing room.

"I know I won't," she said, as tears slid down her cheeks when she looked at Faith. "I'm pregnant," she whispered. Faith felt as though her heart had stopped when she heard her.

"Are you sure?" she whispered back, and Annabelle nodded.

"Totally. Two months. I don't know how it happened. I stopped taking the pill, in case we want a baby in the next year, and it happened the first month. I'll be five months pregnant in July," and she was already changing shape. Faith felt as though she was going to keel over. She'd dealt with that before, but on a smaller scale, not for a million-dollar wedding, with parents like Miriam and Jack Albert, who were so invested heart and soul in this wedding.

"I didn't think I'd gain weight this fast," Annabelle said. "My sister had a baby with her boyfriend, and it didn't show for six months. But she's anorexic." Annabelle had a much fuller figure, and Faith could see now that her bust was much bigger than it was before. She hadn't noticed until then.

"How did your parents deal with that?" Faith asked her.

"It's okay now, but it was a mess at first. My parents didn't speak to her for a year, and then they saw the baby and fell in love with her."

"So, what are we going to do now?" Faith asked her, as they hung out in the dressing room, talking. Faith helped her take the dress off, and Annabelle put her leggings back on, with a baggy sweater. "I think you have to tell your parents. You can't let them go on with a wedding like this and not tell them. It's going to be obvious that you're pregnant in July." Faith could easily see them canceling the wedding, but it wasn't right to keep a secret like that from them. She would lose her commission, but that wasn't the important thing now. "I assume you're keeping the baby," she said, and Annabelle nodded.

"It's the only thing Jeremy is happy about. He never wanted a big wedding, and the whole thing got out of hand. I knew my parents would do that. They can't help themselves. They love to show off and splash money around. Jeremy didn't even want to get married. He doesn't believe in it. His father has been married twice and his mother has been married six times. He just wanted to live together and forget all the paperwork and rituals. My father threatened him if he didn't marry me, and said he wouldn't let me see him anymore and would cut off my allowance, but if we got married, he'd buy us a beautiful house. Jeremy didn't want to deprive me of a home, so he agreed so we'd get the house. And he's going to hate every minute of the wedding. It's all my parents' friends and my dad's business associates. But Jeremy is thrilled about the baby. We want four or five kids. And the house my father bought us is gorgeous, just down the street from them. It has six bedrooms and a pool. We'll be able to live there forever. So going through the wedding is the price we have to pay," in addition to the million two her father was spending, Faith thought. "I was actually starting to enjoy it, but now this happened. I've known for about a month. I keep meaning to tell them, but it's never a good time. I won't be able to hide it by July. It's almost starting to show now," and it was still early at two months.

"Annabelle, you have to tell them," Faith insisted. "It's not fair not to. Your father is spending a fortune on this. You have to give him a chance to cancel it if he wants to. Or maybe he'll want to throw the wedding anyway, or you can have the wedding after the baby. But they have a right to make that decision." Annabelle nodded, she knew what Faith was saying was true.

"I'll tell them tomorrow. Whenever the time seems right. My mother is due back tomorrow, and my dad's been out a lot. I want to catch them together so I don't have to say it twice. Jeremy is afraid they'll take back the house. But if they do, he says we'll manage. I can move in with Jeremy.

He has a studio apartment, but it would be hard with a baby. I can't believe I'm going to be a mom in seven months. Maybe it will give some real meaning to my life. I've never even had a job. My father didn't want me to work. Jeremy has a trust fund from his grandparents, which gives him some income. He used to work for his father parttime, but he hated it. They're in industrial refrigeration. Air-conditioning for office buildings and hotels. So now he works at a skate-board shop, which drives my father crazy." Faith could see why, but she just listened. Annabelle and Jeremy sounded like children, and now they were going to have one, but their parents' money would protect them and make life easy for them. She wasn't sure that was such a good thing. Whenever she heard stories like Annabelle's, it made her grateful that she had never had children. She still didn't want them. She didn't know what she'd have done in a situation like this, but one thing was certain, Annabelle's parents had to know about the pregnancy.

"Call me if I can do anything to help," Faith said, and hugged her before she got into a cab to go back to her office. Violet was waiting for her. Faith had told the manager of the store to hold off on any alterations until they heard from her. If the wedding went forward, they were going to need a very different dress, and the whole world would know that she was pregnant. It happened more and more these days, and she wouldn't be Faith's first pregnant bride. There had been early pregnancies from time to time that were easy to conceal. And a wedding two years earlier, with a bride who was pregnant with their fourth child. But it had been an informal garden wedding of a very liberal family, not an elaborate extravaganza like this one. Whatever they did now, there were going to be stressful days ahead, and she couldn't guess how Jack and Miriam would react. It didn't sound promising to her. She was anxious to hear what Annabelle's parents said, and decided to do, once they knew. She could see the Albert wedding disappearing fast.

Faith thought about it all the way back to her office, and when she got there, Violet told her that Doug Kirk had called. Violet had gone back to the office when Annabelle started to cry about the dress.

Faith called Doug back immediately. He said he was calling for the list of stores she had suggested for Phoebe's dress. He wanted to take her shopping that afternoon. The wedding was only two months away and she hadn't done it yet.

"Would you like me to come?" Faith offered, and he laughed.

"I can manage it, but you're welcome to come too. Phoebe can never make a decision, so she can use the help." He said their first stop was going to be the bridal salon at Bergdorf, which would have been her choice too, and would give Phoebe plenty of options. Listening to him, she decided that Phoebe might need an ally.

"I'll meet you there," she said, not giving him a choice. Something kept telling her that Phoebe needed protection from him. But if that was true, why was she marrying him? He acted like her boss whether in the office or away from it.

Faith arrived a few minutes before they did, and had the manager pull some gowns by designers she thought would look good on Phoebe with her tall, slim figure. She looked serious when she arrived with Doug, and he looked over the choices and nodded, and told Phoebe which one to try first. There were six gowns waiting in a dressing room for her to try, and Faith offered to go into the fitting room with her. She nodded gratefully, and looked the dresses over. She didn't seem excited by any of them.

"It's going to be a tough choice," Faith said, as Phoebe got undressed. "You're going to look gorgeous in everything."

She tried the dress on that Doug told her to put on first. She smiled when she saw herself in it, and Faith followed her out to show Doug. He didn't ask her if she liked it, and said it was too serious. He didn't like the embroidery, and told her to take it off. She went back to the dressing room, and tried the next one. She told Faith she didn't like it at all, and it was scratchy and uncomfortable, and the undercorset was too tight.

"They can loosen it if you love the dress. Anything can be altered," she said to reassure her, thinking of Annabelle that morning with the dress that wouldn't close because her body had expanded. Nothing was too tight on Phoebe, she was in perfect shape.

"That's better," Doug said, smiling. "I like it, but I think we can do better."

"It's uncomfortable," she said in a low voice, and Doug ignored the comment as though she hadn't said it, which shocked Faith. What Phoebe thought really didn't matter to him.

"Next," he said, and Phoebe put the third one on. It was magic. She lit up like a Christmas tree and looked like a fairy princess in it. It was easy to see she loved the gown. She came alive wearing it. She looked exquisite. It was an Oscar de la Renta, and looked as though it had been made for her. She floated out into the waiting area to show him, and he frowned as soon as he saw the look on her face. "Hideous! Take it off!" he said harshly, pointing back toward the dressing room.

"I love it," she said softly. She looked as though she was glowing, which he purposely ignored.

"I hate it. I'm not going to look at you in that gown on our wedding day." Faith could tell he was saying it to be mean, and Phoebe had tears in her eyes when they got back to the dressing room.

"I really love it," she said to Faith. Her heart ached from what Doug was doing to Phoebe. It was hard to watch. He was tearing her down, and bullying her. "Maybe I could buy it myself. Doug pays me a good salary and I have some money saved." Faith looked at the price tag, and it was surprisingly reasonable for a wedding gown. She showed Phoebe, who nodded and looked hopeful. "I have to check my account, but I think I could do it." She wanted the dress and Faith thought she should have it. It was cheaper than the others. But it wasn't about money. It was about power and control.

Phoebe tried three more dresses to humor him, but it was obvious that the third one was the one for her and that she loved. The fourth one fit her badly, and Doug said he liked it a lot. The fifth one made her look like a Folies-Bergère dancer, with feathers on it. And the sixth one was extremely plain to the point of austere. It had a high stiff neck, an overlay of lace on a heavy taffeta dress, and a long train, which was surprisingly heavy. Phoebe looked miserable in it. It covered her from chin to fingertips, and she could hardly move in it, with a corset that looked like torture.

"That's the one!" he said, beaming. "That's it. I love it!"

"I can hardly walk in it. It's really heavy, Doug, and the neck is too tight."

"I want to marry you in that dress, Phoebe." He made it sound like an order, and made it clear she had no choice. "I'm paying for it, and I have to look at you."

"I like the third one better," she tried again, gently. "I feel so pretty in it, like a real bride."

"You look like a Victorian queen in this one. A czarina. I'm buying you this one, Phoebe, and I expect you to wear it." As Faith listened to him, she knew why he had come along, to force her to buy what he liked, not what she did. And he didn't want her to look too pretty or love her dress. It was sick.

"What if I pay for it myself? I think I have enough," Phoebe offered with a hopeful, pleading expression.

"If you want me to show up at our wedding, you'll wear what I tell you to," he said in a frightening tone. Faith waited until Phoebe had gone back to the dressing room, and tried to talk to Doug in a pacifying voice.

"I think it would mean a lot to her to have the dress she loves. A bride needs to feel special and unique on her wedding day. And I think the other dress is quite uncomfortable."

"If she wants to marry me, she'll wear the dress I pick for her," he said coldly, and at the look in his eyes, Faith decided not to make things worse, and rejoined Phoebe in the dressing room. She was looking longingly at the Oscar dress he wouldn't let her have, and then at the one she had hated and he loved.

"I guess, since he's paying for it, I have to wear the one he wants me to," she said sadly, and Faith decided to take a chance and say something to her.

"Phoebe, I was engaged to a man like Doug once. I was afraid that he would control me all the time if I married him. Do you ever wonder about that with Doug?" She shook her head in answer. It was Faith's first attempt to wake her up before she made a terrible mistake. It was all so clear, except to Phoebe.

"What happened? Did you marry him?" she asked Faith.

"No, I didn't, and I never regretted it. Once I was out of it, I realized just how much he did control me. Make sure that doesn't happen to you," Faith said, trying to get through to her, but Phoebe only nodded and left the dressing room without saying a word. The dress Doug wanted her to wear needed no alterations and he handed the salesgirl his credit card, and told her to send it to his apartment. The neck Phoebe said was too tight didn't matter to him.

Phoebe thanked him, and they left the department a few minutes later.

"It's a good thing I came with you, or you'd have bought that ugly one you loved." She didn't comment and they rode down the escalator in silence. Faith felt desperately sorry for her. It had been a sad hour watching them, and seeing Phoebe's dreams elude her. "Well, that's done," he said with satisfaction. "Let's go back to the office." She nodded and they got into a cab, and Faith went back to her office, thinking about them, and about Annabelle. She had two unhappy brides at the moment, and no idea how it was going to turn out for either of them. She just hoped that Phoebe didn't marry Doug, but she didn't know how to stop her. She was in his clutches. And Annabelle had a major drama to deal with. Faith suspected Jack would be furious with his daughter.

"How did it go?" Violet asked her when she got back to the office. Faith sat down with a sigh and looked at her.

"Incredibly depressing. She found a dress she loved that she looked exquisite in, and he wouldn't let her have it. He picked one that looks like an iron maiden covered in lace. It was dismal-looking, and very uncomfortable, and he told her that if she wants him to show up at the wedding, she'll wear what he tells her to." Faith had tears in her eyes when she said it, remembering the look of despair on Phoebe's face.

"She can't marry him," Violet said in a grim voice. "He's crazy."

"I think he might be, but she has to want to get away from him. I tried talking to her about my ex-fiancé who was like him, and it went nowhere. I think she loves him and wants to please him. It could be disastrous for her." They both knew it was true, but had no idea how to stop it, and Faith was sure they couldn't. She had seen situations like that before. They usually ended in divorce, but only several years later. Doug was one of the most controlling men she'd seen. And Phoebe was so gentle and meek, she was easy prey for him, which was why he was marrying her.

They both looked upset when they went back to their offices to catch up on work. But Faith was haunted for the rest of the day by the vicious look she had seen in Doug's eyes, and she was terrified for Phoebe, and very sorry about the dress. She was starting her married life with threats and disappointment. It was no way to begin, and Faith was afraid where it would end.

Chapter 5

At six the next morning, the day after Faith had shopped for wedding dresses with Phoebe, and Annabelle had admitted to her she was pregnant, Faith's phone rang as she waited to start her ballet class. She answered and all she could hear was sobbing, and for an instant, she was terrified it was Hope, and something had happened to Angus or one of the boys.

"Hopie? Is that you? Baby, what is it? Talk to me."

"It's me, Annabelle," she said, sobbing, and Faith could guess what had happened. She had told her parents she was pregnant, and they had either thrown her out, or canceled the wedding, or both.

"Oh, Annabelle, I'm so sorry," she said, with deep feeling for her, and relief for her sister at the same time. "You told them about the baby?"

"No, I couldn't. My dad's been out a lot lately, and my mom had him followed by a detective. They took pictures of him. He's having an affair. He has a girlfriend! He has an apartment for her and everything. She's two years younger than I am. My mother knows it all. They got in a horrible argument, and she made him leave. She says she's going to divorce him and cancel the wedding. I didn't want the stupid wedding anyway, but now it's all ruined. And I never even got to tell them about the baby. My father left the house, and my mom says she's going to take everything. It's such a mess, Faith. How can he have a girlfriend? How can he do that?"

Faith knew it was easy for him. As easy as it had been when he tried to get her to have dinner with him. She could guess that he had cheated on Miriam before, but this was serious, and very unpleasant three months before his daughter's wedding. And on top of that, an out-of-wedlock grandchild on the way and they didn't even know it. Faith could see a canceled wedding in her future, and so could Annabelle. She was sorry about it now. She had gotten used to the idea. If only she could figure out something to wear five months pregnant.

"Maybe things will calm down," Faith said, trying to console her. But it didn't sound as if that was likely to happen, with a mistress tucked away in a secret apartment, a girl half his wife's age.

"Do you think they'll cancel the wedding?" Annabelle asked her.

"I think it's possible," she said honestly. "Let's wait and see what happens. A lot could happen in the next three months. Let me know if there's anything I can do."

Faith lay in bed and thought about it. They had two major problems on their hands right now in the Albert household. Annabelle's pregnancy, and her father's girl-friend. And Annabelle still had to tell them. The explosion over his mistress had come at a most inconvenient time.

Faith was still mulling it over, when her phone rang again. Her ballet teacher was due to call any minute. Faith wondered if she should cancel on her. More tears and more sobbing, and this time she thought it was Annabelle, but after straining to hear what she was saying, it was Phoebe.

"Oh my God, Phoebe, what's wrong?"

"It's over. It's all over. Everything. He broke the engagement and says he's canceling the wedding. He ripped the ring off my finger last night and threw me out of his apartment, bare-foot, without my purse. I had to walk to the apartment of one of the nurses I work with. I'm at her place now. I couldn't walk all the way back to mine. And I didn't have money for a cab."

"What happened?" Faith was stunned.

"We went to dinner last night, and the waiter was very friendly. He didn't do or say anything wrong. He was just nice, that's all. Doug is very jealous. He had a fit and made me leave the restaurant and wait outside. He accused me of cheating on him. He said he thought I had given the waiter my number so I could see him again. I would never do anything like that. As soon as we got home, he took the ring, and pushed me out the door, and locked me out of the apartment. He said it's over and he's canceling the wedding. He doesn't want to be married to a slut like me. He called me a whore." Faith cringed at the vision of it. Poor Phoebe.

Faith's stomach turned over as she listened to her. This was far worse than anything she'd ever been through. The man was a sociopath, and Phoebe had to get away from him, as soon as possible. And his canceling the wedding and throwing her out was a blessing. She wanted to convey that to Phoebe, to give her some perspective.

"Phoebe, listen to me, maybe this is for the best. That's not normal behavior. Healthy, sane people don't treat other people that way. He controls you. You can't marry someone who treats you like that. Can you get some counseling, or go to a group for abused women? Do you want me to take you?"

"No, I don't want him to know I told you. I can stay here with my friend. But, Faith, it's over. . . ." And she wouldn't have to wear the ugly wedding dress he picked out for her, Faith thought. "I never cheated on him, I swear." Faith heard her ballet teacher call her on Skype and had to ignore her.

"I believe you. But you can't let him treat you like that. You have to get away from him," Faith said, feeling desperate for her.

"I love him," she sobbed miserably, and all Faith wanted to do was help her to get free of him.

"You can't marry him, Phoebe, he'll hurt you."

"I didn't flirt with the waiter, I promise. And I didn't give him my number." She was obsessed with the things Doug had said to her, and trying to prove her innocence. Faith knew she was innocent, but she also knew she was in grave danger if she stayed with Doug. She had to get away from him, and let him end it. Faith could hear that all Phoebe wanted was for him to take her back. She was signing on for a lifetime in hell if she did.

"Just stay with your friend this weekend, and see what happens." It was the same advice she had given Annabelle. They were both in explosive situations, but Annabelle was not in danger. Phoebe was if Doug took her back. She hoped he wouldn't.

"He canceled our wedding," she said again, and couldn't stop crying.

"Could you go home to San Diego for a while, until things calm down here?"

"I'll lose my job, but he'll probably fire me anyway. And what would I tell my mother and sister? He said he was going to tell them I'm a whore." Faith winced listening to the words. He was cruel beyond belief, and crazy.

Phoebe got off the phone finally, and Faith sent her ballet teacher a text to apologize and cancel, then made herself a cup of coffee. She called Hope and told her what had happened.

"Wow, that's heavy stuff with the doctor. And it sounds like you may lose two weddings."

"I'm more worried about the girls than I am about the weddings, especially the nurse."

"He sounds totally nuts," Hope commented.

"I think he is. She doesn't want to see it. She says she loves him," Faith answered her twin.

"That's not love, that's abuse. It sounds like he has completely sucked her in," Hope said wisely.

"He has," Faith agreed.

"Do you want to come out this weekend?" she offered.

"I'd better stay here, in case anything happens. I have two small June weddings I need to put the finishing touches on, and I have to work on Violet's wedding."

"Has Dad called you, by the way?" Hope asked her.

"No. Why would he? Is something wrong?" Sometimes she forgot about him entirely. He was so removed from her life.

"He called me right before you did. He's in town for a few days. He wants us to have dinner with him and Beata. The nanny is off, and I really don't want to. Angus said he'd stay with the kids if I want to go, but to be honest, I don't. Beata is such a bore, and we never hear from Dad except when he shows up, and never lets us know he's coming. It's a lot of effort for nothing." Faith didn't disagree with her. Their father put so little effort into being one, but Faith always felt duty-bound to see him when he showed up.

"Don't leave me stuck with him. I don't know why I feel obliged to see him."

"Because you're nicer than I am," Hope said. "I'll come in if you want me to."

"Maybe he won't call me," Faith said hopefully, but as soon as they hung up, he called and extended the invitation she always felt was a command performance. It was always all about him, and what was convenient for him, with total disregard for whatever was happening in their lives, even though they were adults now, with Faith's job, a family in Hope's case, and responsibilities.

He extended the same dinner invitation to her that he had to Hope. He wanted to have dinner at Cipriani, his favorite restaurant. The only mercy was that it was so loud they wouldn't be able to speak to one another. He and Beata liked going to chic, fashionable places. Being in a noisy restaurant would spare him the trouble of asking either of his daughters what was happening in their lives.

He didn't really care. He never called them, and only saw them a few times a year, when he came to New York for other reasons. And Beata wanted to see their friends, not his children. He hadn't even seen Hope's baby yet, and he was a year old. He had never been to their home in Connecticut. It wasn't on his familiar path, and he said it took too long to get there.

Faith accepted his invitation as she always did, wondering why she bothered, except that he was the only father she had, and she thought she should. She sent Hope a text after she hung up, and told her time and place, and Hope texted back that she'd be there, but she was doing it for Faith, not her father. Hope never let her down.

Their father was already at the restaurant when they arrived. He and Beata were seated at a corner table. The twins kissed their father and were dutifully polite to Beata, who made no pretense of being interested in them. She thought that Hope was a boring housewife and Faith was some kind of a misfit since she wasn't married. They exchanged the usual banter, most of which their father couldn't hear. And he politely asked about their mother.

"She's fine," Faith answered him, "she's getting married." He looked surprised. Faith had said it loud enough so he would hear her.

"I'm surprised she's still trying. Marriage isn't her strong suit. Three strikes, you're out," he said with a cynical grin, which annoyed both twins, who always staunchly defended their mother. His only accomplishment in that department had been marrying a baroness for her money, which they thought was the only reason why he hadn't left her. There was no warmth between them.

"We think she got it right this time. He's a very nice man, he's French, but he lives here," Faith filled him in.

"Then I'm glad for her. Give her my best," he said coolly. Their dinner arrived then, along with the whole dinner crowd, and conversation became impossible, which was a relief for all of them. Faith realized halfway through dinner that he saw them as much out of obligation as they did for him. There was no mutual enjoyment involved, or even interest on his part. It was just a duty he performed when he came to New York. It made her realize too how much nicer Jean-Pierre was, and they genuinely hoped it would go well for their mother this time.

She had accepted the invitation to be married at Hope's farm in Connecticut, and Faith was organizing the small family wedding for them. They were going to be married at the local church near the farm, and then they were having lunch prepared by a local caterer. It was going to be small, but the girls wanted it to be perfect and special for her.

Hope had ordered cold lobster and caviar, their mother's favorites. And Marianne had bought a new white silk suit at Chanel for the occasion. She was hiding it from Jean-Pierre so he didn't see her "wedding dress."

Dinner with their father ended early, as it always did. They paid lip service to seeing him again soon, which might not be for six or eight months, or even a year, when he showed up in New York again, without advance notice so they could plan. And Beata said goodbye to them as stiffly as she always did, and looked immensely relieved that it was over. She made it very clear that she considered dinner with Arthur's children a wasted evening, one she would have preferred to spend with her New York friends, or at some social event they were invited to.

"Why do we do that?" Faith asked Hope as they walked away, and went to collect Hope's car from the valet outside.

"I do it for you," Hope said simply, "and I think you do it because you still hope a different father from the one we've got will show up. He doesn't give a damn about anyone but himself. I don't think he even likes Beata. She's just his insurance policy for his old age so someone will take care of him and pay his bills."

"He's been paying those dues for a long time," Faith commented. "I don't know how he stands her. The human iceberg."

"I don't know how Mom put up with him for twelve years," Hope said. She really didn't like him. He had disappointed them all their lives.

"He was better-looking then, when he was younger," Faith said, and they both laughed. What they said about him was all true. "And you're probably right about why I see him. I just figure he'll get nicer with old age, but he doesn't. He's still the same selfish asshole he's always been."

"Now at least you make sense. I think when you have a serious man in your life again, you won't care if you see him anymore. It might be a relief."

"You may be right, if that day ever comes. I can't imagine having a serious relationship again. I don't want to be disappointed." Faith hadn't been lucky with men. "You've got to give Mom credit for trying again."

"I think what you said to Dad is true. She got it right this time. Jean-Pierre seems like a really nice guy. I was surprised, and Angus loved him."

"She deserves to be happy," Faith said to her twin. They hugged when the valet delivered Hope's car, and she dropped Faith off at her house and drove back to her family in Connecticut. Faith gave her credit too. Hope had done it right the first time around. She was married to a great guy, and she was happy with her flock of unruly boys.

Hope texted her two hours later when she got home. She

always did so Faith wouldn't worry about her. They still had the same powerful bond they'd always had. Faith texted her back, thanking her for coming in for their duty dinner.

Faith told their mother about it when she called her the next day, minus the nasty comment about marriage not being her strong suit.

"Did you tell him I'm getting married?" She was curious to know.

"I did. He said to send you his best, which isn't saying much from him. He doesn't improve with age," Faith said honestly.

"Poor guy. He really missed the boat in life, and everything that matters. I don't think he even likes the woman he's married to. He's just impressed that she's a baroness."

"It doesn't compensate for how dull she is." They both laughed then, and she told Faith she'd found her wedding suit.

"You'll look beautiful, Mom," Faith said.

"Thank you for organizing it. I know how busy you are this time of year."

"I may be a lot less busy soon," she said, and told her about Doug and Phoebe's canceled wedding, and the Albert wedding that was poised to go down the tubes too.

"I'm sorry to hear it," her mother said. "And I hope that young nurse doesn't marry the doctor. He sounds terrifying."

"He is. I hope that wedding stays canceled. I'll have to start winding everything down on Monday when I go into the office. He hasn't officially told me it's off yet, but I assume he will. Since he hired me, I have to wait to hear it from him."

Her smaller weddings were still on track, and going smoothly. Annabelle called her that afternoon.

"Any news?" Faith asked her, but she thought it was too soon to know. Even if they were separated, they could still give their daughter a wedding.

"Mom says she's calling her lawyer on Monday and telling him to file for divorce. I don't know if she will, but it's what she says. Dad sent me a text to tell me he loves me." His own life was a mess, but Faith was sure that he still loved his daughters, unlike her own father, who had ice in his veins. It was always slightly depressing seeing him. It was a reminder of all the times he had disappointed them when they were children, both before and after the divorce. It was no wonder she didn't want to get married, after everything she'd seen. Being a wedding planner was her way of wanting to correct it with other people's fantasies, and making it work for them. But she wasn't brave enough to try it herself and doubted that she ever would be again. Marriage just looked too high-risk to her. Look at the Alberts, and Doug Kirk, and her own parents. It was hard to believe that anyone could

Danielle Steel

make it work. Jean-Pierre had been married to his wife for forty-four years, and her mother said that he had loved her. Hope and Angus were happy, and she hoped they always would be. But the odds didn't seem great to her. She could make people's weddings perfect, but not their marriages.

No one notified Faith officially that the Albert wedding was off, but it was Sunday, and Annabelle still hadn't told them that she was pregnant. That was going to cause another explosion when they found out, and might be the deathblow to the million-dollar wedding that Annabelle hadn't wanted in the first place, but wanted now. She said even Jeremy was hoping they wouldn't cancel. It all seemed to depend on her father now and what he did about his girlfriend. She was still shocked about that, and hoped it wasn't serious and he didn't marry her. The last thing she wanted was a twenty-seven-year-old stepmother, who was probably a gold-digger. She had always thought her parents loved each other. She and her sister had talked about it all weekend, and her sister said she had always suspected he cheated on their mother, and apparently, she'd been right.

Faith called to check on Phoebe on Monday. She was still at her friend's apartment and hadn't gone back to her own. She was embarrassed to admit to her roommates what had happened. Doug had texted her not to come to work, and said he would send her the salary he owed her. The wedding was still off.

"At least you won't have to wear the wedding dress you hated," Faith reminded her.

"I would have worn it for Doug," she said, still devastated over what had happened. "The one I liked didn't suit me anyway. Doug said I looked cheap in it."

"You looked beautiful, Phoebe," Faith said quietly. "I think that's what he didn't like about it." Phoebe couldn't allow herself to believe that. It was so complicated and so sad, all Phoebe wanted was for Doug to come back. And Faith hoped with all her heart, for her sake, that he wouldn't.

Chapter 6

Of the three big weddings that Faith had been working on since January, the only one that was going smoothly was Alex and Morgan's. Everything about it had been magical from the start. They got the caterer and florist they wanted. The borrowed house for the ceremony and reception worked ideally.

They were going to decorate the ballroom with topiary trees of orchids and lily of the valley, and a garland of them over the doorway for the ceremony. And a canopy of white flowers over the garden for dinner afterward. The band they wanted was available, the invitations were beautiful and were due to go out on the first of July. Alex had a friend who was doing the photography. They had chosen the wedding cake they wanted, and they'd been fitted for their white linen suits during a weekend in London. The suits were ivory, and both men were going to look incredibly handsome in them. They were going to exchange simple gold wedding bands. Every detail had been thought of. The wedding was still almost four months away, but everything was in order.

The two weddings of the older couples in June were going smoothly. Her mother's family wedding lunch in Connecticut was in good order too. Violet was all set with her little French restaurant in Gramercy Park, and Faith had ordered the flowers, and was giving them to her as a gift. Violet's parents were paying for the reception at the restaurant.

What was utter chaos were the Kirk and Albert weddings. Phoebe had reported to Faith that the wedding and engagement were canceled, but she had received no written official notice from Douglas, who was technically her client. She wasn't sure whether to cancel the suppliers, or leave them in place. She wondered what he was up to, if he was just manipulating and tormenting Phoebe, or if he was truly canceling it. The wedding was two months away, and if he waited much longer to cancel, he would lose his deposits and be charged penalties if he did. He seemed too smart for that, which led her to believe he was just torturing Phoebe, who had heard nothing from him since the text he had sent telling her not to come to work. He had sent her a check for the salary he owed her, but she was no longer being paid, and had no income. Fortunately, she had some savings she could live on, until she found another job if she had to. But she couldn't stay out of work for long, especially since she sent money home for her mother. She wasn't sure whether she should start looking for another job or not. All of which he was well aware of, since he knew her circumstances. Faith was afraid that all of it was her punishment for supposedly flirting with a waiter, which wasn't true.

The biggest mess of all was the Albert wedding. Miriam had called Faith and told her the whole sad story, crying the whole time. She was hysterical, and also furious with her husband. She was threatening to cancel the wedding, which would punish Annabelle as much as it would Jack, as Faith pointed out to her. Miriam's edict to him was that he give up his girlfriend immediately and act like a husband, or she was filing for divorce, and a great deal of money would be involved. The couple hadn't seen each other since the night she threw him out, and were communicating only through lawyers. Miriam refused to speak to him, although Jack had tried and sent her an apology and told her he loved her. But he was staying with the girlfriend.

In the midst of all of it, Annabelle added fuel to the flames and confessed to her mother that she was pregnant. She didn't feel she could wait any longer. It was showing much more quickly than she'd expected. It was the final blow to her mother, who was profoundly shocked, and couldn't imagine her daughter at a nearly royal wedding visibly pregnant, and in July it would very definitely show. She would be five months pregnant. Miriam finally broke her silence with Jack, and called him. She wanted to know if they should cancel the wedding. Everything was out of control now, most of all their daughter. She was due in November. And even if they canceled the wedding, Miriam wanted her to get married. She didn't want her grandchild born out of wedlock.

Jack was as shocked as she was, and didn't know what to say. They had been through the same thing with their older daughter, who had divorced one man and had a baby with another, unmarried. They didn't want Annabelle following in her footsteps.

After speaking to Jack, Miriam asked Annabelle what she wanted to do. Being visibly pregnant in front of five hundred guests was not what they wanted for her. They thought the whole thing would be embarrassing, but Annabelle surprised her. She said she wanted to go through with the wedding, even if it was bigger than she had wanted. But she only wanted to do it if both her parents were present. And Miriam wouldn't allow Jack in the house or anywhere near her unless he got rid of his girlfriend. So, everything hinged on him now. And just in case her parents managed some kind of truce, Faith took Annabelle to a young designer she knew and explained the problem. She worked up some sketches, and designed a gown that bared her shoulders, and the entire wedding gown floated down from there in a large A-line, so nothing showed and the train flowed from her shoulders too. She did it in a heavy silk faille with enough body and structure not to cling to her. It was very stately looking and very dramatic. So if the wedding went ahead, she would have a wedding gown to wear that fit her, and she would look like a bride. It was very elegant and very regal, and Annabelle liked it better than the first one.

Jeremy was ever present, and supportive of Annabelle and her mother in the crisis, and he was far less opposed to the wedding now that Annabelle was having their baby. And he was acting like a responsible husband.

The only one without a dress, days away from her wedding, was Violet. Her forays among inexpensive stores and designers had turned up nothing she wanted to wear. They either looked cheap or didn't suit her. She had even looked in vintage shops and found nothing.

"What are you going to do?" Faith asked her, she was sorry that she hadn't found a dress.

"I think I'm going to rent one," Violet said, trying to be a good sport about it. "I checked out a couple of places this weekend. They're not bad really. Not what I would have picked to buy, but it costs next to nothing to rent a wedding dress, and I'll only wear it for a few hours. I don't need to buy one." In truth, she thought many of them looked tired, a few had stains on them, and none were brand new, with a fresh, crisp look. The problem was that in order to keep their overhead down, they used an inexpensive dry cleaner, but by now Violet had no choice but to rent a dress, or rush out and buy one she couldn't afford, and spend two years paying for it, which seemed stupid too.

Talking to her about it gave Faith an idea. She went up to her storeroom in the attic that night, and dug around for a while, and finally found the box she was looking for. Her mother had packed it for her, and Faith hadn't seen it in sixteen years, since her ill-fated wedding that never happened, when the groom fell in love with a male ballet dancer and canceled the ceremony. Faith could still remember how devastated she had been. She could almost taste it. She opened the box and seeing her wedding dress brought it all back in a rush, but it was for a good cause. She and Violet were about the same height, and wore the same size. The dress had been inspired by a 1920s wedding dress that Faith had fallen in love with. It had slim lines, and showed her ankles, which seemed like a good length for a daytime wedding. It was made of exquisite French lace that had been embroidered, and tiny pearls had been added. She carefully took it downstairs and in the morning she asked Violet to come upstairs to her bedroom and showed it to her.

"Oh my God, Faith, it's gorgeous. What are you going to do with it? Were you planning to wear it?" It was like a work of art, and on the one hand it looked bridal, and on the other it was just a very beautiful dress one could wear to any very special occasion. Faith had forgotten just how beautiful it was until she saw it again. And it had a simple veil trimmed in lace the same length as the dress.

"No, I'm not planning to wear it. I hope you are. It's never been worn. Try it on. See if it fits you." Faith was smiling at her.

"I can't wear that," Violet said, looking at it with awe, afraid to handle it, it was so beautiful.

"Don't be silly. It's sixteen years old, not a hundred. It just looks vintage." Violet hesitated at first, and then couldn't resist. She took off her denim skirt and white blouse, kicked off her shoes, and slipped into the exquisite dress. It fit her as though it was made for her. She looked like a porcelain doll in it. "Vi, you have to wear it," Faith said to her. "It's magnificent on you. It never looked as good on me. It's been here waiting for you. I want you to wear it."

"Are you sure?" Violet asked her breathlessly, her eyes wide in her pretty young face.

"You need to get shoes for it. Ivory silk would be best,

or satin if you can't find silk." Faith wanted to see her get married in the dress that had been wasted until now. She had held on to it for long enough, and the sad memories that went with it. It was time to set them free, and give the dress a life it had never had. They packed it carefully back into the box, and Violet took it down to her office, and carried the box as though it contained spun glass. Her wedding was complete now. She had the dress. The look on her face was worth all of it.

"What are you doing about your vows?" Faith asked her. She liked the traditional ones, but there were also some classics that were out of favor and Faith had always loved.

"Nothing," Violet admitted. "I have no imagination."

"You should check the binder, there are some great ones in there. I've always loved the line 'with my body I thee worship.' It seems so respectful and so tender," Faith said, smiling at her.

"I love that," Violet said with a shy smile. "Maybe I'll have the priest put that in. And we're going to go with 'love, honor, and cherish' not 'obey.'"

"I agree with that. I've heard that other line used in some royal weddings. Check out the others too. You can take it home tonight and study it. Homework." Faith was having her bridal bouquet made for her of lily of the valley. It was going to be a beautiful little wedding after all.

Violet's was the first one in their summer wedding season. Then Faith's mother's, and the others scheduled for June, among them the Kirk wedding, which remained a mystery until two days later when Doug called Faith himself. He apologized for not getting back to her sooner, and she assumed he was calling to advise her of the cancellation. The deadline for deposits was very close.

"I've decided to forgive Phoebe," he said somewhat grandly, which annoyed Faith profoundly.

"For what?" For things she'd never done and sins she'd never committed? And what about his crimes against her? Except that Faith knew Phoebe had already forgiven him and wanted him back. "Are you calling to cancel?" Faith said hopefully.

"No, I'm not," he said, and Faith considered it the worst news so far. She wanted Phoebe to be free of him, so he couldn't manipulate her anymore. She realized now that his whole "cancellation" of the wedding, as he told Phoebe, had been a fraud, a hoax. He never canceled his club or the important suppliers. Faith suspected that he had never intended to leave her, just to frighten her and break her heart.

"Have you told Phoebe this news?"

"No, I haven't," he said proudly.

"When are you planning to tell her?"

"I don't know yet." He was still controlling and manipulating.

"Do you figure she needs a little more punishment?" Why keep her believing it was over, when he knew he was coming back? It seemed so cruel to Faith. But that's who and what he was, a torturer, and Phoebe was his prey.

She felt sick about it when she thought about it that night. She hated the idea of Phoebe going forward to an unhappy fate. There was no way Phoebe could be happy with a man like Doug, nor could anyone else.

Phoebe called Faith, jubilant, the next day. He had finally called her, waited another day to do so, and had told her that he was now "willing" to marry her again, as though it was some enormous favor he was doing her. Doug called Faith again to confirm it, and she would have liked to hang up on him, but she didn't dare.

"I'll get the ball rolling again," she said to Doug in a somber voice. He was tormenting a woman who couldn't defend herself. He was worse than a schoolyard bully. Phoebe didn't deserve that kind of treatment, at his hands or anyone else's. Faith was so distressed to hear the news. She wasn't worried about the wedding. A wedding only lasted a day. The damage Doug would inflict on Phoebe could last a lifetime. Faith had escaped that fate, and she had hoped Phoebe would as well.

Chapter 7

Despite Annabelle's frequent and often tearful reports, and a few hysterical calls from Miriam, officially the Albert wedding had not been canceled. There were threats that it would be, and it was beginning to look unlikely that it could happen with the father of the bride having a girlfriend, his wife threatening to divorce him, and a pregnant bride. But Faith decided that the wisest course, if by some miracle it did happen, was to continue as though everything was still on track. If she didn't, the whole wedding would collapse like a soufflé and become irretrievable. So she continued to meet with the florist and his designers, stayed in touch with the band, protected the order for the wedding cake, kept a firm grip on the tents they had ordered, and kept the reservation for the porta-potties, and everything else they had booked for the wedding, china, crystal, and silver rentals, chairs, and the fireworks show of course. Unraveling all of it would be a nightmare if they had to cancel, and a considerable amount of money would be lost in non-refundable deposits. Faith would face it if she had to, but it seemed best not to let anything go, or it would be swallowed up by other events, and if the wedding was then on again, they wouldn't have all the elements they needed, which Faith had ordered so well in advance. Now it was all chaos.

Miriam had confided in Faith when she called her, and told her all about Jack's twenty-seven-year-old girlfriend. She was a minor actress and trade show model, and Miriam claimed that her private detective had discovered that the girl had been a stripper in Vegas when Jack met her three years ago. She was two years younger than their youngest daughter. Jack paid the rent on her apartment, so it was obviously more than a fling or a brief affair. She had been around, in the background, for several years, and Miriam had only begun to suspect it recently. He "traveled" more than he used to, went to evening events without his wife, and had been "working late" several nights a week, which he had never done before. She had told him to end it with the girl immediately, or she would file for divorce, and the settlement she wanted was astronomical. They had nothing when they married thirty-six years before, so they had no prenup, and Miriam had every intention of taking every penny she could get to punish him for cheating on her. Faith believed her when she said it. Betrayed women were nothing to mess with, and Miriam was no softie and no slouch when it came to money, and she had a good idea of what Jack was worth.

She was almost as upset about Annabelle's pregnancy. She was going to bring disgrace on the family, which her sister had already done with an elopement, a divorce, and a baby born out of wedlock. Annabelle was her pride and joy, and now she was following in her sister's footsteps. Going forward with the wedding with Annabelle visibly five months pregnant made her cry every time she said it. Her conversations with Faith were fraught with tears, sobs, threats against her husband, and laments about her daughters. Faith actually felt sorry for her, although she hadn't felt close to her before. Miriam sounded distraught and was coming unglued.

The only small silver lining was that her future son-in-law, whom she hadn't particularly liked, was being wonderful to all of them, supportive of Annabelle, and very kind and helpful to Miriam, doing anything he could to make things easier for her, errands, odd jobs around the house, answering the phone and screening calls. She said he was talking about getting a real job now that he was going to be a father, and giving up his part-time job at the skateboard shop, which

Jack had been trying to get him to do for months. He was suddenly becoming more responsible. But it was small compensation for everything else that was happening to her.

Annabelle told Faith that she had no idea what was going to happen. Even if her parents didn't cancel the wedding, she didn't want to have a big splashy wedding with parents who weren't speaking to each other. And Miriam said it was too humiliating to have a wedding and see everyone they knew while she was well aware that he had a girlfriend stashed away in an apartment in the city. And what if others knew or had seen him with her? Her sense of having been publicly ridiculed was complete. It bothered Annabelle less to be pregnant at her wedding than to have her parents at war during the entire event.

At least they had ordered the dress that would work, so if it did go forward, she'd have something to wear. The dress was due to be finished in June, in time for the Fourth of July wedding.

While they waited to find out the fate of the event, Faith gave Annabelle the binder of wedding vows to look over, and pointed out her favorites. She stopped by the office a few times just to say hello when she was in the city to see her friends or go shopping. She was still wearing baggy clothes and had only told her closest friends she was pregnant. It didn't bother her not to be married yet. She thought that if they canceled the wedding, they might get married on that date anyway. She liked it as an anniversary for the future. Jeremy was on board about getting married now, with a baby coming. Before that, the need to get married didn't make much sense to him, except as an excuse to give a big party, which didn't mean anything to him. But a baby did, and he was being very attentive to Annabelle, and was excited about being a family.

Morgan and Alex's wedding was in good shape too. They were so impeccably organized and so easy to make decisions with that they had rapidly become Faith's favorite clients. She loved working with them. She had mentioned her binder of vows too, and quoted some of her favorites to them, some of which they liked better than others. They were very traditional and didn't want any of what Alex called "modern mumbo jumbo" in the ceremony. Faith preferred classic wedding ceremonies too.

She was working at her desk, going over some details of the Kirk wedding, when Violet told her that Morgan was there to pick up the binder of wedding vows, but didn't want to bother her if she was busy. Faith's hair was loose and she was wearing a sweatshirt and jeans since she didn't expect to see anybody, when she went out to give Morgan a hug, and was startled to see him with a tall, very handsome man, who looked faintly like him, but was slightly older. He had chiseled features and bright blue eyes, and he smiled when he saw her. Morgan gave her a hug and introduced them.

"This is my brother, Edward, my best man at the wedding, and generally the best man I know. His law firm is moving him from Chicago to head up the New York office. We're looking at apartments today. We just saw one in the neighborhood, so I thought I'd pick up the binder you told me about with the vows." He was already holding it. Violet had just handed it to him.

"That sounds exciting. The move, I mean, not the vows, although they're nice too." Faith and Edward exchanged a smile. She was startled by how good-looking he was. He was a bigger, taller, more athletic version of his younger brother, and Morgan was handsome too.

"It is. It's a big change for me. I've lived in Chicago all my life. It's good to shake things up once in a while. I have a son at Columbia Law School who thinks it will be great to have a place to crash and bring his friends. It'll be nice to be in the same city again. He's always studying, so he doesn't get home to Chicago often now." Faith wondered how much older Edward was than his brother. They were a handsome family. "I hear you've been doing a great job with the wedding. I'm looking forward to it," he said pleasantly, with a smile.

"We all are. They're my favorite clients." She smiled broadly at Morgan. He looked happy to see his brother. Morgan rarely went to Chicago now either, he never had time, with all the seasons, collections, and fashion shows he did.

They chatted for a few minutes, and then they had another apartment to see, so they left. Violet raised an eyebrow after they did.

"Wow, he's a hunk."

Faith nodded agreement. "So's Morgan. Their wedding is going to be just gorgeous."

"I like the best man," Violet said in a teasing tone, and Faith grinned. "Is he single?"

"I have no idea. Maybe we should have given him a questionnaire to fill out."

"He's pretty cute, Faith. What about for you?"

"I'm not shopping for a guy," she corrected her. "We have enough trouble on our hands with the Albert wedding about to explode, and now the Kirk wedding back on. I wish it weren't. Phoebe Smith is headed for trouble. I was hoping she'd bail before she marries him." Violet nodded, distracted from the handsome brothers for a minute.

"Do you think she will?" Violet asked her.

"Sadly, no, I don't. I think he has her totally under his spell, with the addiction of abuse. She's hooked. She should have run like hell when he dumped her, but she didn't.

And now she's back in it. She even hates her wedding dress, but she's going to wear it because he picked it. I think she's in for some very hard times." Phoebe was the only one who didn't see it, and refused to open her eyes. She resisted waking up from the nightmare, even when he broke their engagement for a while. Faith had given her a copy of their selection of vows too, and she was sure that Doug would insist on the unpopular one no one used anymore of "love, honor, and obey." She was sure of it.

It was Violet's last day in the office before her own wedding. She was taking the rest of the week off to make her final arrangements, spend a bachelorette night with her girlfriends, get her hair done, and all the little details before her wedding day. Even if it was a small wedding, it was still a very special day for her.

She hated to leave Faith shorthanded, but Faith had insisted she take the time off.

Faith gave her a big hug that afternoon when she left for the day. She was attending the wedding, and was planning to go to the restaurant in the morning, to make sure that the florist was doing what she'd ordered and that no problems had come up. Then she was going to the church to see Violet marry Jordan. Faith saw more weddings than most people, but she was never blasé about it, and this one meant a great deal to her. Violet was excited about wearing her dress.

Her grandmother had done a few minor alterations, shortened the hem just a touch, and tightened some buttons. Everything was ready for the big day. Violet loved the veil that went with Faith's dress. It was a wisp of the finest French tulle, and the back of the veil reached the hem of her dress, with delicate embroideries and pearls that matched the ones on the dress. They looked perfect together.

For the honeymoon, they were going to stay at a romantic inn in the Berkshires in Massachusetts for a few days, which Violet said was all they could afford, but they were excited about it.

"Are you nervous?" Faith asked her before she left. She looked so bright-eyed and happy. She had the look of a real bride.

"Not nervous, just excited. I keep telling myself it won't make any difference. We're already living together, and we know each other so well. But I think it does make a difference. It's a big commitment, but we're ready. We just don't want kids right away. That's a commitment we're not ready for. We agree on that. That's just too scary, and we're too young to take that on. Financially, it would kill us." They were both twenty-nine, the same age as Annabelle Albert, but so different, responsible, and so much more grown up.

"There's no rush for that. Enjoy each other for a few years first. Kids are a lot to take on. My sister handles it well, she has a nanny, and her husband helps, but it's still a lot. It's not the same once you have kids. I wouldn't know, but I see it among my friends, or I used to. My old friends who married young have kids who are in college now. My sister started a lot later, at thirty-seven. I thought she was crazy to have so many so soon, but she seems to be enjoying it. I'm glad it's her and not me. Just enjoy being a bride. That's all you have to think about right now. It's such a special time." They hugged again, and Violet left a few minutes later, and it made Faith smile after she left, thinking that the next time she saw Violet would be on her wedding day. She was such a sweet girl. And she was going to miss her for the two weeks she'd be off after the wedding. Faith just hoped that nothing dramatic would happen while she was gone.

Faith spent the next few days tying up details on their upcoming weddings. They had the two small luncheon weddings coming up, and the Doug and Phoebe wedding was the next bigger one they had scheduled, in June. And her mother's wedding to Jean-Pierre before that. Faith was looking forward to that now too. Her objections had dissolved once she'd met him, and they seemed like a good match.

Her mother was so happy these days. She and Jean-Pierre got along beautifully and did everything together. He was planning to give up his apartment after they were married, since he no longer used it. Hers was bigger and more comfortable and felt like a home, and they liked being uptown. His had been meant to be temporary when he rented it. He had been there for ten years, but it still had a temporary feel to it. His long-term home was still in Paris. They were going to France on their honeymoon so Marianne could meet his ninety-eight-year-old mother. She was in relatively good health, still went to the opera and the ballet, and was living in a home for the elderly. Jean-Pierre went back to France regularly to see her. He had a widowed sister who lived nearby and visited their mother more often.

The morning of Violet's wedding, Faith got up early. She skipped her ballet routine that day and dressed for the wedding before she left to check on the restaurant. She was wearing a light blue wool dress and matching coat and felt like the mother of the bride as she got ready. She thought about wearing a hat for the church ceremony, but decided it was too dressy. She wore her hair in a bun, as she almost always did. Long ago, she had worn it down a lot, but it no longer fit her image as the all-knowing wedding guru.

She was relieved to see that the florists were already at work when she got there. They had boxes of cut flowers. She had ordered white roses and lily of the valley. The air was heavy with the scent when she walked in. There were long-stem roses for the entrance, two topiary trees to make the entrance to the restaurant look fancier, and a garland of white roses over the door. There were two long tables set up in the restaurant instead of the usual rounds. Violet had rented the long tables, and white tablecloths to go on them, and once the flowers were set down, it looked like a wedding, no matter how small the place was. Faith had sent two large arrangements of white roses to the church. Violet's bridal bouquet of lily of the valley was being delivered to her home, with bouton-nières and corsages of white roses for Jordan, her parents, and her two attendants. Faith had thought of everything, as she always did, even without Violet's help. She wanted everything she had done for her to be a surprise.

The owners of the pretty little restaurant were vastly impressed by what Faith had done. The flowers and the touches she added had transformed the place. It looked romantic and smelled heavenly with the delicate scent of the lily of the valley blended with the roses.

The wedding cake had been delivered while she was there too. Violet had decided that a real wedding cake was too heavy for their budget, so she had decided not to have one, which Faith thought would be sad, so she had taken care of that too. She had used a baker who was a Frenchwoman she knew who did exquisite cakes. The one they delivered had latticework and real flowers all over it, on three tiers. It was a work of art. Inside it was rich French vanilla, which Faith knew was Violet's favorite.

She left the restaurant fifteen minutes before the ceremony, and everything was done. The two musicians were just setting up, with a keyboard and a violin, which would be romantic, and there was a small area where they could dance once they removed their usual tables. The paintings on the walls were landscapes of France. It had a very authentic feel to it, the owners were French, and so was the food. Violet had picked the menu with her parents.

Faith walked to the church, pleased with the work she'd done. It was a sunny day with a light breeze, and seemed like a perfect day for a wedding. Not all brides were as lucky.

When she got there, Faith slid into a third-row pew on the bride's side, not wanting to intrude on the family. The organ was playing the music they'd chosen and within minutes the small group of wedding guests arrived, and smiled at one another as they sat down. A few minutes later, Jordan and his brother emerged from a side door and took their places at the altar. Jordan looked nervous, and so young with the lily of the valley boutonnière Faith had sent him. The music got louder, the priest came to stand at the altar, and everyone waited. Then suddenly Violet was walking down the aisle on her father's arm, beaming, as she looked ahead to the man she was about to marry. She stood next to Jordan when she reached him. Her father gently lifted the short face veil to the back to reveal her face to the groom, and then took his place in the front pew next to her mother. Violet was wearing the beautiful dress that Faith had never worn. The music stopped, the congregation was invited to be seated, and the ceremony began.

Faith watched with tears in her eyes as they said their vows, and was surprised when she heard the vow she had always loved so much. She didn't know that Violet had decided to use it, as they pronounced to each other ". . . with my body, I thee worship," and then went on to "love, honor, and cherish." A moment later, they were husband and wife, Jordan kissed the bride, and they came down the aisle arm in arm, beaming as a brand-new young couple, embarking on the greatest adventure of their life. She smiled broadly at Faith as she walked past her, and Faith shook hands with her parents and congratulated them on the receiving line, and embraced Violet and Jordan, and smiled into Violet's shining face.

"You're a gorgeous bride," she told her, and Violet whispered to her.

"Thank you for the beautiful dress." She looked exquisite and the veil was perfection with it. People milled around outside, greeting one another, and slowly made their way to the restaurant, where they were offered champagne as soon as they walked in. The piano and violin were playing, and the restaurant looked like a little garden with the flowers all in place. Many of the guests walked through to the garden and stood outside drinking champagne until lunch.

Violet came to find Faith there as soon as the bridal party arrived, after taking photographs outside the church.

"Oh my God, Faith, the flowers, they're incredible. It looks so fancy. It looks like one of your weddings. You have a magic touch."

"It was hard work doing it without my assistant," she said, and Jordan came to thank her too, once Violet told him that the flowers, the music, and the cake were all gifts from Faith. He was a nice young man, and he looked so proud to stand at Violet's side as her husband.

The lunch was delicious, and authentic French. It was four o'clock in the afternoon by the time she left the restaurant, and five by the time she got home after doing some errands. It had been a lovely afternoon, and a beautiful little gem of a wedding. A cousin of Violet's had caught the bouquet and was delighted. Faith had taken a step back as it flew past her, as she always did. The last thing she wanted was to catch the bouquet. She was grateful to have shared such a special moment with Violet, and had enjoyed the relatives she sat next to.

She realized when she got home that she hadn't turned her phone back on after the wedding, and it had been off since that morning. She turned it on, and eight messages from her mother popped up. It was unusual for her to get so many. She called her immediately, but it went straight to voicemail, and then she listened to the messages her mother had left. All Faith could make out was that something had happened to Jean-Pierre and they were going to Lenox Hill Hospital.

Faith picked up her purse and coat and headed out the door, and five minutes later she was on her way to the hospital. She asked for Jean-Pierre Pasquier by name at the emergency room, and was directed to cardiac ICU, where she found her mother sitting in a waiting room looking pale and frightened.

"What happened, Mom?" she asked, as she slipped into a chair next to her. She was wearing the same clothes she had worn to Violet's wedding.

"I don't know," Marianne said, looking distressed. "We were taking a walk in the park, which we do every day, and all of a sudden he got light-headed. We sat on a bench for a few minutes and I thought he was better, and then he felt faint on the way home, so we took a cab, and he said he was having palpitations. He's had some mild episodes like it before, but this was worse, and he hadn't had anything like it for a long time. He says it used to happen from stress. They're doing tests on him now. He didn't have a heart attack.

They checked when we came in. We've been here for hours, waiting. They just took him a little while ago, so they must not be too worried."

"It's probably nothing, Mom," Faith said to reassure her, and hoped that it was true.

The cardiologist on duty came to see them an hour later, and he explained that Jean-Pierre had been having arrhythmia, which he described as an "electrical problem." His heart was just out of sync for a short time. They could give him medication for it. They were planning to do a procedure in the morning, an electrical cardioversion, to restore his heart's normal rhythm and set it to a regular beat again. It was done with paddles to administer a shock to the heart, and didn't sound too dangerous, but Faith suspected that it might be a bigger deal than they were saying. They were able to visit Jean-Pierre in a room then, and he apologized to both of them for being so much trouble. He looked embarrassed and very pale.

"Don't be silly," Marianne said to him. "I was so worried about you. How do you feel now?"

"Tired," he admitted to her, and he looked it. "You should go home with your daughter and get some rest. We've been here all day," or a good part of it. "They're going to do a minor procedure tomorrow, to get things back on track. It's nothing."

"I'll be here when they do it," she said firmly, and Faith walked away to the window, to give them some privacy. She could see how much her mother cared about him from the look on her face when she got there. She loved him, and was terrified that she might lose him.

The cardiologist came back to check on him again before they left. Jean-Pierre told him he was getting married in a month when they asked what was happening in his life at the moment, and the doctor explained that good stress, like something exciting happening, can be as disturbing to the body sometimes as bad stress. But he said that after the procedure, he should be fine. If he had recurring episodes, they could start him on medication. In the long term, one day he might need a pacemaker if this was a chronic problem. But they were a long way from there at the moment.

Marianne and Faith left half an hour later, and Faith offered to go to the hospital with her the next morning, and she insisted it wasn't necessary. They said it would only take a short time. They were going to keep him for another day after that, for observation, and then he could come home. He didn't have to change his lifestyle or his diet, and the procedure should take care of it. If not, they would address it. It reminded Faith of the fragility of life, and that her mother marrying a man who was ten years older might not have a happy ending. One day, it wouldn't for one or the other of them. But she hoped they would have a long time together.

"I know what you're thinking," she said to Faith, she had thought the same thing. "I love him, and I'll settle for as little or as much time as we get. It's worth it to be with him."

"I understand, Mom," Faith said. She really seemed to have found her soulmate. She just wished that she had found him earlier. But Marianne seemed to have her eyes wide open, and wasn't going to let the uncertainty of life stop her, or cheat her of the happiness she had found for as long as they had it.

Faith talked to Hope about it when she got home, and she was shocked. Their mother hadn't called her, probably because they were so far out of the city. In a dire emergency, she would have eventually.

"She really loves him," Faith said, in a sober tone.

"I'm glad. And he loves her too," Hope answered.

"Let's just hope they have a long time together," Faith said. "I'm happy they're getting married. It means a lot to both of them."

"It's nice that we're doing it here, at the farm, and we'll all be together," Hope said and Faith agreed.

For the merest instant, she envied the strong, simple, sure love her mother felt for Jean-Pierre. She had never loved any man with that certainty and doubted she ever would.

The procedure went well the next morning, and appeared to solve the problem. After another twenty-four hours of observation, they let Jean-Pierre go home to Marianne's apartment, and he said he felt much better. But it had been a reminder of their mortality, and how precious, fleeting, and fragile life was. It made them more grateful than ever that they had found each other, no matter how late in the day it was.

Chapter 8

Violet came back from her honeymoon looking relaxed, blissful, and glowing. They'd had their few days at the inn in the Berkshires, and spent the rest of the time at home, relaxing and doing projects together. Faith had given her two weeks instead of one. Jordan had taken two weeks off too. Violet said that being married did make a difference. They felt more settled, and more sure of each other. She compared it to the difference between owning a house and renting one. If the roof leaked, you fixed it in a house you owned, as a renter, you complained to your landlord and if it remained a problem you moved out.

"Good point," Faith said, smiling at her.

She had brought the wedding dress and gave it back to Faith in a box lined in tissue paper, carefully folded, with the veil. It had been an honor to wear it, and suited her so well.

"You keep it," Faith said gently. "It's yours now. You wore it at your wedding. It's a piece of your history."

"It's your dress, Faith. It's too valuable, I can't keep it," Violet insisted.

"I'm not taking it back. I want you to have it," Faith said again, and Violet could see that she meant it.

"You did so much for us for the wedding. The flowers, which were gorgeous, the cake, the music. You made the wedding."

"You and Jordan made the wedding, by how happy you were. It was a blessing for the rest of us just to be there. And the food was delicious. I have to take my mother and her fiancé there. I think he would love it. It's real French cuisine."

"And it wasn't insanely expensive. You found that too," Violet reminded her. "You should go into wedding planning, you're so good at it," she teased her.

"Nah . . . too crazy . . . too stressful," Faith answered, and headed for her office. She left the box with the dress in Violet's office for her to take home. Faith was never going to wear it, and she never had. It was Violet's now, and belonged with her.

As Doug and Phoebe's wedding approached, he called Faith with some new detail to attend to every day. Phoebe never called her, but Faith reached out to her. She offered her the binder full of vows, in case she was working on hers.

"No, we're just going to go traditional," Phoebe said breezily. "Love, honor, and obey." Faith stopped for a beat when she heard her say it. She had predicted it to Violet, but it hit Faith hard when she heard Phoebe say it.

"'Obey' is pretty much out of the wedding vocabulary now, and has been for a while," Faith said quietly. "That's a little strong for most women today. Don't you think? How about 'love, honor, and cherish'?" She tried to suggest it gently.

"Doug likes 'obey,' he said his parents said it, so he wants us to say it too. I don't mind." Faith wanted to scream "But you *should* mind!" But she couldn't say it to her.

Phoebe came in with a check from Doug a few days later. It was for some of the extra things he'd ordered recently, like a video of the wedding, which Faith had arranged.

Faith offered Phoebe a cup of tea and they sat down in the living room. She wanted to make sure she was okay. She normally had a good relationship with her brides, but Phoebe was a special case, and she wanted to keep a close eye on her for signs of Doug's control and abuse.

"How's everything going?" Faith asked her, as they chatted. "You're getting down to the wire, a few more weeks." Phoebe didn't look worried as she relaxed on the couch. She was back in her job at his office, after he had deprived her of several weeks' salary, to make his point, in his fury about the waiter she swore she hadn't flirted with, but he said she did.

"It's all fine now. Doug has calmed down. He's really excited too." She smiled at Faith.

"How are you feeling about the dress? You know, since you didn't need any alterations, we could always take it back and we can switch it for the one you loved." Phoebe looked panicked when Faith said it.

"I can't do that. Doug would be so upset. He loved the one he bought, and he *hated* that one I liked." Faith remembered it all too vividly, and how lovely she had looked in it.

"I want you to feel like the most beautiful bride in the world on your wedding day," she said warmly, and she could see worry in Phoebe's eyes.

"I don't want to do anything to upset Doug. Everything is back to normal now." But Faith could sense that normal for him was not normal for anyone else.

"You know, Phoebe, you can decide right up until the last minute if this is what you want to do. You have free choice here. Marriage is a very big step." She was speaking to her like a mother or an aunt. "It doesn't matter how far you've come, if something in your gut tells you not to do it, you can listen to that. You have to really."

Phoebe shook her head and avoided Faith's eyes. "I'm sure," she said quietly. "Doug is the man I want to be married to. I know he's right for me." Faith wished she didn't feel that way, but she could see that there was no getting through to her. She was going to marry him no matter what. She was too afraid not to, and to lose him, and maybe to be alone. She wouldn't have been for long. She was a very pretty woman. But there was no way to rescue her if she didn't reach out, and try to save herself. She seemed nervous after Faith questioned her, and a few minutes later, she left. Faith walked into Violet's office, frowning.

"I think I just blew it. I tried to talk to Phoebe, and inquired if she has any doubts. She looked terrified as soon as I asked. She wants this marriage desperately. I don't know why."

"Maybe she doesn't even know she's being abused. She may think it's like this for everyone," Violet said wisely.

"I think he terrified her when he canceled the engagement, and she's afraid he'll do it again and she'll lose him. It would be the best thing that could happen to her. I've never had a wedding I felt so uncomfortable about. I feel like I'm leading a lamb to slaughter."

Violet shuddered. "I hope not."

"Me too," Faith said, and went back to her desk. She had tried and gotten nowhere. Phoebe was so much in Doug's control, she was unreachable.

Marianne and Jean-Pierre got married on a perfect June day on Hope and Angus's farm. The sun was warm, there was a gentle breeze. They got married in the local church after the morning service, and then they went back to the house for caviar and champagne before lunch.

Faith had arranged for flowers at the tiny local church. Hope had ordered beautiful bouquets to put around the house. Marianne wore her new ivory silk suit, and the girls had dressed for the occasion. Faith wore a pink Chanel suit, and Hope wore a long beige pleated skirt and a silk V-neck sweater to match. They wore high heels, and both men wore coats and ties. Jean-Pierre was somewhat formal and very French, and had worn a dark blue suit for his wedding, white shirt, light blue Hermès tie, and beautifully polished shoes. He'd had a haircut the day before, and Hope had her hairdresser come out to do her mother's hair the morning of the wedding. Jean-Pierre surprised Marianne with a beautiful diamond wedding ring, since she didn't want an engagement ring. She expected a simple gold band, and was surprised when she saw the diamond Cartier band.

She was glowing the morning of the wedding, and was nervous on the way to the church, but as she stood next to him and said her vows, and then he said his, they both looked peaceful, and as though they were completely sure of what they were doing. And she used the vow that Faith loved, and had shared with her: ". . . with my body, I thee worship." Faith's eyes filled with tears as she listened to them, and she and Hope held hands. They were there to support their mother, and they trusted her decision and the man she'd chosen to marry. This time it was right.

Jean-Pierre's health had improved since the minor procedure he'd had to regulate his heart. It had corrected what was necessary, and he hadn't had a problem since, which was a huge relief to Marianne, and the best wedding gift of all.

The lunch was as delicious as the caterer had promised. Faith had ordered the best caviar. They had oysters to start, and lobster for the main course with salad and excellent cheeses to follow. There was a beautiful little wedding cake with snow-white icing and chocolate inside. Hope had bought a bride and groom to put on top, which made the bride and groom smile.

They sat in the sun afterward and the men took off their jackets and ties. Hope had put all three boys in little white suits, and they played near them, before the two younger ones went for their naps, and Seamus went to watch a video with the babysitter while his brothers slept.

It was an absolutely perfect day for Marianne, with the people she loved most. Their wedding day had a peaceful feeling to it, as though they both felt they had come home at last.

They were leaving for Paris in three days, they were going to spend a week there, and then were going to the South of

France for ten days at his house there, before the summer invasion of tourists. They were planning to spend the final weekend in Venice, which was one of their favorite cities, and then back to New York. They would be away for three weeks in all, and after their honeymoon, they had been invited to visit friends in Palm Beach and Newport and others in the Hamptons. They were going to have a busy summer, visiting friends and enjoying their new married life. In France, Jean-Pierre's mother had said she was eager to meet his bride. It made Marianne feel young when he said it. Everything felt bright and new. Even at their age, it was a fresh start.

The caterers had just left, and Marianne and Jean-Pierre had gone for a walk. They had changed into country clothes, and they wandered off on the paths where Hope liked to ride.

"It was a sweet wedding," Faith said to Hope, smiling as she thought about it. "Thank you for doing it here. It's more personal than if we'd done it at a restaurant in New York. I think she loved it."

"I did too, and I think he's really a good guy. I hope his health holds up. That would be terrible for Mom if he gets sick and she has to nurse him."

"He seems okay now," Faith said thoughtfully. "It was scary when he wound up in the hospital. Poor Mom was a wreck."

"It's bound to happen someday, he's ten years older than

she is," Hope said. "Let's just hope not for a long time," and then she smiled at her twin. "I've got some news," she announced proudly.

"What's that?"

"I'm pregnant again. A Christmas baby. A girl, I hope, this time."

"Already?" Faith looked surprised, and as though she wasn't convinced it was good news. Hope was disappointed by her reaction. "Oliver is only one. That's a lot of kids, Hopie. Four? What does Angus think about it?"

"He's thrilled." She smiled at her sister. "We can handle it, and we can afford it. It wasn't an accident."

"Can you manage four?"

"I think so. It won't be that different from three, and Angus and I will pitch in more. Other people do it." Faith nodded. It was true, they did. She got up to kiss her sister then and gave her a hug.

"Actually, this makes sense. You can have my share too. Do you think you'll have more after this?"

"I don't know. I'll be forty-three when it's born. Maybe we'll be done. Angus always said he wanted six. I thought he was kidding."

"I sure wouldn't want a baby now," Faith said with a shudder, "or at any age. I made the right decision for me. So, I'll be an aunt again. Have you told Mom yet?"

Hope shook her head. "She'll probably get all wound up and think it's too many. It'll be fun when they're a little older, and we can travel with them, and do more than we can now. They're still babies."

"And you'll have another one by Christmas." She grinned at the idea. "It always seems so mysterious to me. Presto magic, there's another person in the room."

"It feels like a miracle every time," Hope said, smiling. And Faith sensed that they actually might have one or two more babies.

"Are you feeling okay?"

"Fine. I've never had any problems with any of them. I'm going to wait a while before I tell everyone. If you tell people too early, it feels so long."

They chatted for a long time, until their mother and Jean-Pierre came back from their walk. And after the sun went down, they went inside, and relaxed and chatted until dinner. Angus lit a fire, and the men huddled in a corner, talking business and sports, while Marianne and the girls talked about everything from fashion to politics. It was nice sharing Marianne and Jean-Pierre's wedding weekend with them.

They had leftovers from lunch to eat for dinner, and Angus cooked steaks on the barbecue. They each had another piece of wedding cake, which they all agreed was delicious.

"I'm glad you didn't want a big wedding, Mom," Hope said, as they put the dishes in the kitchen sink for now, to be dealt with later. "It's so cozy, being here with you."

"That's how I wanted it," Marianne said, smiling broadly. "Thank you for letting us do it here, and making it so nice for us." Jean-Pierre had told her, which he had said repeatedly before, how lovely her children were. He loved the warm family atmosphere between them, and how well they got along.

When they finally all went to their bedrooms that night, they were all coasting on the warm memories of the day, Marianne and Jean-Pierre saying their vows in the tiny church, and the elegant family luncheon afterward. And there was enough caviar left for all of them for breakfast. Everything had gone off without a hitch, using Faith's usual suppliers. None of which was surprising, since it was a Faith Ferguson wedding. Hope teased her about it, as they stopped and said good night on the landing, and then went in opposite directions to their bedrooms.

The next day Faith and Angus went riding. Marianne still rode occasionally, but she didn't want to leave Jean-Pierre on his own, and she didn't think he should do strenuous exercise so soon after his fainting episode.

They finished the caviar at lunch, and in the late afternoon, a car and driver came to pick up Faith, and Marianne drove back with Jean-Pierre in the passenger seat, chatting with her and enjoying the scenery. They were both in great spirits and looking forward to their honeymoon. And when they got to her apartment on Park Avenue, he commented that it felt like home, now that they were married.

"It's funny. I didn't think it would make a difference but it does. Everything between us feels more real now. I wish I had met you sooner," he said.

"You came into my life at the right time," she answered. "Maybe we wouldn't have been ready before this."

He smiled at her and put his arms around her. "You're a wise woman, Marianne Pasquier," he said, and she smiled at the sound of her new name.

"I like that."

"So do I," he said, and followed her to what was now their bedroom. "I want to make good on that vow we made yesterday," he whispered, and she looked over her shoulder at him, and smiled. The years faded away as he said it, and they felt young again, with the future and all their hopes ahead of them.

Chapter 9

When Faith got to her office the Monday after her mother's wedding, she felt as though she hit the ground running and never stopped. She had details to finalize on Morgan and Alex's wedding. She called Morgan at his office, and he sounded distracted, which was unusual for him. He confided to her after a few minutes that their surrogate's egg retrieval was complete, he and Alex had both done their part. Her eggs were being fertilized now, and they would wait to hear if the fertilized eggs had implanted and if she was pregnant. The process had begun. If it worked the first time, they would have a baby in their arms in March. And if she wasn't pregnant this time, they would try again. She had done this twice before for others successfully. She was a married woman with two children, they couldn't afford

143

more, and she felt she was doing something important for people who wanted children desperately, and preferred surrogacy to adoption. Alex and Morgan had decided that they preferred this route. It was a costly process but they felt lucky that they could afford it. For now, they were more interested in their baby than their wedding.

"By the way, my brother was very impressed by you. It's going to be a big change for him, moving here from Chicago, and he doesn't have a lot of friends here, except through work. Maybe you could come to dinner with him sometime at our place."

"He seemed very nice," she said politely. And it never hurt to meet a new friend. She liked Alex and Morgan immensely.

"My nephew is a nice kid too. He stays with us for the weekend sometimes, but he spends most of his time in the library, studying. Law school is tough. My brother was like that when he was young too. He was a terrific student, a lot better than I was. I barely made it through Parsons."

"I was the student at our house," Faith said, smiling. "I used to write all Hope's papers for her. No one ever knew. She hated school. She only did two years of college at NYU, and dropped out to model. She never went back."

"Is everything falling into place for the wedding?" Morgan asked her.

"Beautifully," she reassured him.

"I've had my head so full of this baby process, I haven't been able to think of anything else. Alex too. I think we'll both feel better once we know she's pregnant. But nine months is going to seem like forever." She didn't tell him that her twin sister was pregnant again. She was still adjusting to the idea herself. Four seemed like so many kids, even though the three she had were adorable and beautiful children. It was so much responsibility, and once they were older it was fertile ground for so many problems. She was surprised Hope wanted more. She had thought she would stop at three. And Hope thought Faith worked too hard, so they each had their own worries about the other.

"I'll give you a call about dinner when Edward gets here," he said about his brother. "He's going to be flying back and forth a lot for the next month or two. He takes over the New York office right before our wedding in August." And that seemed just around the corner too.

Annabelle Albert dropped in to see Faith on Tuesday afternoon. She was in the city to see her doctor, she looked very big to Faith, but she said the doctor had told her it wasn't twins. They had just found out it was a boy, and Jeremy was even more excited now than he had been.

She lowered her voice then. "I think my father might be leaving his girlfriend. My mom really wants him back. But only if he leaves the girl. If he does, I think she'll go ahead with the wedding. She's calming down a little about the baby. She's been so upset about Dad, she's not as mad at me, and she's starting to like Jeremy. He's been so great ever since Mom and Dad split up. And he's thrilled about the baby.

"I haven't seen my dad since he moved out," she said, "but he texts me a lot. I think he feels bad about everything that happened. My mom hasn't seen him either. She refuses to, until he's dealt with the problem. She won't even talk to him. Anything she has to say to him goes through their lawyers. It seems pathetic. It was so stupid of him."

She was in town for a fitting of the second dress she was having made, after she saw the doctor. It was almost finished, and she said it was beautiful, but huge. So was she.

"It's about the same size as the tent Mom is having made," she said, and laughed. "The doctor says I've gained too much weight. Mom says she did too. And so did my sister." She was four months pregnant, and looked more like six or seven. Faith couldn't imagine what she'd look like by November, when she was due. In contrast, Hope didn't even show.

She realized with some amusement that her wedding business was turning into a baby factory, between Annabelle, and Alex and Morgan waiting to find out if their surrogate was pregnant. She'd had pregnant brides before, but not as obviously so. They either got married quickly, as soon as they found out they were pregnant, or they waited until after the baby was born, because they didn't want to walk down the aisle visibly pregnant. Annabelle said she didn't mind. She was upset about it at first, but after her parents' separation, it didn't seem like such a big deal now. People would talk about it, but they always found something to talk about, and she and Jeremy were happy about the baby, which was all that mattered. And the new wedding dress she was having made was incredibly elegant, even more so than the first one, which was sexier. The second one was magnificent and suited her now. It was regal.

In the last week before Doug and Phoebe's wedding, he drove Faith absolutely crazy. He called her daily to check on every single detail. He called her twice a day about the guest list and the RSVPs, which went to Faith. There were some people who still hadn't answered, but that was standard at every wedding. She had Violet calling them to try to press answers from them. They needed to know for the seating. There were a hundred and twenty-six people coming so far, and they were still missing another forty answers. Doug was pushing her to get definite responses, but some people were just slow to respond, and there was nothing Faith could do about it. She couldn't threaten them into answering.

Doug insisted on speaking to the florist himself, the wedding cake baker, and the band. He called the club almost daily too. He complained to Faith that no one at the club called him back, but she was sure that by now they were utterly fed up with him.

He told Faith that he had gone back to Bergdorf with Phoebe to make the dress even tighter than it had been. He thought that the neck fit her too loosely, and the waist needed to be cinched in more. Faith felt sorry for her. The dress had already been strangling her when he bought it for her. But she was sure now that Phoebe had done what he wanted. He had his own vision of how the dress should look, and the bride in general. Phoebe had to conform to his vision of her, not her own. She was going to look like a Victorian school-teacher in her wedding dress, with a corset under it so tight she could hardly breathe, a waist which cut into her, and the neck was so high and so tight that it almost choked her. Since he was tall himself, he wanted her in towering high heels, which would be hard to walk in, and to dance in afterward. Her feet would be killing her, something Faith always urged brides to avoid.

He called the hairdresser himself to make sure that her hair was done the way he wanted. He didn't leave anything to chance, and he pounded so hard on her suppliers that Faith was afraid they wouldn't work with her again. He got in an argument with the hairdresser and fired her. His club had finally flatly told him to stop calling. He was furious about it, and said that after the wedding, he was going to drop his membership. He was always at war with someone about something.

He had turned out to be so different from what he had presented at first. Faith hated dealing with him herself, she couldn't wait for it to be over. She had never felt that way about a wedding before. But beneath the obvious tension he created around him, Faith still felt there was something very dangerous lurking, some kind of character disorder. Since Phoebe showed no sign of wanting to leave him, or even stop his obsessive control over her, there was nothing that Faith could do about it. And once married, Phoebe would be at his mercy and on her own.

Two days before the wedding, Faith did a walk-through with the club's catering manager. She went over all their dinner choices and preferences. She checked the table linens that the club was intending to use. Some were not as clean as they should be, with spots in plain view. She was planning to check the actual table settings as soon as they set them up the morning of the wedding. She reassured Doug about every detail, but he continued to call her to check "just one more thing," until she couldn't stand it anymore, and had Violet take his calls and say she was busy.

The day before the wedding, Faith met Phoebe at her apartment for a last look at the dress, so there wasn't some unfortunate surprise the day of the wedding, like a missing button.

Faith buttoned up the dress for her, and poor Phoebe looked like a mummy. Doug had had it altered to be so tight when he went to the fitting with her that she could hardly walk in it, and she was being suffocated by the chin-high lace collar with bones in it to keep it stiff. There were sharp stays in the collar and corset. It looked like it was painful to wear. Faith suggested to Doug that they have it loosened slightly, which he insisted wasn't necessary and Phoebe went along with it. She was too cowed into submission not to.

She had decided to walk down the aisle alone. There were no important male figures in her life who she could have asked to walk her down the aisle. Her sister was stuck in San Diego with their mother, as Phoebe had suspected would be the case, and their mother was too ill to come. Phoebe would have loved to have the wedding in San Diego so her mother could see her get married, but Doug had insisted on New York, where all his friends were. Phoebe had none, other than the nurses she worked with, whom Doug wouldn't let her invite. He said it was too awkward for him, because they were his employees. But even Phoebe understood that he thought they weren't fancy enough and would hurt his image.

He hadn't allowed her to invite her roommates either. The only friends at the wedding would be his.

Phoebe stayed at her old apartment with her roommates the night before the wedding, so Doug wouldn't see her, and Faith met her there to help her dress. She had already been to the club early that morning to see everything get set up. Faith was wearing a long, simple navy blue silk dress that she often wore to weddings. It was totally innocuous and let her blend in with the crowd, and didn't make her look as though she was competing with the guests.

She found Phoebe looking panicked and her roommates were out. Since they weren't invited to the wedding, they hadn't stayed to help her dress. Faith had wanted to book a hairdresser and makeup artist for her, as she did for all her brides. But after firing Phoebe's hairdresser, Doug wouldn't let her. He said he preferred her looking natural to being overcoiffed by a hairdresser who would make her look like a hooker. She had pinned her hair up in a simple French twist, and she looked beautiful, even without professional assistance. She was so pretty that nothing dimmed her looks.

"The club is looking terrific," she told her to reassure her, and Phoebe nodded, and looked into Faith's eyes. Faith saw sorrow and fear there, and disappointment.

"I thought today would be different," she said sadly. "I wanted my sister and my mom to see me get married, and the girls I work with, and my roommates. They're all mad at me for not inviting them, but I couldn't. Doug wouldn't let me. The dress is so tight, I'm not sure I can get down the aisle without someone to hold on to. What if I trip or look stupid?"

"You won't, just walk slowly," Faith said gently. "Would you like me to walk you down the aisle?" she offered. Phoebe hesitated and then she nodded.

"Would you?"

"Of course. I've done it before."

"Doug wants me to walk alone, but I don't think I can in that dress. It had a slit in the back, but he had it sewn up. He said it looked vulgar." He had done everything he could to make her feel uncomfortable and insignificant. He couldn't even wait until after the wedding to control and torture her. He had turned their wedding into an event that only he would enjoy, and his associates and friends. The bride was of no importance, except as an accessory to him.

In spite of everything he'd done, she still looked beautiful in the austere dress. She looked regal as she stood there, nearly choked by the tight Victorian neck. She could take only the smallest of steps. Faith used her own makeup to accent Phoebe's eyes, and put some blush on her cheeks. She was as white as the bridal gown she was wearing. Getting into the car Faith had waiting downstairs with a driver was nearly an Olympic event, which took both of them to get her in. She had to fall backward and swivel onto the seat, with no breathing room at all, and the slit sewn up nearly to her ankles. Getting her out at a side entrance to the club they used for brides was easier. Faith just pulled her straight out to a standing position, and then she hobbled in on Faith's arm, in the painful high heels.

She had said from the beginning that she wanted to get married in a church, which Doug had vetoed early on, since he was an atheist.

Violet was waiting at the club to help them, and she said that Doug had called her on her cell every three minutes to question her about the final details. It was an entirely different event from Violet's warm, elegant little wedding only a month before, in the gown Faith had given her.

"You look beautiful," Faith whispered to Phoebe, just before they left the waiting room, and she smiled.

"Thank you for doing everything for me," she said softly. "This is harder than I thought it would be without my mom. I don't think I'll know anyone here. I haven't met many of Doug's friends. He usually goes out without me." Faith wondered again why he was marrying her, and she wondered even more how Phoebe had allowed herself to get into this position with a man who controlled her every move and breath. The only consolation was that she couldn't imagine her putting up with it for long. At some point, it would all be too painful to tolerate for another minute, and she would explode. Faith hoped that moment would come soon. But in the meantime, they had a wedding to get through.

Violet gave them their cue when the music changed, and Faith took small measured steps, with Phoebe's hand tucked into her arm for stability. She made it look as though it was supposed to be that way. They walked through the door down a narrow hallway to where she would start down the aisle, and Faith could see people staring at her. Despite everything Doug had done, she was a beautiful bride. Her unadorned simplicity only added to her beauty, in the agonizingly tight, plain dress.

"We're halfway there," Faith whispered to encourage her, but Phoebe's eyes were locked into Doug's by then. The way he looked at her told Faith that he could control her just by the look in his eyes. She moved toward the man she was about to marry like a robot. She was no longer holding on as tightly to Faith, she almost seemed to glide above the ground, despite the tight dress and high heels.

Faith delivered her to him safely, without mishap, and he looked at Phoebe with no mention of how beautiful she looked, which most grooms acknowledged when they saw their bride. Everything about Doug felt like some form of sociopathic behavior that Faith had completely missed in the beginning but was obvious to her now.

She adjusted Phoebe's veil, and then stood back, and disappeared down a side aisle, just close enough to help if she was needed, but out of the guests' immediate field of vision. Part of her job was to be invisible, but always within easy reach if needed.

The guests had been standing while Phoebe made her way slowly down the aisle, and were invited to sit down by the minister. Doug had compromised to allow her to have him at the wedding. The ceremony was brief, as Doug had wanted it to be, with as little mention of religion as possible. They used the old version of the vows with the word "obey" in them. Faith almost flinched as she heard it. And what seemed like moments later, they had been declared man and wife, and Phoebe's fate was sealed. Doug walked her back down the aisle, moving a little too quickly, so she had to take tiny flying steps to keep up with him and she almost tripped. Then they stood in a reception line, with Faith directly behind them to keep an eye on things while their guests filed by to congratulate them. Immediately after, Doug disappeared into the crowd to greet special friends and associates, and Phoebe was left standing alone, holding her bouquet of white orchids, and looking lost. Faith immediately came to join her and handed her a glass of champagne. She took a long swallow, and seemed a little less frozen a few minutes later.

Faith kept her company until Doug returned right before they sat down to dinner. The guests in black tie looked very elegant and so did Doug with a new tuxedo he had bought for the occasion. Phoebe looked uncomfortable in the stiff, tight dress.

"Having fun?" he asked her, which sounded almost like a joke to Faith. How could she be having fun when she knew not a soul at her own wedding, and the groom had deserted her for the last hour? They walked into the club's ballroom, and the flowers looked beautiful. They were a little less lavish than Faith would have liked, but Doug had kept a tight hand on the price. He wanted quality, but not a lot of it. But the club provided a handsome setting, and Faith was sure that no one noticed, or was as particular about the flowers as she was. Phoebe didn't seem to notice the décor at all. She was overwhelmed. So many strangers, Doug rushing around the room to chat with people he knew well, and others he wanted to touch base with and welcome, and it never dawned on him to take Phoebe with him. The wedding seemed to be his show, rather than their special day, to launch their future together. To Faith she seemed more like an appendage than part of the central focus of the event. It was Doug's wedding, and she was an accessory. Phoebe was more relaxed when he finally came to sit next to her.

Faith was standing discreetly just beyond a doorway where she could watch everything from her vantage point, while

Violet was actively involved with the catering manager and the musicians to ensure that it all went smoothly. Faith had trained her well.

There were speeches that celebrated Doug's accomplishments, and a couple of clever, funny ones that roasted him. No one mentioned Phoebe, except to wish her well, because no one knew her. And in a room full of strangers, in a dress that was acutely uncomfortable, and was even harder to sit in than to stand in, Phoebe looked unapproachable and bland, almost like a mannequin. People smiled at her, and admired how attractive she was, but Faith was shocked to notice that no one spoke to her. It was up to Doug to include her and bring her into the fold. He set the example, and made no effort to share the spotlight with her.

Faith wasn't surprised, but she was sad for her. The wedding was everything she had feared it might be. Like everything else, it was all about him. Faith noticed that Phoebe wasn't eating, and saw her eyes fill with tears a few times. She was thinking about her mother and sister, and wished that she could have shared it with them, or gotten married in less formal surroundings with her old friends, but Doug would have hated that. Most of the wedding guests were physicians he was associated with in some way or wanted to impress. It looked like a medical convention when she saw how many had "Doctor" in front of their names, in some cases both husband and wife. Faith wondered how many of them were really his friends. But it was a beautifully done event in an impressive location, and they were all happy to be there.

Doug had the first dance with Phoebe, which was an important moment at every wedding, large or small, as people gathered around to watch and admire them, and wish them well. Doug had chosen a formal and elegant waltz, and had taught her the steps. He glided her smoothly around the room with measured grace, and moved just a little too fast for her, which made her look as awkward and uncertain as she felt.

They were going to Bali and Vietnam for their honeymoon for two weeks, which Doug said he had always wanted to do, and they'd have a week on the beach to relax, and then he was going to a medical convention in Beijing and Phoebe was flying home alone. Faith knew she was stopping to see her mother in San Diego on the way back since he'd be gone anyway. She was looking forward to that as much as the rest.

All Faith hoped for her was that somehow it would turn out all right, that he'd be kind to her, and eventually soften some of his rigidity and open his heart to his new wife. She didn't think it was likely, but maybe he could learn, and the kindness Phoebe brought to his life would soften him.

Now that Phoebe had done it, Faith hoped it would go well for her. She was a lovely girl and deserved a loving man to appreciate her. It was hard to imagine Doug in that role. But maybe they'd all be surprised. In that case, Faith most of all. She couldn't remember a bride she had been as concerned and worried about in all the years she'd been doing weddings, or a union she'd been as hesitant about.

The wedding looked and went exactly as Doug had wanted it to. It wasn't a warm event, but it was a pretty one. He had wanted to impress the assembled company, and he had. Faith overheard snatches of conversations of people saying what a wonderful time they'd had. No one mentioned the bride. It was the exact opposite of many of the weddings she did, where the bride got all the attention, and the groom little or none. Before the minister had discreetly disappeared, he had asked Faith to sign the marriage certificate as a witness. Doug's associate was the other one. She felt almost guilty signing it. It should have been a family member or a friend.

Most of the guests stayed until the very end. Phoebe tossed her bouquet from a balcony before they left, and an older woman caught it and seemed delighted. Then Doug and Phoebe departed in a shower of rose petals and rice outside the club. They climbed into a chauffeur-driven Rolls Doug had hired, and they looked very glamorous as they drove away. The handsome doctor and the beautiful blond bride.

Faith saw her sad, serious face through the window, and went back inside to monitor the end of the reception with a heavy heart. The outcome seemed predictable. She hoped that she was wrong.

On Monday morning, Faith was at her desk signing off on the final bills for the Kirk wedding. It had come in at almost exactly the price she had quoted him. Everyone had stuck to their estimates, which was the beauty of using suppliers she knew well. She could count on them to do what they said, on time, and charge what they said they would. They never let her down, which was why her business ran so well, and her weddings smoothly. She didn't use fly-by-night companies who might cheat her, or fail to show up.

She had just finished signing the last check when Miriam Albert called her, and she took the call immediately. She figured it was the call she'd been dreading, telling her the wedding was off. She had to know now, it couldn't be avoided. It was three weeks away.

She kept the tone light when she answered. And she expected to hear tears at the other end.

Miriam got right to the point. "The wedding's back on." It had never been officially off, although Miriam had threatened many times to cancel it, instead of enduring the public humiliation of giving a wedding with a husband who was cheating on her and living with another woman. "He moved out of the apartment, and he wants to come home." She sounded breathless. "The little whore left for Italy yesterday. My private eye confirmed it, and if he comes back to me, I'll kill him if he goes near her again. He says he wants to come home, and make it work with us again." Faith had a feeling that the amount of money Miriam intended to take from him had more to do with his renewed devotion than his passion for his wife. But whatever worked for them. She was happy for them if they could share a wedding rather than a divorce. The recently inflicted wounds needed healing, which would take time, but Miriam sounded happier and seemed to believe that his intentions were sincere. Faith knew that Annabelle would be relieved if her parents got back together.

"I'm really happy to hear it," Faith said to her, "not just for the wedding, but I know how traumatic this has been for you and Annabelle." The added bonus was that it had given Miriam a chance to get to know her new son-in-law and discover that he was a good guy, even if untraditional, and she liked him, which was a good thing since he was going to be the father of her new grandson, which made Jeremy a person who would be in their lives forever. He really would be a member of the family now. Even if he and Annabelle got divorced later, he would still be in their lives as the father of her son.

"Jack swears he'll never do this again," Miriam said, sounding hopeful. "He'd better not, I'm going to check up on him. I'll never trust him again." It seemed a sad way to live to Faith, but given what had happened, and his invitation to her, Miriam's lack of faith in him seemed justified. He was not a man who could be trusted around women, and apparently never had been. "I want the wedding to be gorgeous. Spend whatever you want to, it should cost him. We've all been sitting on the edge of our seats, waiting to see what would happen and if we'd have to cancel."

"So were we. I was hoping you could work it out, for your sake and Annabelle's. She's been very worried."

"I know she has, and that's not good for her or the baby." Her sudden concern for Annabelle's unborn child was new too, and also an offshoot of her breakup with Jack. "I guess we just have to live with it. Jeremy's a good boy. He wants to find a real job now, and he's been very sweet to me and my daughter. They deserve to have a nice wedding in spite of her father's bad behavior. Why should she suffer for it, and be deprived?" And then she thought of something. "How bad is the new dress she's having made?"

"It's spectacular. She looks like a princess in it. I actually like it better than the last one, and it's so voluminous you really don't see anything of . . . er . . . her condition."

Miriam laughed then for the first time. "Her 'condition' is enormous. She looks like she's having triplets. I looked like that when I was pregnant too. Some women just gain a lot of weight. You lose it later," although Miriam had never lost it all, and Annabelle might not either. She'd had about ten spare pounds on board when she got engaged. And she'd added to it considerably with the baby, and was gaining rapidly, but the new dress concealed it.

"The important thing is that you and Jack are okay. That's great news," Faith said diplomatically, and she meant it. It was better for everyone if the family stayed together. The fallout and damage from a divorce would have been greater than anything else. With Jack back in the fold, it somehow made Annabelle's pregnancy just what it was, an unexpected early pregnancy and not a tragedy. Added to her parents' divorce, it would have been a catastrophic family situation. Now they were just dealing with a premature pregnancy. Lots of people had them, and with the distraction of a fabulous wedding, people would lose interest in it rapidly. A scandalous divorce over an ex-stripper would have held their attention a lot longer.

"Do we need to reconfirm everything?" Miriam asked her, ready to write more checks if she had to, on her husband's bank account.

"We're fine the way things are. I didn't cancel anything because I didn't know if you were going to cancel or not."

For a while it looked like a sure thing that they would, but Miriam had never confirmed it. She was waiting to see what Jack did about his girlfriend. She sounded willing to give it another try now, if he had really left the girlfriend, and wasn't going to meet her somewhere after the wedding. If he did, he'd pay a heavy price for it, and he must have known it. Faith was sure he had had to pay the girl something too. She wondered if she got to keep the apartment to live in after her trip to Italy, and if not, he would have compensated her for that too. So everyone had come out ahead for the moment. Miriam was getting Jack back, he had avoided a very costly divorce, and Annabelle was getting her million-dollar wedding. And whatever the stripper got, it was between her and Jack, and Faith was sure it had been generous.

"So it's full steam ahead. Fasten your seatbelt, here we go, Faith. And I have to get my dress altered. I lost twelve pounds with all this mess going on. The dress I bought is too big now."

"Well, that's always a welcome bonus," Faith said cheerfully, and thanked Miriam for letting her know.

In truth, she had let a few things slide that she should have confirmed by then. But no real damage had been done, and she could tighten it all again quickly. It would have been a huge, costly endeavor to cancel, but Faith would have done it if she'd had to. It was great news that she didn't. And it was plainly obvious that many forces had been at work to bring Jack and Miriam back together, many or most of them financial. But Miriam had the upper hand on this one. Jack had no intention of losing more than half his money, and their marriage was a long one. Miriam didn't want to lose her husband. And Annabelle didn't want a wedding given by parents at war with each other. So everything was back on track again.

As soon as she hung up, she walked into Violet's office. She was putting together a proposal folder for two new clients they had seen for December weddings. There was life after the current crop of brides and grooms. And there would always be another wave. It was one of the great advantages of Faith's line of business. There would always be people getting married, and the dramas that went with it. Normally, it was a happy line of business, except for the occasional snafu like this one.

"The Albert wedding is back on," Faith announced to Violet from the doorway. "We're good to go."

"With three weeks left to do it," Violet said, glancing at her calendar. But they had laid the groundwork for it months before. The breakdown of Jack and Miriam's marriage had given all of them a chance to think about what mattered to them. Clearly the wedding did, and that was the only part of it that made the wedding make sense. In the real world, there was nothing sensible about a million-dollar wedding. But they didn't live in the real world. Jack Albert could afford it, and they were all on board now. It was all Faith needed to know to go forward. It was not up to her to judge them, or to comment on what someone else might have done with the money. She had a job to do now, to give them the most fabulous wedding she could, according to their wishes. It was what she did best, and why they had come to her in the first place. Faith only owed them one thing, to give them the biggest, splashiest, most extravagant, most beautiful wedding in the world. She only had three weeks left to do it.

She was working on the security logistics for the Albert wedding when Morgan called her the next day. She had schedules, spreadsheets, and timetables all over her desk, and she was trying to figure out what the cost of their over-time would be.

"She's pregnant!" he screamed into the phone, and for an instant, Faith wasn't sure who it was, and then figured it out. Their surrogate was pregnant. The countdown to fatherhood had begun.

"Congratulations!" she said. "Well done!"

"She's due in March. I can hardly wait. Alex wants to start doing the nursery. I think we should wait to make sure she doesn't lose it," he said, but Faith could hear he was over the moon. They had wanted this for a long time, had gone about it seriously and responsibly, and now it was happening. They had been together for ten years and had been discussing starting a family for the last five. She was happy for them. They were both good people with integrity, solid values, warm hearts, and a stable life. In Faith's opinion, they would be terrific parents.

Chapter 10

The three weeks between the day Miriam Albert told Faith the wedding was definitely on and the Fourth of July, the date of the event, literally flew by. Violet and Faith worked at full speed, confirming, solidifying, double-checking, attending to details, verifying, making site visits to Long Island almost daily. It took three days to set up the main tent for the reception, the catering tent for food prep, another tent for late-night dancing with the second band, the flooring that went into them, the electrical lines, the chandeliers, and the generators that powered it all. Furniture was removed from the house to make more room for guests if they went inside. There were porta-potties, trucks with all the rentals they'd ordered, chairs for the reception and the ceremony. The florist began setting up at five A.M. on Friday.

There were hedges filled with white orchids, paths lined with delicate topiary trees, sculptures made of tightly packed white flowers, and two enormous white horses, well over life-sized, made of white roses. They stood nuzzling each other. And there were white swans on the front lawn made of orchids, which would be the guests' introduction to the wedding.

Five hundred and forty-seven people had accepted, out of six hundred and fifty invited, and Annabelle no longer cared how big the wedding was. The one guest she wanted present, and to give her away, was her father. He had moved back in the previous weekend, was home early from work every night. He had returned with an amazing diamond bracelet for her mother. Nothing was mentioned about the tornado they'd just lived through. They put it behind them, and the central theme, the only one at the moment, was the wedding.

Jeremy was stunned when he saw what the preparations looked like, first the construction of the tents, then lining them, the addition of air-conditioning, and then the building of the flower sculptures. Each supplier had their own work area and huge staff. There were easily a hundred people on the property creating and installing. There were trucks lining the road, and they had obtained permits to allow them to do so. All of it had been orchestrated and was being chore-ographed by Faith and Violet. Violet was manning the phones, and Faith was the on-site producer, driving everyone hard, and exacting perfection from them.

Jack and Miriam were amazed by how well Faith did her job, it was why they had come to her for Annabelle's wedding. Although it was fully visible by then, and obvious what it was, the subject of her pregnancy never even came up. It had been entirely eclipsed by her father's affair. There would be plenty of time to celebrate the baby later. For now, it was all about Annabelle and Jeremy. Faith was trying to focus on the bride.

She came out to the front lawn to admire the orchid swans with Faith when they were finished.

"They're exquisite," she said gratefully, and Faith smiled. They had been her idea, in lieu of the ice sculptures she had done at another wedding.

"I'm happy you like them. The florist thought I was crazy. Now he wants to copy them to use again."

"They're fantastic," Annabelle said. The dress had been delivered. She had tried it on and it fit perfectly. It fell from her bare shoulders in rich panels of heavy French silk faille, with a long train behind her, and the delicate veil floating over it. No one was going to care if she was pregnant, and there were lots of other things to look at. The two giant white horses made of roses were the most beautiful things any of them had ever seen. They looked like they were made of snow, and their pose, nuzzling each other, was unusual and romantic. They looked almost real, despite their size.

When the tables were set and the cloths were on them, Violet set down the place cards and table numbers. There were escort cards and charts in various places so people could find their seats with the help of a map on the board. All of that had been calligraphied. Every detail had been thought of and attended to in the most creative way.

Annabelle checked out what they were doing, as it all began to take shape. It was going to be the wedding of the century, and Faith had used her father's generous budget well.

There was a rehearsal dinner that night, given by Jeremy's parents, who were wealthy too, but less willing to go overboard, and they refused to give a dinner for nearly six hundred people, which seemed excessive to them. They limited it to family and people who came from a great distance, and had dinner for a hundred guests at a small exclusive hotel. They appeared to be nice people who lived well, but not on the grand scale of the Alberts. They loved their son and liked Annabelle, and were visibly overwhelmed by the scale and lavish ostentation of the wedding. And Jeremy's mother admitted in a moment alone with Faith that they had been upset at first by the unexpected pregnancy, but had made their peace with it. It was a relaxed, fun event that all the young people enjoyed.

The Wedding Planner

It ended early, as rehearsal dinners were meant to, according to Faith's etiquette book, and there was no dancing. Jeremy stayed at his parents' house that night, so he wouldn't see Annabelle the next day before the wedding.

On the day of the wedding, a fleet of hairdressers, makeup artists, and manicurists arrived to do Miriam's and Annabelle's hair and makeup, and the bridesmaids' and her sister Eloise's, who was her matron of honor. They were bowled over by the preparations they saw going on outside. They spent the afternoon getting ready, and Annabelle and her mother had a tearful moment when she put on the dress. She looked breathtaking in it. Faith and Violet were there to help them. Faith was wearing her navy "uniform" as she called it, and looked sober and appropriate. Her hair was pulled tight in a low bun on her neck, as she wore it most of the time. She looked beautiful because she was, but remained as neutral as possible so as not to draw attention away from anyone in the wedding party. Annabelle's dozen bridesmaids looked well-coiffed, were carefully made up, and were wearing matching taupe-colored organza gowns, which were simple and very chic. Jack had paid for those as well, as part of the budget. Her sister's was a slightly darker shade. Faith had helped pick them as well, in a color that everyone could wear, and their satin Manolo Blahnik shoes were dyed to match, with cognac-colored rhinestone buckles. All the bridesmaids looked very elegant.

The guests were invited for seven o'clock, with the wedding due to start at seven-thirty. No alcohol was served before the ceremony, according to tradition. Cocktails would be served on the vast front lawn, with dinner sometime between nine-thirty and ten, with the dance band starting to play at the same time. Jeremy and Annabelle had picked their favorite songs.

All five hundred guests had been seated by seven twenty-five. Annabelle needed a few more minutes to compose herself. She had borrowed her mother's pearl and diamond earrings, she was wearing a blue satin garter under her dress, and Faith handed her a penny to put in her shoe for good luck. She carried one at every wedding to give to the bride, since everyone forgot that part of the rhyme, "and a sixpence in her shoe." She had given one to Phoebe too, and to her mother when she married Jean-Pierre. Her mother had been amused by the detail, and put it in her Chanel pump for good luck.

The bridesmaids headed down the aisle, which was a long white satin runner that led all the way into the tent set up for the ceremony. It was precisely seven forty-five as Annabelle came down the aisle on her father's arm, looking elegant and magnificent. She was smiling shyly as Jeremy caught sight of her, coming through the white curtains of the tent. She was a beautiful vision, and Jack had tears in his eyes as he handed her over to Jeremy, lifted her veil, and patted his son-in-law's arm. Miriam was crying as he took his seat beside her, and dabbing at her eyes with a lace handkerchief. She looked beautiful too in her emerald green satin gown. Her new diamond bracelet was on her arm, with emeralds on her ears. To look at the Alberts, no one would have suspected the recent trauma they'd been through. Somehow, Miriam had managed to save their marriage and her dignity, in spite of everything that had happened, and Faith respected her for that. There was more to her than just flashy clothes and big diamonds. There was a strong woman with a heart and guts, determined to hang on to her husband.

The ceremony went flawlessly, performed by a minister they knew, and Annabelle had chosen the same vow that Faith's mother had when she married Jean-Pierre, and it had special meaning when Annabelle said it, with their unborn child as an additional bond between them.

". . . With my body, I thee worship . . ." Jeremy repeated the same words after her in a voice quavering with emotion. The ceremony was very touching. They hurried down the aisle together, as their friends cheered them, after they became husband and wife, and Jeremy kissed her on the lawn in front of the two rose horses and told her she was the most beautiful woman in the world.

Faith and Violet exchanged a smile from their positions, with their radios in their ears. After turbulent months leading up to it, the wedding was going well. From then on, it was a jubilant celebration with excellent wines, delicious food, a band that everyone danced to, and a livelier one later in the evening. The wedding cake was a magical creation. There wasn't a single thing that Faith wasn't pleased with, and the Alberts told her several times what an amazing job she'd done.

The photographers from *Vogue* covering it had been very discreet and left early. The one Faith had hired for the Alberts had four assistants and took photographs of everyone all night.

The party went until four A.M., and as she always did, Faith stayed until the bitter end. The breakdown crews were ready to get started when she left. The bride and groom had left around three. Annabelle hated to leave, but she was exhausted. One of her friends caught the bouquet, and her sister had left with one of the groomsmen at around two.

Faith offered to drive back to the city. Violet was exhausted, and ten minutes after they drove out of the Alberts' gates, Violet was sound asleep, and didn't wake up until Faith dropped her off at home.

Faith had that great feeling of peace and well-being she always got with a job well done. It had been one of the most challenging weddings she'd done, and it couldn't have gone better. She had smiled when she saw Jack and Miriam on the dance floor and he kissed her.

The wedding cake had been particularly beautiful, with miniatures of the two white horses on top. She had thought of everything, and Jack and Miriam had thanked her profusely before they left and retired to their room, well after two A.M. It was the young people's turn then. Faith wished that all her weddings could be as successful as this one, despite all the dramas they'd been through, with Annabelle's baby and Jack's infidelity. But she rarely got to work with a budget as large as this one, and she knew she wouldn't again soon.

The fireworks show had been particularly impressive at midnight, and added to the festive atmosphere.

As she got undressed in her quiet house, it was almost six A.M. The sun wasn't up yet, and she could hear birds chirping, already awake, waiting for the dawn. She knew she'd remember the night, and the Alberts, for a long, long time.

She got a small box from the Alberts on Monday. It was sitting on her desk when she got to the office at ten o'clock, and Violet looked mysterious about it. Jack had dropped it off himself on the way to work.

Faith opened it, and a very narrow diamond bracelet sparkled up at her, with a note from Jack and Miriam, "To the best wedding planner in the world. It was fabulous! Love, Jack and Miriam."

She looked at Violet in amazement. No one had ever given her a gift like it before. Violet helped her put it on. It was a delicate fine line of diamonds, a tennis bracelet.

"You earned it," Violet said with deep respect. "I've never seen a wedding like that."

"I had a healthy budget to work with," she said, deeply touched by the generous gift. They were nice people, even if rough diamonds themselves, but she had come to like them in the end, even Jack with his philandering, and roving eye. She had a feeling he wouldn't get away with much from now on.

"It wasn't about the money," Violet said to her. "The flower horses were incredible, and the swans. It all looked so beautiful, and it was fun too. I loved it."

"So did I. And I think Annabelle and Jeremy did too, even though they didn't want a big wedding to begin with. They were good sports about it. I tried not to make it too daunting, and to give the whole thing a very personal feeling, which wasn't easy with nearly six hundred guests."

"It was magical," Violet said, as Faith sat back down, wearing her bracelet. It had been a totally unexpected gesture, but it meant a lot to her.

She was still smiling, and she didn't see Violet go back to her desk, with tears running down her face. She had something to tell Faith, but she didn't want to spoil how happy she was.

* * *

Morgan and Alex called Faith two days after the wedding. They knew that her big Long Island wedding had been that weekend, and they asked her how it was. She described some of it to them, and was proud of the flower horses, but she had to move on from her moment of victory and concentrate on theirs now. It was only six weeks away, and she wanted it to be just as big a success for them. They were focusing on their wedding again, now that they knew their surrogate was pregnant, and they had a long wait ahead of them until March. Two of the embryos hadn't implanted, which was a relief, so they knew they were expecting a single baby, and it was a girl. They had been nervous about having triplets or twins, but their surrogate had been willing to take the risk, when they put three fertilized embryos back in. But they had seen on a sonogram that she was only pregnant with one. Everything they had done was state of the art and very technical, but the specialist they were using had great results, and it had gone well so far.

They invited her to dinner that Friday night, and she accepted with pleasure, and said that she would ask them any new questions she had then. She had an easy week ahead, recovering from the Albert wedding and wrapping that up.

She was looking forward to seeing them.

* * *

She had told Hope all about the Albert wedding and sent her some photos of the décor she'd taken with her cellphone. She decided it was her prettiest wedding so far, even more so than the big wedding she'd done the year before, which was bigger but not as artistic or as personal, and she'd never felt as close to the bride. With the Alberts, she had found herself in the midst of their family dramas, and felt close to them as a result.

Alex and Morgan had told her she could wear jeans to dinner. They were going to eat casually in the garden, and when she arrived, she was surprised to see Morgan's brother, Edward, there. They hadn't told her he was coming, and she wondered if it was a setup, which made her mildly uncomfortable, although she had met him once before.

"I hope you don't mind my intruding on your dinner," he said pleasantly. "I only found out last night I had to come to a meeting in town this morning, so I asked the boys if I could come over and hang out. I'm going back tomorrow, so it was my only chance to see them, and my son is in the Hamptons for the weekend, so I was at loose ends."

"Not at all." She smiled at him. They chatted a little. He said he had found an apartment, not far from her house. He liked it, and it was convenient to his office. He liked to start his day by walking to work before being chained to his desk all day. Morgan said he was an avid tennis player and had won championships in his youth.

"Thanks for the warning." Faith smiled broadly. "I can hardly hit the ball. Sports were never my strong suit. I was the student, my twin was the athletic one. She still is."

He found it fascinating that she was a twin, even though they weren't identical. She said she loved it. Over dinner she showed them some of her photos of the Albert wedding, and all three of them were impressed.

"You're a creative genius if you designed that décor," Edward said admiringly. "Those horses are unbelievable, they look real."

"My florist is an artist. All the credit goes to him," she said modestly. "I just had the idea. He brought it to life. Everyone loved it." She showed him the swans too.

"I wish we could have something like that, but there's no room in the house we're borrowing, even with a ballroom."

"Your wedding will be just as special, and it will represent the two of you," she told them. And it would be more classically elegant and less theatrical, which suited them.

They talked about a variety of subjects over dinner, and it was relaxed and pleasant in the candlelit garden. They had pasta and salad for dinner, and cold chicken. It was a perfect simple meal for a hot night. When they got to dessert, Alex gave a big sigh and said they were wrestling with a difficult decision. Faith was worried that something bad had happened with the surrogate.

"We weren't sure which route to take, adoption or surrogacy," Alex explained, "so we decided to sign up for both, and take whichever option came to completion fastest. We both liked the idea of a baby via surrogacy being genetically ours, or one of ours. But we were equally open to adopting a baby we're not biologically related to. The adoption process took longer and neither of us wanted to wait three or four years for the right one. We've been ready for a while. We found a wonderful surrogate, so we went with her."

"Did something happen?" Faith asked, looking concerned. She thought maybe she had lost the baby, or maybe they discovered something bad about the surrogate, that she did drugs or had some other risky behavior, or was going to oppose them legally, now that she was pregnant with their daughter. And they were already attached to the idea of their baby girl.

"Yes, something did happen," Morgan answered. He hadn't had a chance to tell his brother yet. "We got a call last night from a private adoption agency we used in Florida. They have a baby who sounds perfect for us. A boy. The mother is a young girl from a responsible family. She's a freshman in college, same boyfriend since she was sixteen, nice parents, everyone is respectable and college educated, her father is a doctor. She got pregnant, and I never understand how that happens, but she didn't figure out that she was pregnant until she was five months along. She's athletic and naïve, and was in denial.

"She said she wanted to keep it, but now she and the boyfriend broke up and she realizes she can't do this on her own. He met another girl at the college he's attending, so it's over with them. They're kids. It sounds like they both have a lot of growing up to do before they have children. They're babies themselves. She and her parents have decided that the best thing for the child, and the mother, is to give the baby up to people who can give the child a good life, and the baby's father agrees.

"Florida is one of the better states to adopt from. It's simple and relatively fast. There's no revocation period in Florida. The consent for adoption is permanent and irrevocable from the moment it's signed. The agency has two other couples who are interested, but it's the wrong time for both of them. It is for us too. We already have a baby on the way, and we didn't want two at once, like twins, although we would have accepted it if it happened, but we were relieved it didn't. This baby is due in two weeks, and she could have it any day. They need to know right away. They'd like to set the wheels in motion for an adoption before she gives birth. The sensible thing is to say no, but we don't know what to do." They both looked very serious, and it was obvious that they were wrestling with the decision. "Something about this baby feels right to both of us. But they'd be eight months apart. We want a second baby, but not right away. This would be instant family for us immediately, and we're not even set up for a baby yet." They looked at each other.

"We'd be parents in two weeks. We wanted some more time for us. We've planned everything so carefully. It just seems so fast, and so soon. March gives us time to be organized about it. Can you even get ready for a baby in two weeks? We've already passed our home study, so we're preapproved. In Florida, the mother can sign the consent for adoption forty-eight hours after the baby is born. We'd have to wait about two weeks for the paperwork to clear in an interstate adoption, and then we can bring the baby home. And three months later, the adoption is final. And with no revocation period in Florida, the birth mother can't change her mind, which is a scenario we've always been afraid of with an adoption. We spoke to her father and he says she's made up her mind that it's the right thing for the child to give it up.

"It makes me feel like we're stealing someone's baby. She wants to know where it is, in the future, so they can meet one day, a long time from now, but she wants no contact, which is also a clean situation for us. I don't want to adopt the mother too."

"Sounds like real life to me," Edward said with a wry smile. "Real life happens to you when you're making other plans.

Morgan knows what happened to me. I was in college, kind of like this girl. Nineteen years old, and my girlfriend got pregnant. She was so afraid of her parents that she didn't tell anyone, not even me. Fast-forward, we got married, and we had Wesley when I was twenty. His mother was a sweet girl but we had nothing in common except him. The marriage lasted two years. We parted ways when we graduated, and got divorced. And it wasn't a happy two years. Children are better off being raised by grown-ups than children. Wes had a bumpy start. His mother got into drugs after college. She got off them eventually, but it took a while, so he bounced between two sets of grandparents and me. I was in law school then, and I couldn't take care of him. Eventually his mother got custody again, but she's still immature and a little crazy, even now. He and I didn't really get to know each other until he was in his teens. We're close now but it took a long time. I had a lot of growing up to do when he was born. So I think this girl is making the right decision. The question here is what's the right answer for you?

"I shouldn't put my two cents in, but I will. You're going to be terrific parents, whether you start that clock in March or July. You're ready. You're both responsible and mature. You want two kids, but what difference does it make if they're a year apart, or two or eight months? This sounds like kind of an ideal situation that doesn't come along often. Will the baby disrupt your life? Hell, yes!" He smiled. "Constantly, for the next forty or fifty years. Nothing will ever disrupt your life as much as your child, or bring you as much joy. So this one showed up early. If you want my vote, I would say yes, grab this baby boy and run, and in March, the family you want will be complete. Diapers all at one time, and you're done." He laughed and Morgan grinned.

"My brother always has a way of summing things up, and hits all the pertinent points. We kind of feel that way too. We just weren't expecting it. It kind of tosses all our plans into a hat. Do you think we should postpone the wedding and just do it?" he asked them both.

"Why postpone the wedding?" Edward asked him. "You'll have more to celebrate. You're all excited about the wedding. Do it! So you have a baby upstairs. So what? Your children will surprise you both for the rest of your life. This one is just starting early. You have to do what your gut says. No one can give you the answer to this. Talk to each other and follow your hearts." It was good advice. He was a warm, sensible, practical man, and Faith liked him and what he said.

She had waited until then to chime in, not sure what to say. "I've always loved being a twin, if that helps. Eight months apart is a little like that. We're very, very close and I'd be lost without her. She's my best friend."

They both nodded and looked pensive. Edward and Faith both stayed late, and he gave her a ride home in a cab when they left.

"It's hard to know what they should do," she said thoughtfully. "Life is always that way. Everything happens at once. You either have too much or too little."

"Do you have kids?" he asked her, and she shook her head.

"It never felt right for me. Two broken engagements. I never got married. I guess I'm selfish and spoiled and independent. My twin sister is having her fourth and she loves it. I think I like being an aunt better than a mom, it's too much responsibility." He admired her honesty. "My brides are my children, until the wedding, and then they're on their own." She smiled. "They grow up fast."

"It was hard having a child at twenty. He's the only one I have. Sometimes I regret it, and sometimes I don't. It's what you said. I'm spoiled and independent. You have to give up so much to be a good parent. I was nowhere near ready to have a wife and child at twenty. I made a total mess of it. But the boys won't. They're ready. I hope they do it, and adopt this baby."

"So do I," she said, thinking about it. "See you at the wedding, and thank you for the ride." She smiled at him when they got to her address. It had been a nice evening.

"Maybe I'll see you at the christening before that," he said, and they both laughed. They couldn't guess what the boys would do.

He had the cab wait until she got safely into her house, and she thought about Morgan and Alex, and wondered what they would decide. In his new apartment a few blocks away, Edward was thinking about her. He liked how brave and spunky and honest she was, and how creative. The wedding she showed them was spectacular, and the rose horses she had designed were a work of art. He was hoping to get to know her better. She would be nice to have as a friend, and he was glad he'd met her.

Morgan and Alex lay in bed talking for a long time that night, about what to do about the baby they'd been offered.

"Do you feel ready?" Alex asked Morgan, and he thought about it.

"I don't know. Sometimes. Sometimes I think I'll be a really good father, and other times I'm terrified that I'll make a mess of it."

"You won't." Alex smiled at him. "I think all parents feel like that. We're not going to be any more ready in March than we are now," he said. He had a point.

They fell asleep talking about it, and the phone woke them at six A.M. Morgan answered, it was an unfamiliar voice at the other end.

"I'm sorry to wake you. This is Dr. Greenville, in Miami. The agency contacted you about my daughter, Heather Greenville. She's expecting a baby boy. I know you were considering it, and I don't know what you've decided. The agency gave me your number. She's due in two weeks, and she just went into labor. We're at the hospital now. First babies take a while. I wanted to let you know in case you're thinking favorably, if it's important to you to be at the birth. I don't mean it as pressure, I just wanted to give you the chance to be there, if it's meaningful to you." Morgan looked shocked and stared at Alex with wild eyes.

"That's very kind of you, Doctor. Could you hold on for a minute?" Morgan covered the phone with his hand and looked at Alex. "The girl's in labor. The baby's coming. They want to know if we want to be at the birth."

"Now?" Alex looked as though Morgan had thrown a bucket of cold water at him, as he nodded.

"Let's do it," Morgan said, feeling brave. "Are you okay with that?" Alex grinned at him and nodded.

"Yes," he said, and leapt out of bed, while Morgan told Dr. Greenville that they were coming and would be there as fast as they could manage. He told Morgan which hospital, and said he would see him in a while.

Then he added, in an emotional voice, "Thank you, for my daughter's sake, and the baby's. God bless you."

189

There were tears in Morgan's eyes when he responded.

"We have a baby due in March. I think this is what they call Irish twins," he said, laughing through his tears. And they hung up seconds later. Morgan rushed into the bathroom to brush his teeth and throw water on his face. He dashed into his closet to get dressed. He slipped into jeans, a blue oxford shirt, and Gucci loafers. Alex was wearing a T-shirt, jeans too, and grabbed a blazer. Morgan looked at him.

"Why are you so dressed up?"

"I'm going to be a father, I have to look respectable," he said, and Morgan laughed.

"I love you. We're both crazy, you know that, don't you?" Alex grinned and nodded, and three minutes later, they grabbed their wallets and rushed out the door. Alex smoothed his hair down, he had forgotten to comb it. They found a cab and headed for LaGuardia. The driver got them there in twenty minutes for a big tip. They caught a 7:20 flight to Miami that was boarding and grinned at each other when they sat down. Their life together had always been an adventure, and it certainly was now. The wedding they were planning was nothing compared to this. This was BIG.

Morgan grabbed his cellphone and texted his brother and Faith the same thing. "Baby coming. Flying to Miami. Love, Dad and Dad."

Chapter 11

The flight landed at Miami International Airport at 9:50 with no delays. They took a cab to the hospital, and rushed to the information desk when they arrived.

"We have a baby in the maternity ward. Where is it?" Alex said. He had been wound up since they landed. Morgan was feeling calmer.

"Has the baby been delivered?" the woman asked him.

"No, she's in labor. Where is that?"

"If your wife is in labor, she'll be in labor and delivery." She told them where to go and they ran to the elevator.

Alex looked at Morgan after he pressed the button for their floor. "Do I look a mess?" He was wearing the blazer he had grabbed on the way out.

"Yes," Morgan said, "we both do. I didn't comb my hair,

and you spilled coffee on your shirt on the plane. I think we're supposed to look a mess when a baby is coming. It's part of the deal. Guys do it all the time."

"This is so grown up. Are we ready for it?" Alex asked him.

"Yes," Morgan said, sounding certain, which calmed Alex.

"I thought when we got our baby, it would be all neat and organized and we'd bring her home in a little pink outfit in her new car seat. We look like we just got out of jail."

"We can still do that in March. This is different," Morgan said, as they reached their floor and hurried to the nurses' desk. They could actually hear a woman screaming from one of the labor rooms in the distance. It felt like a TV show to both of them.

"We're looking for Dr. Robert Greenville and his daughter, Heather." The nurse at the desk smiled as Morgan gave her their names.

"They're expecting you," she said quietly with a smile. "You're in plenty of time, things are going slowly. She's still in early labor." She took them into a little prep room and handed them surgical pajamas, and pointed to the sink where they could scrub up, and there was a locker for whatever clothes they didn't wear. "I'll let them know you're here."

They started scrubbing at the sink, and then slipped the pajamas over their jeans and shirts. Alex put his blazer in a locker. They put on what looked like shower caps, and paper covers over their shoes, as Alex looked at Morgan in a panic.

"Are we delivering the baby?"

"I hope not," Morgan said with a grin.

"I thought we were just going to see it in the nursery after it's born."

"I'm not sure what the plan is." As Morgan said it, a nice-looking man in his mid-forties and the same surgical gear entered the room, and looked at them both.

"Thank you for coming. I'm Heather's dad." He shook hands with both of them, and Alex felt like an adult again. "She's still in early labor. Her mom is with her now. They're going to give her an epidural, but it's too soon, so she'll have to weather it for a while. She went into labor just before I called you. First babies can take a long time, but the epidural will make it easier. If they give it to her too soon, the labor will stop. Heather is willing to have you in the room if you'd like to be there, as long as you stay behind her head. She's only eighteen. This is rough on her. I'm an obstetrician, but I'm not delivering the baby. I'm just here for moral support, and to make sure the birth is handled well. She's glad you're taking the baby. She wants to know he'll have a good home. The agency spoke very highly of you both."

"He will have a good home," Alex said solemnly, and Morgan nodded. They followed Dr. Greenville from the room and into another room a few doors down. There was a pretty young girl in the bed in a hospital gown. She looked about fourteen years old, and had long blond hair. She looked at Morgan and Alex. She was covered with a sheet and a blanket, and there were monitors that were hooked up and beeping.

"Are they more doctors, Dad? Is something wrong?"

"No. This is Alex and Morgan, the two men we talked about from New York. The baby's dads." There was a lump in his throat as he said it. His wife was sitting next to their daughter in the same garb they were. She was a very pretty woman and looked young. Heather was holding her hand, and winced with a sudden pain. The monitor showed that she was having a contraction. Her father explained what the monitors were, one for the contractions, another for the baby's heartbeat, which he said was steady and strong. The contraction was a big one and she started to cry and asked for the epidural. Her father said it was too soon. A nurse came in and asked everyone to step outside while she checked Heather to see how things were progressing. Her mother stayed with her and the three men stepped into the hall.

"We don't want to intrude if our being there makes it harder for her," Morgan said. This was suddenly all very real, and getting the baby out was going to be difficult.

They planned to be at the surrogate's delivery but didn't know much about the process yet, or what to expect. They were going to take a class in January. But now they were unprepared.

"It was her idea to call you and ask if you wanted to be here when the baby was born," her father told them.

"We don't have to be in the room if she doesn't want us there," Alex added. "Can't they give her something for the pain?" He hated to think of her suffering, and she would go home empty-handed, while they took her child. Suddenly the reality of what all this meant came home to both of them. Their surrogate had a husband and two children of her own, and had been through surrogacy twice. There was a contract. They were paying her. She was twice Heather's age. This was very different, this was a teenager going through childbirth, scared, in pain, and giving up her baby to strangers, two men she'd never met. It seemed very hard to both of them, although they were grateful to be there, and to her for suggesting it. More than ever, they realized now what a big deal this was. It wasn't just a plan or an idea. It was a person, a young girl who had carried this baby for nine months, and maybe loved it and its father, and was now giving the baby to them. The most precious gift she would ever give anyone for the rest of her life. They wanted to make it as easy as they could for her, and they both felt a surge of deep gratitude to her, and love, although they didn't know her.

The nurse came out a few minutes later, and said they were making progress. She was at four, and Robert Greenville explained what that meant to Morgan and Alex. Her cervix was dilated to four centimeters. It had to get to ten before they could deliver the baby and it could come out. The contractions were forcing it to open, and were doing their job.

"She should try to rest between contractions, so she doesn't wear herself out," he told them. The nurse had dimmed the lights in the room, and Heather had her eyes closed, as her mother sat quietly on a chair by her side. The three men were silent as they walked into the room. Morgan and Alex took their place in the corner behind her bed in two chairs a nurse had put there for them, and watched the monitors from afar. Morgan pointed when the one monitoring the contractions suddenly spiked and Heather opened her eyes, and gave a shout of pain. The contraction went on for what seemed like a long time. She had been squeezing her mother's hand, and she whimpered and closed her eyes again. Four minutes later she had another big one, and then they moved to three minutes apart. When they got to two minutes apart, the boys could see on the monitor that the contractions were getting bigger and longer and the nurse came in again, to check her. Her father stayed this time, to hear what the nurse had to say. Alex and Morgan left the room and looked at each other as they stood in the hall.

"That looks horrendous. Why don't they give her something? Poor thing. She's just a kid," Alex said, upset for her. She looked even younger than she was.

"Her father said they can't yet, or it will slow it all down." Morgan had the feeling that they were taking part in some kind of miracle, and all Alex could think of was the agony she was going through and hoped they gave her something soon.

Her father came out a few minutes later and reported that she was six centimeters dilated, and they were going to give her the epidural now. The anesthesiologist was on his way. She wouldn't feel the contractions after that. At ten, she could start pushing, and the baby would be delivered. He made it sound so simple, but it didn't look it to them. They agreed to wait outside until she had the epidural, and they could hear her sobbing when her father went back into the room.

The anesthesiologist arrived five minutes later, and was there for twenty minutes before Dr. Greenville beckoned them back in. They had given her a shot in her spine, to administer a local anesthetic on an ongoing basis for the rest of the delivery, so everything below her waist would be numb now. She smiled at them as they walked back to their corner and said hi. She looked much happier than she had a few minutes before. They could see the contractions on the monitor, but she didn't feel them. She was talking to her mother in a soft voice and said she felt a lot of pressure, like the baby wanted to come out.

The nurse came back and examined her under a drape that covered her completely, and smiled when she told Heather she was at ten, and she could start pushing soon. She went to get the doctor, and he came in and nodded at her father. They knew each other. He checked Heather and took over from there, with the nurse standing next to him, and her father went to stand near his wife.

Heather's mother was standing over her then, smoothing her hair back, as they saw a huge contraction appear on the monitor. They put her feet in stirrups with the drape still covering her. Alex and Morgan couldn't see anything except the faces of the people in the room, as the doctor told Heather to push. He asked the nurse to apply pressure with the next contraction and her mother to support her shoulders while she pushed. The contractions were a minute apart, and she had to push every time. They could see that she was exhausted and the nurse put an oxygen mask on her face, and with each contraction, the nurse, the doctor, and her parents shouted at her to push. She did and nothing happened, and the nurse was applying pressure to bring the baby down. The doctor was keeping a close eye on her and her father looked worried.

It felt like they had been there for an eternity, but it was only an hour. She wasn't in pain but she was exhausted and she kept saying she couldn't push anymore. The two doctors exchanged a look, as Morgan and Alex wondered what it meant, and then the doctor spoke kindly to Heather.

"You've got to help us here, Heather. I want you to push as hard as you can. I don't want to do a C-section on you for your first baby. I know you can get this baby out yourself." She nodded, and pushed even harder with the next contractions, and the nurse nodded. The baby was moving down. They were getting results. Heather looked as though she'd been run over by a train, and Morgan was clutching Alex's hand. Neither of them was making a sound, as they stood in the corner of the room, well behind Heather's bed. After another half hour of pushing, the doctor told Heather she was almost there. The baby was almost out, just a few more big pushes and then it would be all over. She managed a superhuman effort, as Alex and Morgan wondered if the baby would ever come out, and all of a sudden, things speeded up. The nurse pushed the drape back slightly so the doctor could see better. With one more monumental push, he said he could see the baby's head. There wasn't a sound in the room, as she pushed again, and the baby slipped out and gave a wail. He had a strong, lusty cry, and Heather's head dropped back on the pillow. They put something for the pain in her IV as soon as the baby was born, and the doctor smiled at the two men in the corner.

"Would you like to cut the cord?" he asked them, and they shook their heads. They were both crying. He was such a big, beautiful boy, and his mother had worked so hard to bring him into the world and give him to them. Their son was a miraculous gift.

The doctor cut the cord, and the nurse gently asked Heather if she wanted to hold him, and she shook her head. She was already groggy from what they'd given her, and she said she didn't. The pediatrician came into the room with a nurse, and she was weighing him.

"Nine pounds, four ounces," she announced, and everyone looked amazed. Heather was dozing from the medication by then, as the nurse finished her job at that end, and then the doctor stitched Heather up. She had torn slightly from the birth, which was no surprise with a baby that size. She was asleep while they stitched her, her parents were conferring quietly. It was an emotional moment for them too, their first grandchild whom they would never see again. Robert was gently rubbing his wife's back. She had been standing next to Heather the entire time. Then the pediatrician asked the two new fathers if they would like to hold their son. Everyone in the room had been briefed on the delicate situation, and had handled it with humanity and compassion for all concerned.

Alex was the first to step forward and hold out his arms, as a nurse handed him their baby, their firstborn. They both realized at that moment that it didn't matter who they were born from, or how they were born, just being there was a gift, and loving the baby boy in the blanket was immediate. They had cleaned him up, and Alex kissed him and gently handed him to Morgan, who held the baby close and looked at him in wonder. They were so happy they had been there and that Heather had allowed them to share this sacred time, which were her first and last moments with the child, who was her son as well. Alex and Morgan would have a lifetime with him, Heather only hours, and she had shared that time with them. Neither of them could imagine a more generous gift.

A nurse led them to the nursery, pushing the baby in a see-through plastic bassinette. They left Heather with her parents. She was going to be taken to the recovery room soon, and would sleep for several hours with what they'd given her.

They took turns sitting in a rocking chair in the nursery holding him, and looking at each other in wonder. With a split-second decision fourteen hours before, this little person was going to be in their life forever, when two days before they didn't even know he existed. It felt like a blessing that had fallen from the sky into their hands.

Robert Greenville came by to see them and the baby and thanked them again.

"How's Heather?" they both asked him simultaneously.

"She's asleep. It was kind of a rough delivery. He's a very big baby, and very beautiful. Someone from the agency will come out to have Heather sign the papers tomorrow, if they discharge her then. Or the day after. You can take him to a hotel with you while you wait for the interstate papers to clear. The pediatrician will let you know when he can fly, but he'll be able to fly by then. The father already relinquished his rights a month ago. He's a good boy. We know him well, and his family. They dated all through high school. The situation just got away from them. She didn't know she was pregnant until too late. They're both kids themselves. It was their decision to give him up for adoption. We think it's the right one."

"What about Heather?" they asked him. "How does she want to handle it now?" They wanted to do what was best for her.

"She said she doesn't want to see him. But her mother and I think she should say goodbye. She's going to have a rough time for a while. This is a hard route to go, but it will be the best one for the child, and in the long run for her too. She's not ready to take this on, neither is the baby's father." The two new fathers nodded, but felt terrible for her anyway.

This was so much to give up, a whole human being that was her flesh and blood. And once she signed the papers, it was irrevocable. Now they understood better all that that meant. "You've both been wonderful," her father said to them.

"So have you and your wife and Heather. I'm sorry it was so hard for her. She was very brave."

"Yes, she was," he agreed. He looked sad, and Morgan and Alex couldn't blame him. It was a happy day for them, and a sad one for him and his family. It seemed like one of the crueler moments in life, and a high price for Heather to pay for a youthful mistake.

Alex and Morgan left the hospital in a daze, and went to check in at a hotel. They checked in to one where they had stayed before when they had come to Miami for a weekend. It wasn't really their kind of city, but they'd had fun. There was lots of music, partying, dancing, a party atmosphere everywhere. The hotel where they stayed was a little more sedate.

Alex looked at Morgan and laughed. "Do you realize we have no clothes?" Morgan thought about it and nodded. They had left New York with what they were wearing, and not even a toothbrush.

"That's actually true." They went to the gift shop at the hotel and bought shorts, a bathing suit for each of them, and T-shirts with the hotel name on it, and toothbrushes, toothpaste, razors, whatever they needed, and went upstairs to their room.

"I feel like I'm in some kind of dream," Alex said. "All that suffering and that beautiful baby, and suddenly I'm a dad, we both are. We've been talking about it for years and now here we are, and we're going to go back to New York in a couple of weeks with a baby someone is just giving us. We don't even have a bed to put him in. We'll have to get all kinds of stuff. I don't even know what we need."

"I do," Morgan said. "Let's order room service. We need to eat." They hadn't eaten all day since the snacks on the airplane. They hadn't wanted to leave the room and miss it if the baby came. They ordered cheeseburgers and champagne, and sat at the table grinning at each other. They hadn't checked their phones all day either. Morgan had a text from Faith, and one from his brother. His brother had written "WTF? Good luck!" and Faith had said "NEWS?" He called her first and told her all about the six A.M. call and the baby, and that he weighed nine pounds, four ounces, and his mother was a sweet girl, and her parents were lovely. Alex got on the phone and she congratulated him too. And then Morgan got back on with her.

"I need you to do us an enormous favor. We have nothing for the baby. Zero. Can you please go to a baby store and buy us whatever we need, undershirts, bottles, diapers, carrier, stroller? I'll pay you back when I get home, and some kind of basket he can sleep in."

"That'll be fun. I'll get a list from my sister, Hope. I'm not too up on baby supplies either," she said, and they both laughed. "When are you coming back?"

"We have to ask the agency. They're going to rush the paperwork, but for an interstate adoption, it takes about two weeks. The birth mother signs the papers when she leaves the hospital. When the interstate papers clear, we can bring him home. And ninety days later, the adoption is final. She's very young. She doesn't want to see him."

"That's so sad. But I'm happy for both of you. This was meant to be. I'll get everything you need."

He thanked her and called his brother next. Edward was back in Chicago by then.

"I'm so glad you decided to step up to the plate," he said. "It felt right to me too." Morgan told him how it had happened with the call from Heather's father at six A.M., all the way to the baby being born, and now they had a son. "You're an uncle."

"It's about time. I like your friend, by the way. A lot. Faith, she's a remarkable woman."

"Yes, she is. You'll see her at our wedding," Morgan reminded him.

"Maybe I'll see her before that. I might not want to wait a month to see her. She's a lovely person."

"I just asked her to buy all the baby equipment we need. I thought I had eight months to get ready. Not two weeks." And they had to buy what they needed for their stay in Miami too.

"Do you know what you want to call him? Does he have a name?" Edward asked him.

"We haven't gotten there yet. Alex and I are still in shock."

"Well, congratulations, baby brother, to both of you. You're going to be a great dad. Better than I was at twenty."

"Wesley loves you, and you're a great dad to him now," Morgan reminded him.

"I came to it a little late. I think we made up for it. But both of you are ready. I can't wait to meet the baby the next time I'm in town."

"He'll be at the wedding too," Morgan said with a grin. "We weren't planning on that either."

"One thing I know," his brother said to him, "is that life is a surprise. That's the best part of it. Enjoy it."

"I am," Morgan said. They hung up a minute later. Clearly, his older brother was right. He had never been happier in his life.

Heather looked worse the day after the birth than she had the day of. She had dark circles under her eyes, and she looked like she'd been crying. She was sore from the birth, and in pain. They were giving her pain medicine, and for most women the excitement over the baby balanced the discomfort afterward. Heather had nothing to compensate her for the agony she'd been through. No reward. Just pain, and loss of the worst kind. She was giving up her child, and the future she could have shared with him. But she knew that keeping him was the wrong decision. It was the greatest sacrifice of her brief motherhood to give him up, because it was best for him.

Alex and Morgan met with the people from the adoption agency on Sunday morning. There were legal documents to sign for the interstate adoption that had to be sent to the appropriate agency in New York. Heather was signing her baby away to them, but the interstate adoption had to be cleared in both states. She could still change her mind now before she signed. She was young, and bruised and battered, physically and emotionally. Even at her age, she had the right to keep her baby and care for him herself if she wanted to. Her parents seemed like kind people, and were supportive of her. Morgan had the feeling that they would help her if she decided to keep the baby. Alex and Morgan didn't want to steal the baby from her. They wanted to reach out for him if she wanted to give him up, but not otherwise.

She was still refusing to see the baby, but she could hold him and see him if she wanted to. It was entirely up to her.

After seeing the adoption agency people, Alex and Morgan spent an hour in the hospital nursery holding him. Then they saw the pediatrician, who said that they could take him home by the time the paperwork cleared. He was a healthy, normal infant, and it was a short flight to New York, and he'd be two weeks old by then.

After they saw the pediatrician, they took a cab to a mall, and bought everything they needed at the hotel and to bring him home. Little pajamas, undershirts, diapers, bottles. There was a long layette list at the store. They needed a car seat for him to leave the hospital, and they bought a stroller to put the car seat in. All of it was foldable, practical, multipurpose, and had no fewer than five or six functions. Morgan couldn't figure it out, but Alex was good at it.

"You have to be an engineer to work this stuff," Morgan complained, collapsing the stroller when he wanted it to stand up, or battling to open it after he had put it in travel mode, and it locked.

"It's not that difficult." Alex laughed at him.

"He'll be in college by the time I can do this," Morgan said, frustrated. "Why can't we get one of those gorgeous giant English prams like the queen of England used for her children?"

"It's not practical. You have to be modern." Alex grinned at him.

"This 'modern' stuff is ugly on top of being impossible to figure out. The damn thing has a drink holder, and I can't see where to put it." They had bought a suitcase to put all the spare parts, equipment, supplies, and clothes in, and Faith had texted them that she had bought everything they needed in New York, from a list her sister provided. They were all set. They had enough for ten babies when they got back to the hotel, with more waiting in New York.

Morgan wrote a letter to Heather that night, telling her what it had meant to them to be at the birth, and to be the parents of her baby now. He promised her that they would keep him safe and love him forever. Alex added a few words too. The emotions he felt were so huge, he found it hard to fit them into words. Morgan was better at that than he was. They complemented each other and always had.

"Do you suppose he'll hate not having a mother?" Alex asked him as they lay in bed that night, watching TV.

"He'll have both of us. That will balance it out somehow. And he'll have a sister. That will add a feminine side to his life too. What are we going to name him?" They'd been thinking about it all day and nothing seemed right so far. They needed it for his birth certificate when they left the hospital the next day. They didn't want to leave it just as "baby boy," they were combining their last names, which would be Phillips-Bates. They couldn't decide what went with it, since his last name would be a mouthful.

"What about Blake?" Morgan suggested, as they switched to another show on TV. Alex thought about it and nodded.

"I like that. It's nice." They'd been talking about girls' names recently and had nothing for a boy. "What about Blake Andrew, as a middle name? It kind of goes together. Blake Andrew Phillips-Bates." It was a big name for a little boy.

They went back to the hospital the next morning, to be there when the pediatrician checked the baby again, and he declared him healthy and fit to leave the hospital. The nurse handed Morgan a folder with the list of vaccinations he needed when they went to see the pediatrician in New York. They suggested that the next visit be in two weeks, when they got home, unless they had a problem before that. There were feeding and bathing instructions. They were given formula to take home. They had brought a car seat with them, to take him back to the hotel safely in a cab. They had brought little blue cotton pajamas with them, and a blue blanket, and a little pale blue cotton cap to keep his head warm. They showed the nurse everything they'd brought and she approved with a smile. She had showed them how to hold, feed, and change the baby.

Then they saw Heather's parents at the nursery window, and Morgan and Alex went out to meet them.

"Would you like to see him?" Alex offered. "He just got checked out to go home." Heather's mother nodded and they both looked sad. They went back to the nursery together, and she sat down in the rocking chair to hold him. He was all dressed and swaddled in the blanket. She looked at him as though drinking his face in to remember him forever.

"Could we take a picture?" Robert asked them, and Morgan replied immediately.

"Of course. What about Heather?" Morgan asked gently. "How is she?"

"Rough. And the hormones after the birth don't help." Her milk hadn't come in yet, and would take another day or so, and that would be hard for her too. She had not chosen an easy path. But she was determined to stay on it.

Her mother, Betty, went to ask her again if she wanted to see him before they left. Heather was checking out of the hospital that morning too, and was going to sign the papers before she did. If she stuck to her plan, she would never see her son again, except maybe when he was a man, if he wanted to meet her, to better understand why she had given him up. It would all make more sense then, if she'd lived her life well, and had other children. Right now, all there was, was an empty space where her baby and her heart had

211

been for nine months. She didn't even have his father to share it with, and console her for what they couldn't do. They had split up when he left for college, and he was in love with someone else. She had texted him that the baby had been born, and they both cried when he called her, but agreed that they were doing the right thing.

Heather had her parents. It was a lot, but not enough at a time like this. This was an adult moment like no other, and she was trying to be equal to the task. It was a hard way to grow up, with a decision that would impact her life forever.

When Betty came back, Heather was with her, much to everyone's surprise. Alex and Morgan were terrified that if she saw Blake, or held him, she would never give him up, and not sign the papers, but they knew they had to give her that chance. They couldn't steal him from her. The papers were waiting in her hospital room for her to sign.

"I'd like to see him," she said softly. "I don't want to hold him. I just want to see his face one time." Alex had given her father the letter they'd written to her. Her parents had been extremely decent about everything, compassionate and kind.

"We took pictures for you," her mother said softly.

Alex and Morgan stood back as a nurse held him, and Heather looked long and hard at him. Her eyes filled with tears that poured down her cheeks, and both men and

Heather's mother were crying. Her father was more composed, but his lips were trembling as he watched his daughter's grief.

"Be a good boy," Heather said to him in a whisper. "Have a happy life. I'll always remember you . . . please try to remember me a little," she said, gently touched his cheek with a fingertip, and walked out of the nursery with her head down, and tears pouring down her cheeks, with her parents walking behind her, as Alex and Morgan watched her go, crying too. Alex put an arm around Morgan and hugged him. They stood there for a few minutes until they calmed down, feeling Heather's pain with her, while Blake slept innocently in the nurse's arms. Heather's father came back ten minutes later with their copy of the relinquishment paper. The representative of the agency was there too to handle the paperwork from then on. Robert, Alex, and Morgan shook hands and then hugged. And then Robert went back to his daughter, and they took their son.

They gathered up all the things they had for him, and went downstairs with the nurse to the van and driver they'd hired and took him back to the hotel to settle him. They sat watching him for the rest of the day, like the miracle he was. Their two days in Miami so far had been the most emotional of their lives.

In the next two weeks, while they waited for the papers to clear, they learned his needs, how to feed him and change him and bathe him once the cord had healed. They slept when he did. When the papers came through, they left for the airport and were both carrying diaper bags, with formula and paper diapers in them, and several changes of his tiny blue pajamas and extra blankets for the plane. He slept through all of it, and woke once for a feeding, which Morgan managed masterfully. Alex changed his diaper. They smiled at each other, over the baby, and then strapped him back into his car seat in the seat between them. They were traveling first class in three seats. The adventure was just beginning for all three of them. And Blake Andrew Phillips-Bates was on his way home, with both his dads.

Chapter 12

When Alex and Morgan got home, Faith had brought over all the clothes and equipment she had bought for them. They put it all in the guest room they were going to turn into a nursery, sooner than expected. They had another one destined to be their daughter's room in March. They put the baby in a little Moses basket in their bedroom, and checked on him every few minutes. They stood looking at him as though they were afraid he'd disappear.

"I feel like a child stealer," Alex admitted to Morgan. "I wonder how Heather is." They had thought of her often in the past two weeks.

"I think her father is right. This is going to be hard for her for a long time." It was the reality of adoption, which is why they had chosen surrogacy first. But at least they didn't have the worry of her changing her mind. The adoption would be final ninety days from the time they got home. They'd heard horror stories of mothers who changed their minds, and took their babies back. They already loved Blake. And Heather had recognized that she was too young to mother him adequately. They were in love with him after only two weeks, and had come to know his needs and what his cries meant. They had an appointment at the pediatrician for his two-week checkup the next day.

They had called for the appointment from Miami, and had called an agency for a baby nurse. They agreed that they wanted one for a few months, and it made sense now to keep her for when their baby girl arrived, and then have her for another five or six months after that. Fortunately, they could both afford full-time help, since they both had big jobs. Blake's sudden arrival was going to be a huge change in their life. But Morgan decided that his brother was right. Whether it happened now or in seven months didn't make much difference. They had both taken three weeks off from work for his arrival, and planned to hire the nurse in the next week, and couldn't wait to send out announcements of his arrival once the adoption was final.

For the last week of their unexpected paternity leave, they took Blake out in his stroller between feedings, bought the baby monitor they had forgotten to get in Miami and wasn't on Hope's list. They got one they could check even if they weren't in the house, so they could use it to check on the nanny once they had one. They were suddenly facing all the issues parents did, but had had no time to prepare for any of them. They hired a baby nurse they both liked on their second day home. She cost a fortune, had great credentials, and they agreed she was well worth it.

Faith had called to check on them the night they got home, and was impressed by how calm they were. They were organizing the guest room as a nursery, were going to order baby furniture from a fancy French store, and were interviewing baby nurses the next day. They were making the adjustment at full speed, as Alex put away the toile de Jouy guest room bedspread they had bought in Paris, and the small antique objects around the room. They were going to put the furniture in storage in case they got a bigger place, which was beginning to sound like a good idea once their second baby arrived. That had been their long-term plan, but now they had moved up the schedule. They had already settled into fatherhood in two weeks and were loving it, and Morgan said it felt like Blake had always been part of their lives. They couldn't imagine their life without him. He was part of them now.

* * *

Faith wandered into Violet's office to tell her the details of Blake's arrival. She hadn't had a chance to tell her yet, and she thought it was an amazing story which illustrated how life could change in an instant, for good or bad.

She told Violet about it, and noticed that she looked very pale.

"Are you okay? Are you feeling all right?" It was a blistering hot day, and the air conditioner in her office had been working on and off. "It's so damn hot." And Violet had been out with the flu for a few days the week before, and didn't look well yet.

"It's not the heat," Violet said, and suddenly she started to cry.

"Oh, Vi, what's wrong?" Faith said, as she came around her desk to hug her. "Did you have a fight with Jordan?"

Violet shook her head. "No, it's worse than that," she said miserably. "I can't believe it. I got pregnant on our honeymoon. I felt sick a few weeks later, and I thought it was some kind of fallout from the stress of getting married, and then I remembered that I forgot to take the pill on our wedding night. I'm three months pregnant. I found out just after the Albert wedding. You were so happy about how it went, I didn't want to spoil it for you with bad news. I didn't want to upset you, and I couldn't believe it myself. I'm due in six months, in February. That's the last thing I wanted. We can't afford it, and I don't want to take time off. I'll work till the last day, I promise, and I'll only take four weeks off after it's born. We'll put the baby in daycare or something." She was desperately unhappy about it, but relieved to have told Faith.

"Good lord, it's an epidemic. Annabelle Albert in November, my sister at Christmas, you in February, and Alex and Morgan's baby girl in March. And the one they're adopting now. I hope it's not contagious. Don't come near me!" She made a cross with her fingers as though to ward off a vampire and Violet laughed through her tears.

"I feel so stupid. Jordan isn't happy about it either. We can't afford it, and I don't want a baby yet, for years. I love my job. And I'll look like an elephant when I help you with all our Christmas weddings." They hadn't been booked yet, but they would start soon. There was one very grand one that had been booked eight months ago, last December. They were going to start working on it in September. It would be at the bride's parents' home in Locust Valley on Long Island, so it didn't involve finding a venue. They had a big garden and Faith was going to fill it with ice sculptures, and try to achieve the effect of a czar's palace. She already had a few sketches to show them after Labor Day, but she wanted to focus on Alex and Morgan's wedding first. And the December bride and her family were at their home in the South of France until Labor Day.

"It'll be fine," Faith reassured her, although she wasn't thrilled either, but Violet was so dedicated and such a hard worker, she was sure she wouldn't let the baby affect her job. Violet said Jordan would pitch in on the weekends when she was busy with weddings. He had promised to help.

She was going to prove to Faith that her pregnancy wouldn't affect her work, although she had had terrible morning sickness for the past month, which was how she'd suspected it. She hadn't had the flu the week before, she just couldn't stop throwing up, though she'd felt a little better for the last few days, but was still very queasy and had vomited a few times that morning. Every day started that way now.

"I have an appointment for a sonogram tomorrow. I'm going at lunchtime. It won't take long. They're just checking to see that everything's okay and make sure my dates are right. They can tell on the computer. It's the first one I've had." She didn't sound excited, just annoyed. It hadn't been good news for her or Jordan, and it was so fast. They didn't even have time to enjoy being married, and now there would be a crying baby in the house, keeping them up all night, and they both had demanding jobs.

Faith tried to be a good sport about it, but she talked to Hope about it that night.

"I couldn't even complain. She's a lot more upset than I am." Faith had told Hope about Alex and Morgan's instant baby when she got the list of supplies from her.

"You seem to be surrounded by babies these days," Hope teased her. "Watch out you don't catch one, or Mom."

"Very funny. I'd probably have twins."

"I hope I do," Hope said. "I'd love a little girl like you. But they've already told me it's only one. They can see it on the sonogram. I hope it's a girl." They had decided to be surprised and didn't know. It was barely showing now. She was five months pregnant, but she was so tall and slim her pregnancies weren't obvious for a long time. Faith had noticed after Violet told her that she already had a little round belly, which explained why she had been wearing loose blouses for the last month. Faith thought it was because of the heat.

The next day, Violet came back from the sonogram looking sheet-white and sick. Faith saw it immediately and asked her if they had seen something wrong.

"Yes, they saw something wrong." She stared at her friend and employer. "Twins. What am I going to do? We can't afford one, let alone two. Jordan will kill me." But he didn't. He was thrilled when she told him over the phone. He couldn't get away from work for the sonogram. She had faced the news alone.

"Are you crazy? What are we going to do?" She was panicked at the thought of twins.

Danielle Steel

"We'll figure it out. I'll ask for a raise. And my parents will give us a loan," he comforted her. He had been upset about the pregnancy, but he thought twins were exciting. "Are they identical?"

"Yes," she said miserably.

"How do they know?"

"There's only one sac. Apparently there are more complications with identicals. They said I might wind up on bed rest for the last four or even five months. Jordan, that's in two months. If that happens, Faith will fire me, she needs an assistant all the time," she said with her office door closed.

"No, she won't fire you. You can make calls from home. Faith loves you and she knows how fantastic you are. Could they see what sex?"

"Not yet, I'll know in a few weeks. They can tell from a blood test." She was too young to need amniocentesis at twenty-nine, and there was no sign in the sonogram of anything wrong. The dates were consistent with hers, but they told her she would probably have the twins early, which would mean January in her case. She was relieved that Jordan wasn't upset, but she was more so than ever. She was not happy at all, and it didn't cheer her that everyone else was having babies too, like Faith's sister, and Morgan and Alex's surrogate and their new baby boy, and the Albert girl.

222

So what? They could all afford them. She and Jordan couldn't, they couldn't even afford one baby, let alone two at once.

Alex and Morgan had adapted to their new circumstances with surprising efficiency. They hired Helen, their baby nurse, on their second day of interviews. She was British with a green card, and they were vastly impressed by her. Her references were excellent. She was experienced, and thirty-eight years old. She seemed to be very careful with the baby. She taught them how to care for the baby, and she was perfectly at ease working for two gay men. She had worked for a gay couple before. Morgan and Alex had hired her for a year.

Helen seemed much more efficient than Hope's nanny, Faith thought when she visited them. The guest room furniture was gone. Blake was still sleeping in the Moses basket, but a crib was arriving on Saturday. There was a chest in the room with a teddy bear painted on it, and all his equipment and strollers and clothes were neatly put away. The nanny was living in and would sleep in his room until the new baby came, and then she'd sleep with her. She was off on weekends, and stayed with her boyfriend in New Jersey. Alex and Morgan were going to take care of the baby themselves on weekends. She didn't take a day off for the first month until a newborn settled in, and wouldn't take any time off till after their honeymoon, so she was there all the time for now, teaching them what they needed to know about their son. They were thrilled, and said she was worth the fortune they were paying her. Faith was impressed. There was no chaos in their home, and the baby only cried when he was hungry. He seemed very easy. They were both back in their offices a week after they got back from Miami. It had been a very busy three weeks for them.

"You guys make it look easy," Faith complimented them when she came to see them a few days after they got home. Blake was three weeks old, and their well-organized life had hardly altered, after the initial shock of his arrival. They talked about Heather sometimes, and worried about her and how she was doing. They still felt guilty about her, but they were in love with their baby.

They were already making plans to christen him in October, with a big party to celebrate it, and the adoption. They asked Faith to be his godmother, and Edward was going to be his godfather. So they would have two good reasons to see each other in the near future, the wedding and the christening. Faith liked that idea, and said something to Hope about how attractive he was.

"Do I smell romance in the air?" Hope asked her.

"No, he's just a very nice guy. He's a lot like Morgan, only

The Wedding Planner

ten years older and not gay. He's divorced and has a son in law school."

"He sounds interestingly eligible. Should I start lighting candles?"

"No, and don't tell Mom, or she'll get all excited. There's nothing happening between us. He's just nice. And what would you light candles for?"

"For you to get married. I don't like your being alone all the time. All you do is work," Hope said with worry in her voice.

"I like my work, and I don't want to get married. It scares me. You and Angus are the only happy couple I know."

"Mom seems very happy with Jean-Pierre." They had both noticed it and were pleased for her. They had a wonderful time on their honeymoon, and he was feeling well, with no sign of his minor heart problem since his procedure.

"They're still in the honeymoon phase," Faith countered. "And her three previous attempts were a disaster, including our father. It took her four tries to get it right. That would kill me."

"Well, see how it goes with Morgan's brother, and don't just cross him off so fast."

"I'm not. We can be friends. We're going to be the godparents of their baby." Hope didn't argue for him any further. She knew that if she pushed, Faith would resist even harder.

225

Faith was busy now with the final details for Alex and Morgan's wedding. Everything was confirmed and in good order.

When Morgan's parents arrived from Chicago, they were thrilled to see the baby, so they had something to celebrate in addition to the wedding. Faith met Morgan's parents, and his mother was thoroughly enjoying the baby. Blake looked like a baby in an ad, and Morgan said he was very advanced for five weeks, and meeting all his appropriate markers. She smiled when Morgan said it. Paternal pride had set in. He was a roly-poly bouncy baby with chubby thighs, and he gave them his first smile the morning of the wedding.

Everyone was excited about the wedding. Helen was helpful in countless ways. She was supremely competent and very British. She helped both grooms get ready, manned the phones, and had the baby dressed in a long gown Morgan had bought at his favorite French baby store. Blake looked dressed for the wedding too. Helen was bringing the baby to the ceremony and the cocktail hour afterward so everyone could see him. She was wearing her official brown uniform with her starched white apron, and all her nursing pins from the fancy nursing college she had graduated from called Norland. That was why she was so expensive. It was the best nannying school in England and was considered to be a college course. She'd had hospital training as well as class-room, and with a green card she was worth her weight in gold. Blake always seemed happy with her. She knew how to entertain him and had him on a good schedule. He was sleeping six hours at night, and she was trying to stretch it to seven. She liked her employers and thought they were wonderful with the baby. She couldn't wait for their baby girl to arrive in seven months.

The house they had borrowed from their actor friend for the wedding was even more beautiful than they remem-bered, once Faith filled it with flowers, candles, and all her magical touches. It was a great deal more restrained and traditional than the Albert wedding, but there was a high level of elegance and stylishness to it that had a mark all its own. The guests were as chic as the two men getting married. There were many women in the crowd, and couples. It was an impressive blend of people, with many in fashion and film production, because of their jobs. There were orchids everywhere, and a fabulous band for dancing in the ballroom after dinner.

The ceremony in the ballroom was very moving, and they used Faith's favorite vow too. It touched her each time. "With my body, I thee worship." They had both loved it the moment they read it. During the champagne reception, where the

Cristal flowed like water, Helen threaded her way through the crowd showing off the baby. Then she and Blake went back to their apartment when the wedding guests sat down to dinner under the canopy of lilies and orchids floating over the air-conditioned garden. Once again, Faith had thought of every touch and detail, and every moment, every flower, was in unfailingly good taste. The wedding had a glamorous, sophisticated look, with very elite guests.

Faith had hired a salsa band for them at their request, for the latter part of the evening. Alex and Morgan were both fabulous dancers. Morgan's parents had retired after the first band. They had been the witnesses at the wedding, for both Morgan and Alex, and Edward was the best man, and looked fabulous in a tuxedo. He was forty-four years old and looked ten years younger.

Morgan and Alex had done the seating themselves, and had put Edward next to Faith, since they insisted that she be seated as a wedding guest, which touched her. She very rarely did that. Violet stayed on duty to keep an eye on the servers, and to make sure that the exquisite cake was brought out at the right time. Faith had had a cake ornament made for them with two men and a baby, which they thought was hilarious.

Once again, not a single detail was overlooked, and miraculously, nothing went wrong. There were no glitches.

Sitting next to Edward was fun, as Faith knew it would be. They danced a lot and liked the other guests at their table. Edward was a fantastic dancer, like his brother. Both grooms danced with Faith, and so did Morgan and Edward's father, before they changed bands to the hotter one. The party went on until four in the morning, with the crowd barely thinning. For the late-night crowd there was a fancy spread at three A.M. of cheeses and cold meats, omelets and eggs Benedict, beggars' purses, sandwiches, potato hulls filled with caviar, and martini glasses filled with mashed potatoes. The food looked as beautiful as it was delicious. Everything the eye rested upon was exquisite and beautifully done. There were a few celebrities in the crowd, movie stars who Alex worked with, and there were two famous fashion designers that Morgan had invited. The grooms and the guests thoroughly enjoyed their wedding. And everyone had admired the baby.

Edward and Faith had a ball together on the dance floor, particularly when they played the samba and South American music. They helped themselves to the three A.M. breakfast and sat down together again. They had been together for most of the evening.

"You throw the best wedding I've ever been to," he said happily, after a mouthful of excellent caviar. "How do you do it?" he asked her, with a look of admiration.

"I love what I do. That always helps." And she loved the grooms in this case and wanted everything perfect for them.

"Being the senior partner of a law firm isn't as exciting, but I love my work too." And he was very bright, with a good sense of humor, which she enjoyed.

At three-thirty, Faith told Edward that she was turning into a pumpkin. She was too tired to dance another step. It had been a long day for her. She had supervised the final installation at six A.M., and had been busy ever since.

He looked suddenly intent and sober and reached for her hand and held it.

"Will you have dinner with me this week?" he asked her, as though it was a serious proposal.

"I'd love to," she said, and he smiled.

"I should probably go too," he said. The grooms had already left by then. People were talking and drinking at cabaret tables more than dancing. The reception was slowly ending.

Edward took her home in a cab, walked her to her door while the cab waited, and stood there until she unlocked it.

"I had fun with you tonight," she complimented him, and he nodded with his slow smile that lit up his eyes.

"I did too," he told her. "Best wedding I've ever been to." She could see that he meant it. He stood smiling at her for a moment and then he leaned down and kissed her. It was a gently sensual kiss, which made her want more. It was an interesting development in their friendship. He took it to a new level after the wedding, with a down payment toward the future. It was a kiss filled with promises yet to be revealed.

He left then, and Faith fell asleep, thinking of him and smiling. It had been a fabulous night and one of her best weddings, for people she really enjoyed and had come to love, which made it even better.

Faith was waking up slowly the morning after Alex and Morgan's wedding, when her mother called her. She drifted out of sleep and came fully awake when she heard the tension in her mother's voice.

"What's up, Mom?" She glanced at the clock. It was nine A.M. and she had gone to sleep at four-thirty. It had been a short night for her, but a great party, and Violet had handled all the details that night, since Faith was a guest.

"We're at Lenox Hill again," Marianne said, deeply anxious. "Jean-Pierre had another episode last night. He has to be on medication now. If it happens again, they'll give him a pacemaker. He doesn't want one, but it may be what he needs. He was fine yesterday, and then last night he had palpitations for no reason. He insisted he was all right, but he didn't feel well, so I brought him to the hospital."

"You should have called me," she said, sitting up.

"Hope said that you had that wedding last night, of the two attractive men with the baby."

"I did. It was fabulous. Another great one. We did it in an incredible double townhouse that belongs to a famous actor." She knew his identity by then but was discreet about it.

"You outdo yourself every time," her mother said proudly.

"It was definitely a good one. The location made it, and two great bands. I danced all night. My feet feel like footballs. I'll be over in half an hour, Mom, and give Jean-Pierre my love." Faith could tell that it wasn't a dire emergency this time, or her mother wouldn't have been talking about other things, like the wedding. But Faith could hear that she was worried. She was so happy. She didn't want to lose him. They really loved each other. She had finally gotten it right.

Faith got to the hospital forty-five minutes later, and found her mother sitting in a chair next to Jean-Pierre's bed. He was reading the Sunday edition of *The New York Times*. He smiled when he saw Faith walk in. She was feeling a little rocky once she'd gotten up, and she looked paler than he did. She was slightly hungover from the wedding.

"You look pretty good," Faith said to her stepfather, and he smiled.

"You do not look pretty good. Are you ill?"

"I went to a terrific wedding last night, with two bands. And I think I had a little too much bubbly. But I had fun."

"That's good. Your mother tells me you work too hard." She nodded. She didn't disagree. "You must take time to have fun too. Every moment is precious." He looked at his wife as he said it. And Faith realized that that was what he meant, to enjoy life to the fullest, every moment, to seize the day, to live and to love and to laugh, and not just work. He seemed to be good at it. Her mother had never looked better. Faith realized what they were doing. They were seizing the moments and the days while they had them. The future would take care of itself. Destiny would decide, as it always does. Faith left them after an hour. They were letting him go home, and they didn't need her there. The scare was over and they said he could leave at lunchtime. They could manage on their own. She had a feeling they preferred it.

She got a call from Morgan while she was in the cab on her way home.

"Best wedding *ever*! We loved it. We're on our way to the airport. Our flight to Paris is in three hours. We'll have some good dinners there, although a lot of restaurants are closed in August. After that we'll head down to Monaco, to get on the sailboat we chartered. It looks like a beauty in the pictures. I can't wait. Helen, the nanny, is in charge here.

233

I gave her your number if there's an emergency. We're going to miss the baby, but he's in good hands. And seriously, thank you for the incredibly beautiful wedding, Faith. And for everything." She had turned out to be a remarkable friend.

"Don't thank me. You paid a fortune for it. I have a hangover today. I think I drank a lot of champagne."

"I did too. It was an absolutely picture-perfect wedding. And the music was great. What time did you leave?"

"Around three-thirty. And then I checked my emails when I got home."

"That's a bad habit. You need to break it."

"Have a fabulous honeymoon. Enjoy yourselves. Forget New York. Leave it all here." She was thinking of Jean-Pierre and her mother seizing the day, enjoying life, loving each other. Good things never came easily, but when they presented themselves, you had to reach out and grab them.

Chapter 13

Faith was sound asleep when her cellphone rang. Because of Hope, her mother, and now Jean-Pierre's erratic health, she left her cellphone on at all times. And with Morgan and Alex on their honeymoon, the nanny had her number for an emergency, so she wanted to be available at all hours. She grabbed the phone, waking out of a sound sleep and answered it with a mumble.

". . . llo . . . yes?" She struggled to wake up. All she could hear was crying. She thought it must be her mother, and Jean-Pierre was back in the hospital.

"Mom? . . . Mom? Is that you? . . ." There were garbled words then, an unfamiliar voice. It sounded like a young woman, not her mother. Thoughts raced through her head. Violet? She lost the babies? "Hello? Who is this? Talk to me," she begged. Whoever it was was in deep trouble.

"It's me . . . Phoebe . . ." She tried to compose herself, and hiccupped on a sob. "I'm sorry to call you in the middle of the night. You were right. He's crazy."

"Who is?" She was awake now.

"Doug. He accused me of sleeping with our next-door neighbor. I've never even seen him. I guess he's some young, good-looking guy. He said I gave him a blow job. He's insane."

Faith was sitting up in bed, listening, and turned the light on. "Did he hit you? Are you okay?"

"I'm okay now. I'm in a safe house. I think he would have beaten me up if I'd stayed. He looked like a madman while he was accusing me. He was shaking with rage. It's not the first time it's happened. He's been like that since we got married." It had been exactly two months since their wedding. "He pulled me out of bed by my hair, and dragged me across the floor to the front door. I was in my nightgown, and he threw me out of the apartment. I had no money, no purse, no shoes on. I was practically naked. I went downstairs and the doorman called the police. They went upstairs to talk to him, while I stayed downstairs. They said he was perfectly calm, and very polite to them. He said we were playing a game and I locked myself out. He wouldn't let me come back to get my purse or my clothes. The police took me to a safe house. That was four days ago, and he hasn't let me back in since. He fired me at work again, and won't pay me what he owes me.

"I don't want my mom to know what happened, she'd be too upset. I called my sister and she wired me some money. I guess I'll go back to San Diego. I don't want him to find me. I just wanted to tell you that you were right about everything you said. He told me what to wear, what to eat, he wouldn't let me see anyone. He said that if I said anything to the nurses I work with, or anyone else, he'd kill me, and no one would believe me anyway. He doesn't know where I am. I said something about you once, about wanting to call you just to stay in touch, and he said that if I ever contacted you, he'd kill us both."

"How charming," Faith said, as rage bubbled up inside her. He had taken this gentle, kind, decent, beautiful girl and tried to destroy her. "You have to get away from him and stay away. He's dangerous, Phoebe. I don't know how far he'd really go, or if he's just a bully, but you can't take the chance."

"I know that now. As soon as I can afford to, I'm going to file for divorce. But I don't know what to do now. I tried calling a nurses' employment agency here. He's blackballed me with all of them. He told one agency I have a serious heroin problem and was stealing morphine. He told another one that I was drunk during a surgery and gave him the wrong instruments. They won't touch me. I called San Diego, and they have no job openings right now, and even if they do, I'll need a reference. I just thought if you know anyone, I'll do anything, wrap packages, open boxes, scrub floors, walk dogs. I need to make some money before I go home. I can't ask my sister again, she's got so much on her hands with my mom, who keeps getting worse."

"I can lend you some," Faith said calmly. It made her think back to when they had come to see her about their wedding. They had been such an attractive couple, and Doug seemed so sane. But even then, she had found him controlling.

"I don't want money," Phoebe said, mortified. "I need work. I'm a qualified surgical nurse in plastic surgery. He's fixed it so no one will touch me, I can't find a job. I'll never be able to work again without a reference from him, and he'll never give me one."

"You need to see a lawyer, and find out what to do about it."

"I'm sorry I called you in the middle of the night. I've been sitting here, thinking about what to do, and I panicked. I've never felt so alone. I'm staying at the safe house where the police took me. I called the girls I used to live with and told them. But I can't pay rent and they don't want me there. They're afraid he'll come looking for me, and hurt them."

"I'm not afraid of him. You can stay here."

"I don't want to be a burden, or cause you any trouble. But if you know of any work I can do, I'd really appreciate it, no matter how menial. I'm in a crisis house. I can't stay here for too long. The spots in the long-term shelters go to women with kids. I guess I could go on welfare. Or work as a waitress or something." She was so upset she hadn't been thinking clearly. All she knew was that Doug was a terrible, dangerous, deranged man. He had accused her of marrying him for the money, and said the story about her mother being sick and poor was probably a lie. She had never asked him for money for her.

"Why don't you come here in the morning, and we'll figure something out?" She was fully awake by then. It was five A.M. "Do you have money for the subway?"

"Don't worry, I'll get there. And I'm sorry. I look awful. All I have to wear is what I got from the giveaway box at the shelter." Faith had an instant vision of Phoebe on her wedding day, in the uncomfortable dress that looked like a suit of armor, and she could hardly walk in it, the one Doug had bought and forced her to wear, instead of the prettier one she loved. All his gifts to her were like a double-edged sword.

Faith couldn't sleep after Phoebe's call, she canceled her ballet class, and was showered and dressed and in her office at seven. She was trying to think of everyone she could call for Phoebe. Her caterers, her favorite florist, the wedding cake baker, some of her old clients who had numerous assistants, often with a revolving door. She was a bright, skilled, highly trained nurse, but she was willing to do anything. Faith made a list. She felt terrible for her. She was such a sweet girl and decent person. She didn't deserve this. She was sure that Doug had singled her out because she was so meek and trusting and naïve, and was totally alone in New York. Phoebe had said that he had pursued her right after she arrived, it had all happened very fast. And she was beautiful on top of it. He was a very sick man, but she'd heard stories like it before, and had spotted it very quickly. Phoebe had been so determined to marry him, and so much in love. She had been taken in by his kindness at first, and then he turned.

She had about a dozen people on her list by the time Violet got to work. She was already starting to show, although she was only three and a half months pregnant, and Faith wondered how long she would be able to work. They had warned her that with twins, particularly identicals in one sac, she could end up on bed rest, even as early as four months into the pregnancy. That was only weeks away. Violet was so dedicated that she swore she would work until the last day before she delivered, but that might not be possible. Faith's mother had been put to bed for three months before she and Hope were born a month early. It happened a lot with twins, along with a multitude of other complications. She worried now about what would happen if Violet was suddenly put to bed on short notice, when they were juggling several weddings. December was always a busy month for them, with people who wanted to get married around Christmas or on New Year's Eve. In that case, Faith would be left high and dry. She relied totally on her, and even now, it was a concern. Because Faith was invited as a guest to Alex and Morgan's wedding, Violet had been the on-duty person and had stayed until four A.M., and came back the next day to oversee the breakdown of the rentals. She had looked exhausted for several days afterward, to the point of looking sick. She never complained, but it was going to get worse before it got better, inevitably. Faith didn't want to have a negative impact on her health, or put her babies at risk.

She told her about Phoebe's call and Violet looked appalled. She had been just as worried about her as Faith before the wedding. For someone not in his thrall, he was easy to spot as controlling in the extreme. She couldn't stand him, and felt sorry for Phoebe.

"Do you know anyone willing to hire at the moment? Or who needs an assistant of some kind? He's fixed it so she can't get work as a nurse. It's a small community, and he got her blackballed with all the agencies. I want her to see a lawyer, to see if we can reverse that. But with no reference from him, it might be tough. People who get fired always say their employer was nuts. But in his case, he is."

"I don't know of anyone right now. But people call us sometimes to see if we know of anyone available." Violet looked pensive.

Faith called Hope to see if she had any ideas.

"We need a baby nurse in December, but that's four months from now, and it sounds like she needs something right away. You really are the full-service wedding planner. You wind up as mother, father, and shrink to some of these girls, not to mention giving them the wedding of their dreams."

"This one wound up with the wedding of her nightmares. It was predictable, but she didn't see it. I tried to warn her. He broke up with her for a while, but she went back to him."

"I hear that most abuse victims do. With tragic results sometimes," Hope said seriously.

"I don't want that to happen to her."

"Maybe she should go back to the West Coast and start over there."

"She says she couldn't get work in San Diego, although she probably could in L.A., but she'll run into the reference problem again. I think she needs to do something else for a while, until this gets resolved and she can go back to work as a nurse."

"I feel sorry for her," Hope said. Not all women were as blessed as she was with Angus, who was a great husband and father and a good person.

"So do I," Faith said. Phoebe had sounded so desperate on the phone.

"How are your two dads doing with their new baby?"

"Amazingly well. The relinquishment is final and the adoption will be confirmed in October. They hired an amazing English nanny, trained by a fancy nannying school in England, *with* a green card. She was married to an American and got divorced. They're on their honeymoon now, on a yacht in the South of France. And baby number two, with the surrogate, is due in seven months. They're terrific guys, and they're going to be wonderful fathers. They seem to be figuring it out and managing nicely. And they're crazy about the baby, who is adorable."

"I'd manage nicely too, with a fancy English nanny," Hope laughed. Her housekeeper was good with the kids and they had had several nannies who had been unreliable and never stayed long. They were young and bored in Connecticut and left for jobs in New York.

Alex and Morgan had hired a supremely competent, high-priced professional. It was worth it to them. They both had demanding jobs and needed someone reliable and outstanding with their children. "They're talking about moving out of the city, after the new baby comes. They're exploding out of their very chic apartment. It just isn't meant for kids. It's a duplex and has a fancy marble staircase, which won't be good when the babies start walking. Too dangerous."

"That's why we moved out here. It's just easier with children, especially if you have more than one."

"How's the baby factory?" Faith forgot to ask her about her pregnancy sometimes. She had done it so often and made it seem so effortless, which she was sure it wasn't. Hope never complained about it, and she knew Faith didn't really care about baby issues. She'd never experienced it and couldn't relate to it. It just wasn't a subject that interested her, although she loved her twin more than anyone on earth, even their mother. Hope felt the same way about her. She had Angus to talk to about their babies, and women friends who had children and infants the same age as hers and got pregnant as often. She didn't need to discuss it with Faith, and never tried. Babies were Faith's blind spot, although she loved her nephews and thought Blake was sweet. But motherhood held no appeal to her.

"I'll keep your nurse friend in mind," Hope said, "if I hear of anyone who needs help."

"Thanks, Hopie. I love you, talk to you later."

When Phoebe arrived and rang the bell at the office, she looked even worse than Faith had expected. It was pouring rain and she was drenched. She stood in the rain, in the mismatched clothes from the donation box at the shelter. She was wearing flip-flops, her long blond hair was matted to her head. She had come uptown on the subway with a MetroCard they gave her at the shelter. But even looking like that, she was beautiful, with no makeup, and the expression in her eyes was the saddest Faith had ever seen. She had seen an ugly side of life in the past two months since she'd married Doug, things no one should ever have to experience. She seemed beaten and betrayed and broken.

"I'm sorry I look such a mess," she said, as she stood dripping in Faith's front hall and set down a wet paper shopping bag, which contained the few things the shelter had given her. It was incredible. Doug wouldn't let her pick up any of her things, and he had torn her diamond wedding band off her hand, and her engagement ring, the night he threw her out. He had done the same thing the first time too, as though she were some cheap floozy who might sell them, or pawn them.

"I just saw my reflection at the subway station. I didn't even recognize myself," she said, as Faith walked her back to the kitchen to make her a cup of tea, and Violet joined them. She was shocked at how Phoebe looked too. It was all reparable, and she'd get back on her feet eventually, but for now she was at the bottom of a black pit, with no idea how to climb out of it.

Phoebe smiled at Violet, happy to see her. She was only

a few years older than Violet and had liked her when they were planning her wedding.

"I hear you're having a baby," Phoebe said to her. "Congratulations." At least that was some good news, instead of focusing on the seamy side of life she had seen. She remembered that Violet had gotten married right before her. Faith had just told her Violet was pregnant before she walked in.

"Yeah, whatever. We don't think it's such great news. We wanted to wait. We had a five-year plan. This doesn't quite fit into that scheme. I've been pretty upset about it. And worse yet, it's twins. I can't even imagine what that will be like, or how we're going to manage."

"I hear it's tough with twins for the first year or two, and it's fun after that," Phoebe said kindly.

"My sister and I were very fun for my mother," Faith said with a sniff, and all three of them laughed. "She survived it. She never had any other kids, though. I guess we cured her of that."

"I'm sorry you've had a hard time, Phoebe," Violet said gently. She didn't want to pry or be indiscreet, but Phoebe looked so sad and disheveled, that it seemed okay to say. She had lost weight and was pale, with a ravaged look in her eyes, with deep, dark circles under them. She hadn't had a decent night's sleep in two months, and the shelter was no picnic either, with a wide variety of abuse victims, some of them recently out of jail, with bad habits of their own. It was a segment of society that Phoebe had never encountered before, and she felt like an innocent in their midst. They could spot how naïve she was from miles away, and some of the women tried to take advantage of it or got aggressive with her. It was a relief to come to Faith's house, where she felt safe. She hadn't felt safe since her wedding.

They talked about job possibilities for Phoebe in the kitchen. Faith wanted to make an appointment for her with her lawyer, and she agreed. She was wondering if Phoebe should file charges against him and a restraining order.

"I can't pay a lawyer till I have a job," she reminded her.

"Just talk to him and see what he thinks you should do. This one's on me," Faith said, and Phoebe thanked her profusely, and went to change into less soaked jeans, carrying the wet shopping bag with her. It was so rain-soaked it was about to dissolve. Phoebe had hit rock bottom since they'd last seen her. This was a post-wedding service Faith didn't usually have to provide, but was happy to for her.

She checked her appointment calendar and saw that she was free until two o'clock that afternoon, and when Phoebe came back downstairs, Faith called an Uber and had Violet call the attorney to get an appointment for Phoebe as soon as she could. She had directed her to a small guest room upstairs. It was a cheerful little yellow room, with a pink bathroom, and it looked like heaven to Phoebe. Faith pulled one of her raincoats out of a closet, and handed it to Phoebe. It was short on her, but she was so slim, it fit, and looked fine.

"Are we going to the lawyer now?" She looked surprised.

"Not yet. We have a little mission to make you feel like Phoebe Smith again, and not the victim of the infamous Dr. Kirk and Mr. Hyde." The Uber was there by the time they had their coats on. Faith grabbed an umbrella and ushered her out the door, and gave the driver the address of Bloomingdale's, which wasn't far away. Phoebe resisted at first, but Faith refused to listen. In under two hours she had sweaters, blouses, T-shirts, new jeans, running shoes, some ballerina flats, and a pair of heels if she had a job interview. They found a few pretty cotton dresses on sale, a jacket, two basic purses, underwear, nightgowns, makeup, and a straw hat that looked terrific on her. They struggled with their bags out the door, got back to Faith's house, and Phoebe threw her arms around her and hugged her.

"I'll pay you back the minute I get a job, I promise."

"No, you won't." They hadn't spent a fortune, and Phoebe felt like a human being again when she put decent clothes on, and was wearing makeup. She looked almost like herself, except for the sad expression in her eyes, but she was smiling again. It was a vast improvement over the condition she'd been in when she arrived. She had checked out of the shelter when she left.

Faith had an appointment with a new bride at two-thirty for a New Year's Eve wedding. She was divorced with two children, and they wanted to charter a yacht for a night for a small wedding. The groom had three children, all teenagers, and they wanted to entertain about forty friends on the boat for a memorable wedding. It sounded simple to arrange to Faith. She walked into Violet's office afterward, where the two young women were talking, and looked up when she walked in. Phoebe was wearing a soft lavender V-neck sweater they had bought that morning, cotton pants the same color, and sandals with daisies on them that she loved.

"I've had an idea. See what you both think. Madame Violet here is a bit of a time bomb at the moment. We hope she'll be able to work right till the last minute, when I take her to the hospital so she doesn't give birth in my office, but the truth is," she said, looking at her, "you could wind up in bed any minute if those twins misbehave, and twins are prone to do that, at any age." She grinned and they laughed. "And Phoebe needs a job now. We could find ourselves stuck if Vi gets put to bed on short notice, which could be a disaster if we're heavily booked. We already have a slew of weddings scheduled in the fall, and one humongous one in Locust

Valley at Christmas, friends of the Alberts, so that's going to be a big deal. And with the best will in the world, I doubt that you'll be able to make it much past Christmas, Vi, and you want four weeks' maternity leave and may need more. And until we get your husband put behind bars or clear your reputation, Phoebe, you're on sabbatical as a nurse. What do you both think if Phoebe comes on board now, learns the ropes here and where everything is, and what we've got on the books, so any time Vi gets put to bed, we're covered. And it will lighten the load on Vi now, so maybe she won't wind up in bed. Thoughts?"

They both stared at her. Phoebe was smiling, and Vi was nodding her head. Violet had thought of it but didn't think Faith would want to pay for two assistants full-time "just in case." "I think it's a great idea. Violet?" She didn't want to do it without Violet's approval. She didn't want her to feel pushed out. "It would just be through March, so seven months, to give Vi time to have the twins, get back on her feet, and then Phoebe goes back to assisting with facelifts or boob lifts or whatever she does that I desperately need and don't want to know about, so please don't tell me." All three of them were laughing and smiling and talking at once. Faith wrote a number down on a piece of paper, folded it, and handed it to Phoebe, as the salary she was willing to pay her. Phoebe looked at it and her eyes grew wide.

"I could get a small furnished studio apartment with that, and have enough left over to eat, shop a little, get a manicure, and go to a movie." It was less than she made as a highly skilled surgical nurse, but it was more than adequate, and she needed the job desperately. Faith was saving her life.

"Yes!" she said, and jumped out of her chair and hugged Faith and Violet. "Yes, yes, yes, thank you." They hugged one another and Faith was smiling too.

"What blesses one blesses all, as they say. Problem solved, for all three of us. Ladies, we have a deal! You're hired," she said to Phoebe. And Violet had gotten her an appointment with the attorney the next day, to find out what steps she should take against Doug, whether to file charges or not, and whether to get an annulment or a divorce, and if she could get damages from him for interfering with her ability to work in her field as an experienced, technically trained, specialized nurse. And Violet had gotten her an appointment to get a new ID card.

She promised to find a studio apartment as soon as she could. She texted her sister that she'd gotten a job as an office assistant for now, and was seeing a lawyer and would work things out. She was going to return the money she'd loaned her. Everything in her life had changed for the better in a single day, thanks to Faith. Even Violet looked relieved and not threatened. She had been worried sick about what would happen if she got put to bed. She didn't want to let Faith down, and it would be fun to have a coworker for a change. And she and Phoebe got along well.

Edward Phillips, Morgan's brother, called Faith that night, and invited her on a real date. He was moving to New York fully in the next week, to take over the New York office of his firm. He wanted to celebrate it with her. She smiled when he suggested dinner at a lively Italian restaurant she knew and liked, not far from them, on Second Avenue. He said he'd pick her up at eight. He said he was looking forward to it. He'd had a text from Morgan. They were in Portofino on the boat and loving it. Faith had been there once with Hope on a trip to Italy, when Hope was modeling in Milan, and they had loved it. It was a romantic little port town with cute shops and good restaurants, and incredibly romantic, all lit up at night with a castle and a church above the port. They had both promised to go back there one day with the loves of their lives, but never had. It was a perfect spot for a honeymoon, and better yet to be on a sailboat. They were doing it just right. The baby was fine in their absence. Faith was calling Helen every day to check to be sure, and Blake was thriving.

The date with Edward was ten days away, and fun to look forward to.

* * *

Phoebe's appointment with the lawyer the next day went well. He was a blunt, matter-of-fact older man Faith had used for years for contracts, and all the legal matters she had.

He explained to Phoebe that she had little recourse in the divorce, since New York had adopted no-fault divorce laws several years ago, and whether she chose to file for divorce or annulment made little difference, except psychologically, and it was up to her. But in addition, he advised her to file a civil suit against Doug for loss of income, loss of wages, fraudulent damage to her reputation, blackmail, threats, assault, and psychological damage to her from the trauma, the loss of all her possessions he wouldn't allow her to reclaim, and the lawyer wanted to get a restraining order against him. The police report from the night he had thrown her out, a deposition from the doorman, the people at the shelter, and Faith would all be helpful to her to reach a settlement with him. He wouldn't want the damage to his own reputation if it came out. He suggested suing for a million dollars, and being pleased if they got half of it. He didn't work on a contingency basis, he charged hourly like respectable attorneys. He said it wasn't a complicated matter to file for her, at the same time as the divorce, and at a guess, he didn't think his fees would come to more than twenty thousand dollars. He thought that Doug would be anxious to settle quickly, to bury the matter before word got out.

She was very happy with what she heard, and signed a retainer before she left his office so he could get started. She owed another debt to Faith, which meant far more to her than her elegant wedding to a madman. She wished she had listened to Faith, but everything the lawyer suggested to her consoled her and she now felt that there would be justice in the end.

Chapter 14

Charles Allbright, the attorney Phoebe had seen, drew up the papers against Doug quickly, and sent them to his office. Phoebe started getting frantic calls and texts from him the day he got them. He threatened her physically in the texts, and she sent screenshots of them to her attorney. Doug didn't know where she was living, so he couldn't get near her, and the restraining order was in force, which reassured her.

In the civil suit he had filed, as part of the discovery, Charles had listed the witnesses who would testify against Doug and corroborate the plaintiff's claims, including the police. Charles had warned her that there would be a reaction, but his attorney would rein him in quickly, faced with a million-dollar civil suit, with people who were willing to testify against him. Charles thought their offer of a settlement would be quick. Phoebe was pleased.

She had found a furnished studio apartment a dozen blocks away from Faith, the weekend after Faith hired her, and she had moved in right away, with an advance on her salary. She was grateful for the haven Faith had provided her, the attorney, and the job. She was loving it, and she and Violet enjoyed working together. They were busy, with new weddings coming in at the end of the summer. Some of them were for summer the following year, some sooner, for the fall and the end of the year. Several were at Christmas.

Faith dressed carefully the night of her dinner date with Edward. It was a warm night, and she was excited about seeing him. Work had been busy, and there was a last vestige of the warm, sensual days of summer. September was just around the corner and always a busy month for her. But she wasn't too swamped just yet, and with two assistants now, both of them efficient, her office was in impeccable order, so she wasn't exhausted or stressed. She was in a festive mood when he picked her up for their dinner date. He wore a blue oxford shirt and khaki slacks with a navy linen blazer, and she was wearing a white eyelet cotton dress and high-heeled sandals, with her long blond hair down, which was rare for her. Hope always said she treated her hair like the enemy and tied it up and nailed it down in a bun, which made Faith laugh and she admitted it was true. She had beautiful long silky hair, which no one ever saw. Edward admired it when he picked her up. It was a beautiful night and nice to see him.

"How did your move go?" she asked him as they Ubered to the restaurant, which was crowded and lively when they got there. It had tables on the sidewalk too. He had reserved one of them. It was one of his favorite restaurants, and hers too.

"It went pretty well," he said of his move. "Nothing got broken or lost. I still have some things to hang. It's exciting moving to New York. I thought about it after law school, but wound up staying in Chicago, now here I am."

They knew enough about each other's jobs, but the personal side intrigued both of them. He told her he had only had the one bad forced marriage at nineteen, which had soured him on the idea of marriage for a long time. When he finally got over it, ten years later, and warmed up to the idea again, he had fallen in love with Julie, a fellow lawyer in his firm, a terrific girl. They were talking about marriage, when she was diagnosed with Hodgkin's disease. He wanted to marry her anyway, but she refused to do that to him. The future was too uncertain. She died three years later at thirty-two. There had been women in his life, but never anyone he wanted to marry after her, and by now, he considered he had missed the boat. That had been twelve years ago. He was forty-four now, and marriage seemed "beside the point" to him. He had a son he was close to now, and had missed too much of his early years because he wasn't ready to be a father. And being married no longer seemed pressing or necessary to him. "Unless I meet the love of my life again. The truth is I'm too damn comfortable now. I like what I do. I play a lot of tennis, see my friends when I want to. I love my job. I'm going to enjoy spending time with Morgan and Alex now that I'm here. He's ten years younger than I am. He was a late surprise for my parents. But he was still a little kid when I left for college, so I missed a lot with him too. I enjoy catching up on that now. I was kind of a late bloomer on the important relationships in my life, after a too-early start on some things, like fatherhood. I'm just kind of coasting now, and enjoying it. It would be nice to share my life, but if it doesn't happen, I'm okay too. I have no burning desires. I have a nice life."

"Me too. And I kind of missed the boat too, but I actually don't care now. I guess I'm a late bloomer too. And a workaholic, according to my sister, but I love what I do."

"And you're fabulous at it, judging by my brother's absolutely fantastic, elegant wedding." He smiled at her.

"Thank you. Two broken engagements kind of soured me on marriage. It didn't seem like such a hot idea after that. Bad choices, bad luck, bad karma, bad guys. The second one anyway. The first one was gay and said he didn't know it till a week before the wedding when he realized he couldn't go through with it, and had fallen in love with a Russian ballet dancer. You can't make this shit up," she said, and he laughed. "It was classic. I think my feelings were hurt for a long time, then the other guy I almost married was a control freak, so I ran. And I just kept running, and one day I figured out that I really enjoyed my life and didn't mind being alone. I've had some minor relationships, but no one I was crazy about. I just kind of bopped along, and as you said, one day I realized that the boat had left the dock, Noah's Ark with all the couples on it, and I wasn't on it and didn't really care. I figured it would have made me seasick anyway. The idea of kids always scared me. It's such a HUGE commitment. How do people do that and not worry that they're going to screw it up completely? It takes courage. I'm not that brave, not about kids anyway, or marriage."

"I felt the same way. I had screwed up with one kid by running away at twenty-one, I didn't want to do that again, and I was afraid I'd blow it again. At nineteen, my eighteen-year-old wife told me I was a lousy husband and I believed her. So the only other time I wanted to try was with the woman who died. The last twelve years have just flown by. I'm like those fridge magnets that say 'Oops, I forgot to get married.'"

Faith laughed. "Me too. I send them to my mother."

"I guess I never fell in love again after Julie. Maybe it only happens so many times in a lifetime. Maybe you only get one shot at it, although I hate to think that's true. But I like the idea of bells and whistles and that's the only time I ever heard them. All the other times I didn't hear a damn thing."

"My mother just got married for the fourth time a few months ago. This one is the right one for her, the bells and whistles guy, and they're so happy together. She's sixty-seven and he's seventy-seven, and they're having a ball and seizing the moment, for however long it lasts. Before this, her marriages were a mess, including my father. But this time, it's a joy to watch them. So maybe we didn't miss the boat. Maybe for some of us it shows up later. I'd rather get the last boat than hop on the wrong one earlier. Maybe there's a special boat for people like us, that shows up at the dock later, after all the riffraff catch the first boats."

He liked the way she put it, and how she felt about her life. She wasn't desperate to find a husband, in fact she sounded like she was leery of the idea, which made her even more appealing. She seemed like if the right guy didn't show up until she was sixty-seven, like her mother, she wouldn't care. And if he never showed up, she was fine too. He had filled the void with being a workaholic too. At least they weren't wasting their time.

She was great to talk to, and the evening flew by. He talked about how much he admired his brother for speaking up about being gay, being open with his family. He felt sorry for Alex too, whose family had been so cruel and rejected him. It was hard to believe people still did that to their kids in this day and age, but some did. It had marked Alex badly, and wounded him, but Morgan and his family had soothed the wounds in time. He thought that it was great that they were having the baby by surrogacy and had had the guts to adopt Blake when the opportunity presented itself. "My brother is a real man," he said proudly, "in the best sense of the word. They're going to be great fathers, not like I was." He still felt guilty about that, and took full responsibility for it, which she liked. He wasn't a coward, and didn't blame others for his mistakes.

"I don't know anyone who's a great father at nineteen or twenty." She gave him a pass on that. He seemed like a very decent, honest, open, warm man, a lot like Morgan, only a little more old school because he was a decade older, which she liked. She liked how traditional he was. He wasn't some wild, unshaven guy with tattoos, rejecting every traditional value he'd ever had, without honor or integrity, who couldn't admit to his weakness and mistakes. We all have them, the flaws that make us human. Faith had never hidden hers either, which made her unsure about children too. She didn't feel self-righteous enough to have them and pretend she was right all the time. It sounded like he had a good relationship with his son now. Edward was modest and open and straight-forward, which she loved, and was rare. Morgan had those qualities too. A kind of moral honesty and uncertainty about life that she felt too. She was humble about her flaws and so was Edward.

It was a dozen blocks back to her house, and they decided to walk in the balmy August night.

"Thank you for dinner. Mine was delicious. And it was nice to talk. There is so much fakery in the world, and bullshit. I love straight talk and honest people. I think it's what I love about Morgan and Alex. I hate phonies. I see a lot of them in my business, people who want to show off with a fancy wedding, but don't care about the marriage and the important stuff," she said as they walked.

"You do a mighty pretty wedding, though," he compli-mented her, and she smiled. "I've never had as much fun at a wedding as I did at theirs."

"I do it better for people I really love, like your brother and Alex. They're great people. We had a couple of dicey situations this summer, but we came through it." She thought of Phoebe when she said it, and they were just approaching her door, when something flew past her head and Edward pulled her close to him as a good-sized rock whizzed by her and broke one of her ground floor windows. She turned to see who had done it, still shocked. Douglas Kirk rushed toward her from behind a car, screaming at her, "You bitch! I saw you on the list of witnesses for that whore I was married to. You're as bad as she is." He tried to rush up close to Faith, and Edward stopped him with a strong arm and a powerful hand and a loud voice.

"Hey, knock it off now. Back up, or you're going to be telling the story from jail." He had Doug firmly by the arm in a viselike grip, but Doug had a free arm to take a swing at him. Edward had him pinned down on the ground in less than a minute, and told Faith in a calm, firm voice to call 911. With the weight of the taller, stronger man on top of him, Doug couldn't move, but he was shouting at both of them, and said to Edward, "Who the fuck do you think you are?"

"I'm law enforcement," Edward said calmly, and Faith looked surprised.

Faith told the police that they were being attacked by a man on the street, and to come right away. Five minutes later, a patrol car arrived, two policemen jumped out, and the policemen grabbed Doug and lifted him off the ground and pushed him into the back of the patrol car. He was still

Danielle Steel

screaming "Bitch" and "Whore" at Faith. She explained the circumstances to the policemen, and Edward got the full story too.

After the police left with Doug and she let herself and Edward into her house, she looked at him with a question. "You're law enforcement?" He grinned when she asked.

"I was a volunteer on the student campus security patrol senior year at Northwestern," he said. "That's good enough, isn't it?"

"Apparently. You did a hell of a job taking him down. Thank you. The poor girl he married really suffered at his hands. We tried to warn her but she didn't listen. He's even worse than we thought." She was feeling shaken, but less so thanks to Edward's protection.

"This won't help his case," Edward said. He had remained calm throughout the attack and all of Doug's verbal abuse. Edward was a good man to have around in a crisis. She felt completely safe standing next to him.

"That was pretty impressive, your performance I mean."

"I'm just bigger than he is," he downplayed it. "I wasn't going to let him anywhere near you."

"I could tell." It was a good feeling, and a stroke of luck having him there. "Would you like a glass of wine?" He nodded. It was one way to extend the evening with her. They could see her shattered front window from where they were standing. She got a bottle of wine, two glasses, and an opener, and he opened it, and poured them each a glass as they sat in the living room.

"I never thought there was risk involved in planning weddings." He smiled ruefully. "Except for the bride and groom."

"There usually isn't." She smiled gratefully at him. "Thank God you were there." He nodded, looking serious. He liked how brave she was, and had acted calmly and quickly, but she hadn't felt as calm as she looked, nor had he. He was like a rock you could lean on, and stand on and hide behind if you needed to. He was smiling, and then he leaned toward her and kissed her, gently holding her face in his hand. She felt irresistibly drawn toward him as he kissed her, as though a force stronger than they were was pulling them together. He kissed her again and put his arms around her and held her tight in the circle of his arms. She felt safe there.

"I'm not ever going to let anyone hurt you, Faith," he whispered. He was her self-appointed protector, and she couldn't stop kissing him and didn't want to, and he felt the same. Passion rose up in both of them that they had both long since forgotten and said they didn't want, and now it enveloped them, and bound them together stronger than any force Faith had ever felt. He pulled away for a minute and looked at her.

"Are you okay?" he asked softly. "With this, I mean?"

"Very much so," she whispered.

"Good, me too," he whispered back, and went on kissing her. The wine was forgotten, and somehow Doug's attack had brought them together, and broken the chains of the past. Later, she couldn't remember exactly when or how, in the haze of passionate kisses, but he had followed her upstairs to her bedroom, their clothes lay in a heap on the floor, having drifted off their bodies, and they made love like starving people, until the sun came up. He looked at her with a smile, and spoke in a hoarse whisper, raw from a night of lovemaking.

"I think the boat just came back to the dock. I don't think we missed it." She smiled and stretched her body against his, as he held her, and was about to tell her he loved her, when they both fell asleep.

Chapter 15

Douglas Kirk's attorney contacted Charles Allbright immediately the day after he had broken the window at Faith's house, assaulted her verbally, and was arrested. His attorney said the doctor wished to make amends and pay for the damage to Ms. Ferguson's home, and that he was under a great deal of emotional stress because of the divorce and Mrs. Kirk's "aggressive position" with the civil suit she had filed. In other words, Doug was running scared and his attorney must have given him hell for running amok, attacking a future witness for the plaintiff in the civil case, and vandalizing her home. Charles guessed that he had advised his client to settle as quickly as possible, and that with behavior like that on record, he was sure to lose the case. No jury would sympathize with him. He was clearly deranged and showing all the evidence of being a sociopath. Faith was convinced now, more than ever, and a jury would be too.

Two days later, Doug's attorney made a settlement offer to Charles of a hundred thousand dollars. Charles consulted his client, advised her, and rejected the offer.

The next offer two days later was for two hundred and fifty thousand, which under advice of counsel, Phoebe rejected too. It was a heady feeling turning down that kind of money, when she could have used it.

Charles advised Doug's attorney then that they remained firm about going to trial in the civil case, and wanted the full amount they were suing for, a million dollars.

A week after Doug had broken the window at Faith's house, his attorney offered Phoebe five hundred thousand dollars and they graciously accepted it, and kept the restraining order in force. For the abuse and torture Phoebe suffered at Doug's hands, she had gained half a million dollars. It didn't make the experience more tolerable and less painful, but it made her feel as though she had been avenged, and the money gave her some freedom and security. She sent some money home to her mother and sister, and Faith helped her to put the rest in an investment account, so it would grow. The legal engagement had been so brief, Charles Allbright only charged her twelve thousand dollars.

The whole operation had been extremely effective. The most important piece, aside from the money, was that Doug was obliged to contact all of the nursing agencies and say that there had been a grave misunderstanding and misstatement on his part on the subject of the abilities and conduct of Phoebe Smith, his surgical nurse, and he apologized for any unintentional shadow cast on her reputation. Her name had been cleared and she could go back to nursing whenever she wanted to, but she was having so much fun working for Faith that she assured her she would stay for the length of time she'd promised, until March when Violet returned to work after she had the twins. Faith was relieved to hear it, and happy her threat of a lawsuit against Doug had gone so well.

The last days of August were magical for Edward and Faith. They decided not to tell anyone what had happened, not even Morgan or Hope, for once. They wanted to guard it and keep it between them like a precious secret. Like an unborn child, they wanted to shield it from air and light, and people's comments, opinions, and assumptions. They called and texted several times a day, and spent their nights together. He left before Violet arrived in the morning, and arrived when Faith was alone at night, and they slept in each other's arms after making love for hours. He could hardly wait to come home to her at night and felt like a lovesick boy. They made each other laugh, cooked together, watched TV together, went to movies, and on long walks in the park on weekends. She wanted him to meet Hope and her mother and Jean-Pierre, but not yet. She wanted what they had to belong only to them for as long as they could manage it. After that they would be under the curious gaze of the world, and other people's jealousy and fears for them.

He was still settling in at the New York office, and with September came a flood of new clients for Faith. It took both of her assistants, Violet and Phoebe, to keep track of it all. Phoebe was learning the ropes surprisingly quickly, and really was a huge help. Violet was hanging in, getting bigger every day but feeling well.

Even though she was only four months pregnant in September, her body seemed to be growing and expanding at a rapid rate. She was big for a four-month pregnancy, but not if you knew it was twins. She was slowly warming up to the idea, not wildly excited or even happy about it yet, but not as devastatingly depressed about it as she had been.

The blood test came back and they were told it was twin girls, and from the sonogram, they knew that they were in one sac, so they were identical. Both Faith and Hope thought it was fantastic that she was having twins, but she hadn't gotten there yet. All she could think of were the downsides, and in Violet's opinion there were many. She tried to avoid thinking about it at all, by focusing on her work. Faith tried to give her all the tasks she could that involved sitting down, desk work, research, phone calls. She gave Phoebe the more active jobs that required physical exertion. Violet wanted to do more, but Phoebe and Faith wouldn't let her. She sometimes went home frustrated at night, but she was grateful that she was still on her feet and could come to work every day. She was terrified of being put to bed and getting stuck there for months. She was going to be even angrier than she already was at the twins, if she got confined to bed because of them, but they were all aware that it could happen.

After Labor Day, Faith got a flood of new clients. She was already working on the big December wedding she'd had on the books for months. They were putting a full-sized skating rink on the grounds of their Long Island estate for the rehearsal dinner. There would be ice dancing with professional skaters, with figure skates for all. The setting would look like Paris at the turn of the twentieth century. And the wedding itself would look like the Russian imperial palace in St. Petersburg, worthy of a czar and czarina. The bride was wearing a white velvet gown with tiny stars on it, trimmed in white sable, with a full-length white sable cape when she arrived, and would remove for the ceremony. Faith had set designers from Broadway helping her build the décor. They were already painting it now. There were to be ice sculptures everywhere, and caviar stations every few feet. The bride's father was Russian of dubious origins, her mother a Polish beauty. The bride was exquisite, and she was marrying a handsome young Russian who worked for her father. The wedding was to be two days before Christmas, with five hundred guests. They had another equally large traditional wedding for a senator's daughter scheduled for New Year's Eve. The Save the Dates had just gone out. And they had a smaller wedding on a chartered yacht.

Then there were all the normal-scale weddings, of young American couples with anxious parents, demanding mothers, quarrelsome brides, and jealous sisters. The two big weddings alone could have kept her busy for the next year, and then she had all the others.

The press wanted to cover the event before Christmas, but the father of the bride wanted no press at all. There was a faintly dangerous flavor to the family of the bride. But the price he was willing to pay made up for it. There was nothing illegal involved or for Faith to do, it was just obvious that the father of the bride had some very unusual, interesting connections. When Faith made her site visit, there were security guards armed with machine guns every-where. They were not her typical clients, and the velvet gown with the sable cape was being made by Chanel for a million dollars. The bride was actually very sweet and the groom was a very nice young man, but Faith was convinced that the bride's father had skills and practices she didn't want to know about.

Faith told Edward about some of the more interesting weddings and clients, without violating any confidentiality. "Your job is way more interesting than Wall Street." And he was stunned by what she could charge as a percentage of the wedding. It was a highly lucrative business and always had been, and a happy one, even if stressful. Faith was artful at not getting involved in mother-daughter battles. No matter whose side you took, as an outsider you would lose, and she didn't want to be in that position. She used extreme diplomacy to avoid it.

Edward and Faith had managed to keep their relationship safe from all prying eyes and tattling tongues for several weeks, despite the obvious joy they radiated. Violet kept telling her how well and rested she looked, which was laughable since they hardly slept, but they were both so happy. Faith couldn't remember ever being this happy, and Edward knew he hadn't been. His staid, work-driven life had satisfied him for years, but Faith satisfied him more and filled him. She nurtured all the empty spaces that had gone neglected and unfed for so long. He opened new horizons to her, they were vistas of the heart, like blue skies on a summer day.

Morgan and Alex came back from their honeymoon a week after Labor Day, just in time for Morgan to start work on Fashion Week. The time on the giant sailboat had been something out of a dream, with well-trained, highly efficient crew members to wait on them night and day, perfect weather in the Mediterranean, fishing and swimming, and stopping at small picturesque ports along the way, or dropping anchor in small peaceful coves. They had spent their last weekend at the Hotel du Cap-Eden-Roc, where their boat dropped them off and left them, and they flew home from Nice.

They were thrilled to find Blake thriving when they got home. He was two months old and smiled all the time. He had chubby little legs and several chins, and looked like a baby in an ad, and he gurgled and cooed all the time. Helen took impeccable care of him, and said he was brilliant. Alex could never quite get out of his mind how his mother had looked when she said goodbye to him, but Morgan had moved on. The baby was theirs now. He never thought of the past. He lived in the present. It was one of the differences between the two men. Morgan was upbeat and positive, always plunging forward. Alex got nostalgic from time to time and was more introspective. But they complemented each other.

They were eager to see Faith and Edward, and had no idea what had gone on between them, or the love that had blossomed like giant sunflowers while they were away. They invited them both to dinner, and they accepted. Faith wondered, the night before, if it was a wise decision, if they wanted to keep their secret. She thought Morgan would spot it immediately.

"So what if he does?" Edward shrugged as they lay naked in bed and he admired her body. She was in flawless shape, with her ballet workout on Skype nearly every day. Edward went to the gym as often as he could, when he had time, but wasn't as dogged about it. He was impressed by how disciplined Faith was. If she said she would do something, she did.

"I just don't want everyone talking about us, and telling us what they think, or interfering," Faith said.

"What are you afraid of?" he asked her gently. He had a way of always cutting to the heart of the matter, and laying her worries bare.

"I don't know . . . maybe they'll tell you that you can do better, or you should have someone younger, or I'm weird because I've never been married. Maybe I am weird," she said, looking up at him with huge eyes, "but I love you. I don't want anyone messing with that."

"They can't. What we have belongs to us. They can't touch it. And I don't want anyone younger, or older." He was two years older than Faith, they were on level ground. "I want *you*. I've never loved anyone as I do you, and nothing is going to change that. I don't want to change you, and you love me as I am. And I don't give a damn what anyone thinks, who approves or who doesn't," he said with confidence.

"Then they'll all start pushing us to get married, and that would ruin everything," Faith said, worried.

"Would it 'ruin everything'?" he asked. "Why? I wouldn't mind being married to you. I think I'd like it." He had been thinking about it lately, and wondering if they should at some point. He already knew he wanted to be with her forever. "But I'm perfectly happy staying like this, if that's what you prefer."

"I'm afraid of marriage. It screws everything up. It ruins everything."

He laughed. "That from the number-one foremost wedding planner in the world?"

"Yes, every time my mother got married, it destroyed the relationship. It killed it. And half the people I do weddings for don't stay married. Some of them have me do their second and third weddings."

"What makes you think the relationship would have lasted any longer if they didn't get married? Maybe those relationships were flawed in the first place. I don't think ours is."

"Neither do I. Let's keep it that way and be lovers forever," she said, and kissed him.

"As long as you don't marry someone else and keep me as a lover on the side. I would not like that." He kissed her neck and sent chills down her spine. They made magic in bed, as never before for either of them, but they loved each other in a simple wholesome way too. Sometimes they laughed like children. It was interesting realizing how afraid she was of marriage, and how against it. He always had been too, but he wasn't afraid of it with her, and he was willing to do whatever she wanted, including keeping their relationship from his brother, but knowing Morgan, he was sure it wouldn't last long. He had a sixth sense about people, and he knew Edward well, and he had never been as happy in his life. That was hard to hide. Why would he? Just to keep her happy, he agreed.

They were invited to Alex and Morgan's home for dinner two days after they got home. Morgan called his brother, and Alex called Faith. It was going to be a simple pasta dinner in their kitchen, which was always fun, just the four of them.

They arrived at the appointed hour separately, Edward five minutes after Faith. They looked surprised and pleased to see each other. Alex and Morgan were full of their trip, with gorgeous pictures of all their stops, and the tiny villages where they went. They had sailed down as far as Sardinia, and back up again, with time to fish and swim in Corsica. They sailed a lot at night, so they didn't waste time in the day. It sounded like a fantastic trip.

During dinner, Morgan asked his brother what he'd been up to, and Edward said he'd been settling in at the office, and it was always challenging when a new senior partner took over. He bored him to death with work details and looked innocent. Faith had been telling Alex about some of the new weddings they had booked, especially the more extravagant ones.

Edward was innocently eating his pasta carbonara, which they had prepared because they knew it was his favorite, when Morgan narrowed his eyes and stared at him. "You're lying to me!" he said to him.

"Don't be ridiculous," Edward said, laughing. "What am I lying about? I just told you your pasta is delicious, and it is, that's no lie." He didn't dare look at Faith. She was laughing too. Morgan was uncanny. He could sense a secret faster than anyone alive, and he knew Edward too well.

"You touched your ear. You always touch your left ear when you lie. You've done it since I was a kid. You're lying about something," he accused his older brother with a Sherlock Holmes look, determined to find out what it was.

"Let's see, what could I be lying about? That work is a little boring right now? No, that's not a lie. Unfortunately, it's true . . . the food tonight is excellent, you're such a good cook . . . that's not a lie. . . ."

"What have you been doing lately?" Morgan said to distract him.

"Not much. I've been home every night, I don't have any good friends here yet, except you two." As he said it, he touched his left ear, and Faith almost choked on her food. Morgan was right. He had a tic he was unaware of. Morgan screamed and pointed at him.

"That's it! You're lying. You've been out getting laid every night. Who is it?"

"First of all, I was not 'getting laid,' and second of all," Edward said, grinning, "it's none of your business."

"Then I'm right!" They were all laughing. "Are you in love?" Morgan loved knowing all the news, and everyone's secrets. They both knew that about him.

"No," Edward said firmly, shaking his head, and then he touched his right ear, and Morgan screamed even louder.

"You touched your right ear. That's only for JUMBO lies. . . . You're in love! Tell me who." Edward was trying to keep a straight face, and Faith was nearly having convulsions, laughing. She hadn't expected Morgan to conduct the Spanish Inquisition. She thought he'd be nosey, not possessed.

"I am not in love," he said, holding up both hands so he didn't touch his ears, and as he did it, he shot a guilty side glance at Faith, and Morgan jumped up from the table and stared at him. "Men my age don't fall in love," Edward said firmly, and Morgan rolled his eyes.

"Touch both your ears for that one. That's the biggest lie of all. You're only ten years older than I am. That's nothing." He looked intently from Faith to Edward, then narrowed his eyes and stared at them after he sat down again. "Oh my God . . . what have you two been doing while we were gone?"

"Nothing," they said in unison, and Morgan looked at them even harder. All four of them started laughing again.

"Oh my God. Oh my God. Oh my GOD! Are you dating, or just sleeping together? What are you doing? It's you two, I know it." Edward and Faith exchanged a look, and they both looked happily guilty, as she reached out and took Edward's hand.

"Okay, Sherlock. You win. I'm in love with your brother. There. Are you happy?"

"EXTREMELY happy." He beamed at them, and Alex was stunned. Morgan was right. "When are you getting married?"

"Never," she said firmly. "I love your brother and I am never going to marry him, *because* I love him. And that's not a lie because I said it."

"Why not?" Morgan looked disappointed.

"Because I don't believe in marriage," she said.

"Oh my God, what are you? Like those drug dealers who sell it, but don't use it. You do the most divine weddings on the planet and you don't believe in marriage?"

"Nope."

"You're a very sick woman . . . cruel. He's my brother. He's a respectable man. He comes from an honorable family, and you're sleeping with him and won't marry him? What kind of woman are you? You're just using him for sex, and taking him lightly? I'm shocked."

"Absolutely." She grinned at her friend, and Edward was smiling broadly at her, enjoying it. Morgan had met his match. "He's my sex slave."

"You're a very loose woman. If I had known you're just toying with my brother, I wouldn't have made you my best carbonara. I would have given you hamburgers, or dog food." He came around the table then and hugged them both. "I love you. You are my two favorite people in the world. Please get married, and have babies. Then we can all go to the park together."

"No babies," they said in unison again.

"Okay, you can come to the park with us anyway. We're looking for a house in Connecticut and thinking of giving up the house in the Hamptons, although we'd miss it," he said, changing the subject. "I'll hate the commute, but I think it would be good for the kids." Alex agreed. "You'd better get married, you know. If you don't, your clients will think you're a slut," he said to Faith.

"Only if you tell them," she responded with a grin.

He hugged them both again when they left, and told them how happy he was that they had found each other. Alex said the same.

In the cab going home, Faith turned to Edward. "See what I mean, everyone is going to bug us to get married."

"No, just Morgan. He's a little crazy that way. He's wanted to get married and have children of his own since he was a kid. I'm glad he is now. It completes him."

She looked at Edward then and whispered, "You complete me." He kissed her, and as soon as they got back to her house, he raced her up the stairs to her bedroom, took off her clothes, and made love to her. Afterward, they laughed about Morgan again.

"In thirty-four years, he has never told me that I have a tell when I lie. I hope no one has figured that out in business."

She rolled over again and kissed him. "I like being the loose woman in your life."

"So I noticed." He grinned at her. It had all been in good fun. So now Morgan and Alex knew about them. It was bound to come out sooner or later. Hope knew about him too, and that Faith was in love with him. Their mother didn't. Faith didn't feel ready to tell her yet. She'd want them to get married too.

Alex and Morgan had Blake christened in September. It was nice for Faith and Edward to be godparents, and even more appropriate now that they were together. But they were good about keeping their secret. Blake looked beautiful in a long lace christening gown from Morgan's family. They had invited a few friends and had lunch at a nearby restaurant, and Helen took the baby home for a nap. He'd had a big morning, and was very well behaved. He slept through his christening because Helen had fed him beforehand.

Marianne and Jean-Pierre were leaving on a cruise at the end of September, and Faith had dinner with them the night before they left. Hope came to town too. She was six months pregnant, and looked bigger by then. She had big, healthy babies. Faith admitted to her mother that she was "seeing" someone, but not that he was turning out to be the love of her life. It seemed like too much to share, and she still felt protective of the relationship.

Marianne questioned her about it, but dropped the subject after a few minutes. She was easier to convince than Morgan that it was nothing serious. Faith didn't want her mother hounding her from now on about getting married.

Jean-Pierre seemed in good form. He looked healthy and rested. His heart was fine. They were going on a month-long cruise in South America. It was spring there, and they were excited about it.

When they said goodbye to them after dinner, and wished them a good trip, they all hugged one another. And when Jean-Pierre hugged Faith, he whispered to her, "I don't know who he is, but you look so happy . . . keep him . . . don't let him go." He smiled at her again over his shoulder as they left. She wondered how he knew. It was as though he had a sixth sense.

Chapter 16

Faith was busy with a number of smaller weddings in the fall. They were all very traditional and elegant. Some older people, some younger ones, none of whom wanted big weddings, but they wanted beautiful ones. Sometimes the smaller weddings were almost as much work.

Faith was concentrating on the two bigger ones in December. Violet and Phoebe were handling the smaller ones together. Violet was doing the desk work, and Phoebe the legwork, and it was working well. She was still having fun at the job.

Violet seemed to get bigger every day. The doctor said that both twins were healthy, and Violet had resigned herself to her fate. Jordan was excited about having two identical little girls, and planned to be at the birth. He had been reading about it, so he'd know what to expect. Violet didn't want to think about it, and she admitted to Phoebe that she was scared, but at least she was still working.

September and October rushed by. It felt as though their mother and Jean-Pierre had been gone only days, when they came back a month later at the end of October. They had had a fabulous trip and met people they liked on the cruise. And Jean-Pierre looked rested and healthy, so did Marianne.

Hope had volunteered to do Thanksgiving at her house in November. Faith was going to do Christmas Eve. Hope's baby was due on Christmas Day, so there was no telling if she'd be there. She was having it in the city, as she had the others, so if she went into labor during Christmas Eve dinner, she wouldn't have far to go.

The big news about Thanksgiving was that Faith had invited Edward to go with her, which would be his first expo-sure to her family. She was nervous about it and so was he. He had heard so many stories about them that he didn't know what to expect. If it went well, she wanted him to come to Christmas Eve dinner at her house. It would be too much for Hope to host it by then, and her mother didn't like giving dinner parties or cooking, although Jean-Pierre had offered to make a leg of lamb, gigot with haricots vert, with lots of garlic, French style. But Faith was just going to have her caterer do it, with their traditional Christmas meal.

On Christmas night she was going to dinner at Morgan and Alex's with Edward. His son was going to be with his mother in Aspen. Wesley never spent holidays with him. Old habits died hard. Edward was happy to spend the holidays with Faith, and follow her traditions. He didn't have any of his own, since he hadn't been married, so he didn't have to entertain his family during the holidays, and both his mother and Morgan were wonderful cooks. Their parents were staying in Chicago to spend it with a group of friends, and not coming to New York. But the brothers would be together, and Alex and Faith, and now Blake. The baby girl due in March was doing well with their surrogate. There had been no problems and they didn't expect any. She was young and healthy, and it was her fifth pregnancy. She said it had been no different from the others. They sent her check every month, and she sent them all her scans and medical reports. It had been uneventful.

Faith was buried in details for the two big December weddings, and Phoebe and Violet were handling the others, with Faith's supervision. They had one at the beginning of November, which Violet was in charge of, and Phoebe was getting very good at handling the details. And Faith was supervising the one on the chartered boat.

They went together to watch the setup of the November wedding in the morning. It was complete by early afternoon. Faith cruised through to make sure it looked the way it was supposed to and they hadn't forgotten anything. She thanked them both for what a good job they'd done, and she was just leaving when she saw Violet wince and double over. She watched her for a few minutes and saw it happen again. Violet sat down, and tried to act as though nothing was happening. Faith walked back into the room to talk to her, after watching her for a few minutes.

"What's happening?"

"Nothing, I'm fine." Violet smiled up at her, and winced again. She'd been on her feet all day, for too long, and the babies were heavy now. She was six months pregnant, and it was still too soon for them to survive if they came early, particularly since they were twins, and would be small. Their combined weight was impressive, but they would be too small and underdeveloped to live outside the womb.

"Violet, tell me the truth," Faith said, watching her. "What's happening?"

"I'm having contractions," she said, looking panicked. "I thought they'd stop, but they haven't."

"How long have you been having them?" Faith asked her.

"A few hours," Violet admitted in a meek voice. "But we were busy."

"Oh God. That's it, Vi. You're done." She went to look for Phoebe and told her what was happening. "That means you're on alone for the rest of it. Can you handle it?" Phoebe looked scared but she wanted to prove to Faith she could do it. She was pretty sure she could. She didn't want to let her or Violet down.

"I can do it," she assured her.

"Do you need me to come back?"

Phoebe shook her head with a grin. "If I need to, I'll call you." The job had been good for her self-confidence after Doug had nearly destroyed it.

"Call if you need me," Faith reminded her. The wedding was at a very exclusive club, she asked the catering manager to get them a cab, and she helped Violet out. She looked terrified, and so was Faith. If something happened in the cab, she wouldn't know what to do. "Should I call an ambulance?"

"No, just get me to the hospital, I'll be fine."

They called Jordan from the taxi, and Violet's doctor, and promised the cab driver a huge tip to get them there fast, which he did. They were waiting for Violet at the emergency entrance when they got there. They took her upstairs immediately with Faith running behind her. They put her to bed and started an IV with medication to stop premature labor.

Doctors and nurses came and went, they checked her repeat-edly, and she and Jordan were in tears and looked tense. The contractions stopped within the hour, and her water hadn't broken, but the doctor was very clear with her. Violet was on bed rest from now until the delivery. In the hospital for the next week, at home after that, using a bedpan, and flat on her back. She burst into tears when the doctor told her, and Jordan said she had to be serious now, or they'd lose the twins. She couldn't get up until two weeks before her due date, and they might do a C-section then.

It was hardcore now. She had run around for six months, and now the jig was up. Faith gave her a hug, and she was still crying with Jordan when Faith left. Faith promised to visit her, and she knew Phoebe would too, when she wasn't busy. Violet just had to do what they told her now, or she'd lose the twins, or they could be born too early, survive severely damaged because they were too premature, which would almost be worse. She needed at least another month with the twins in utero. She'd be stuck in bed over the holidays too, until mid-January, or her due date at the beginning of February.

Faith felt sorry for her when she left the hospital. She called Phoebe at the club to see if she needed help, but she said she was doing fine. Faith felt guilty for letting Violet work as long as she did, but she needed the help and Violet hadn't wanted to stay home and take it easy. But now she didn't want to lose their babies. Bed rest for three months sounded like a prison sentence to her. It seemed like a high price to pay for a pregnancy. Their mother had done it for them too.

Two weeks later, right before Thanksgiving, Annabelle Albert called to say that she'd had her baby boy. He weighed ten pounds and she'd had him by C-section. She was elated. She said he looked like Jeremy, and her parents were wild about him. She said that her parents were still together, her mother was checking up on her dad, and he was behaving for the time being. Annabelle was just happy that she'd had the baby, he was healthy, and her parents were still married. Faith had Phoebe send her flowers at the hospital. Her wedding had gone down in their history as one of the most spectacular they'd ever done. But the one she was doing at Christmas was going to be close to it, and was turning out to be even more expensive. Million-dollar weddings seemed to be becoming commonplace among the ultra wealthy and segments of the population who could afford it. There weren't many, but they weren't as rare as they used to be. And with a forty percent commission to her over and above the cost of a major wedding and twenty-five to thirty percent for small ones, she was beginning to amass a sizable fortune, which she was trying to invest responsibly. She had a financial advisor she trusted, and occasionally she talked about investments with Edward, who was knowledgeable about it too. He didn't know exactly what she made on a wedding, but he could guess it was a great deal of money, given the wealth of her clients. It was a very lucrative business, and she the most in-demand wedding planner in New York.

They called Violet every day, and she sounded depressed being stuck in the hospital. They kept her for two weeks, and then let her go home on bed rest there. She said that if she even stood up to go to the bathroom, she had contractions again, so she had to lie flat all the time now. It was a big treat when she could sit up in bed for a little while. Phoebe had gone to visit her, and Faith went once, but she was busy dealing with all their holiday weddings, and they were short-handed now without Vi.

It was hard even taking a break for Thanksgiving. They had a good-sized wedding two days later, but Faith managed to take Thanksgiving Day off, because no one else was working either, and she was planning to go back to work the day after.

She and Edward drove out to Connecticut in the morning, to Hope's farm. It was his introduction to her family, and she was afraid of what he'd think of them, but he never let her down. He and Angus clicked immediately. Edward loved Hope, especially because she was Faith's twin and he knew how close they were. And Hope loved him. Faith went out to help her in the kitchen when Angus was carving the turkey, and Hope whispered to her, "Marry him. He's fantastic. We love him."

"I love him too, but I'm not getting married. We don't need to. We don't want kids. He already has a son, and I'm too old."

"You're not," Hope objected. "We're the same age, and I'm having one."

"It's your fourth. I'd be having my first at forty-three, at the earliest. I don't want to do that, and neither does he. We love each other, why do we need to get married?"

"So he sticks around," Hope said simply.

"That doesn't mean anything. Dad didn't. He left Mom with us to take care of. If he loves me, he'll stay, and if he doesn't, he'll go. I don't need to put a leash on him, or have a baby to keep him. That doesn't work anyway."

"How's Violet doing by the way?" Hope asked her.

"She's depressed. She hates being stuck in bed. She can't even get up for the bathroom. It can't be much fun. I don't know how Mom did it with us. Baby-making is serious business."

"Tell me about it," Hope said, patting her enormous stomach. "It better be a girl this time. Angus says if it isn't, he wants to try again. Easy for him to say." She grinned at Faith then. "We could be pregnant together."

"Not on your life." Faith laughed at her. "I can't believe you'd have five kids."

"I might. Angus really wants six. He always said so. Maybe the next ones would be twins, and then I'd be done."

"If not, you'd be having your last one at forty-five," Faith reminded her. It sounded awful to her, but not to Hope. They were different, even though they were twins.

Edward enjoyed talking to Jean-Pierre, and to Faith's mother. He thought Jean-Pierre was very interesting, and Angus a great guy. The children sat at the table with them. The Thanksgiving meal was delicious, and the atmosphere around the table was jolly and congenial. Edward said he had enjoyed it, and he didn't think her family was as crazy as she said.

"They put on a good show for outsiders." She smiled at him. "They all loved you. They think we should get married of course. And Hope wants us to have a baby. Angus wants one or two more. I don't know how she does it. I can't think of anything worse than having a baby at forty-five, but she doesn't mind it."

"They seem happy," Edward commented, as they drove back to the city.

"They are," Faith confirmed. "She was a good sport to

do lunch today. She loves her country life as wife and mother. I have trouble remembering sometimes that she was a big model with a pretty glamorous life. She gave it all up for Angus and never looked back. She's too old for it now anyway."

"She's gorgeous, and so are you." He smiled at her. "It was nice meeting them all. Now I know who you're talking about."

She smiled at him and leaned over and kissed him. They went to bed early, and the next day, she got up for her ballet class at six A.M., and then headed for the office. They had a wedding the next day, and she had to do all the prep work with Phoebe. They both missed having Violet's help. But they managed without her, and Faith had hired two more assistants for the actual wedding. They were to follow Phoebe's directions. Faith stayed with her, but was impressed by how efficient she was. On Saturday, the day of the wedding, Faith came home at two A.M. and literally fell into bed next to Edward. She woke him up when she got into bed, and he rolled over, opened an eye, and smiled at her.

"Did it go okay?"

"Yes, except the six-year-old ring bearer couldn't find the rings. We finally did. He left them in the bathroom. His mom made him go before the ceremony, so he forgot them. He was the bride's nephew."

"It's no wonder you hate weddings," he said, "I would too if I went to one or two a week, and had to stay through the whole thing."

"It's always sweet, though. No matter how often you see it, there's always some moment that touches you and makes it all seem worth it, a look in a groom's eye, a special smile between them, a tear on her cheek when she says her vows, a mother looking at her daughter, a father's tears when he leaves her at the altar."

"It's nice that you still feel that way." He smiled at her.

"I may not in three weeks, after the big Russian extravaganza. Those are the hard ones, a million details to keep track of, and then some idiot forgets to deliver the bouquet and no one notices."

"If we ever get married, we should do it at the Elvis Chapel in Las Vegas, so you don't have to do all the work," he said, smiling.

"I like the work," she said sleepily. "The work is the best part, because that's what makes it perfect. I did Hope and Angus's wedding. He wore a kilt, with his family tartan. He looked terrific. I really love him." She kissed Edward then and loved the fact that she could come home now and find him in her bed. They were going to see the tree at Rockefeller Center the next day. It wasn't lit yet, but it was decorated, and she always loved seeing it. Edward wanted to go ice-skating. He added a whole new dimension to her life now in addition to work. Somehow, they managed to fit it all in, and it made their lives richer.

She fell asleep, cuddled up next to him. It was nice to know he'd be there in the morning. In a way, he was a little bit like Angus, a big, easygoing guy, protective as a bear when he needed to be, and fierce as a lion when necessary. The rest of the time he was a teddy bear to cuddle and sleep with.

They had another small wedding the following weekend, which Faith let Phoebe handle alone. They had a big, complicated light show, instead of floral decorations. Phoebe was telling them where to set it up, while they explained that it wasn't possible. There were no outlets where she wanted them to put it. Eventually, they solved it with a series of extension cords. The head engineer came over to thank her for helping before the ceremony started. He had red hair and freckles, and a red heart tattooed on his arm.

"That's what I'm here for," she said pleasantly.

She thought he was cute, but probably young. She hadn't even thought about dating since she left Doug. She hadn't been on a date since before she met him and felt like she wouldn't even know how, and didn't want to. The experience with him was so traumatic, she had no desire to take a chance again. Faith said she'd get over it but she wasn't so sure. She still felt deeply marked by it and badly bruised.

"You're an electrician?" she asked him, and he smiled.

"I'm actually an engineer. I went to MIT, but I'm out of work at the moment, so I do party setups on the side. It's very lucrative. Henrik," he said, and stuck out his hand. "My father's Dutch."

"I'm kind of in the same boat you are. I'm a surgical nurse in plastic surgery, but I'm out of work so I'm doing this as a temp till March."

"Sometimes it's nice to learn something new. But I like what I do, so I'm still looking."

"Me too," she agreed.

"Do you want to go for a drink after the wedding? I have to stay till the end of the reception, then I can go," he said. He was friendly and easy to talk to.

"I have to stay for the whole breakdown, until they load the trucks. That takes until about four or five A.M.," she explained.

"Another time then?" He looked hopeful and she smiled. She wanted to have a drink with him, she just couldn't that night. She handed him her number and hoped he'd call her. He had a nice, easy style and he was obviously smart if he'd gone to MIT. She was impressed by that.

He came to say goodbye to her when he left after the reception.

"Sorry you have to stay. I'll call you this week. Maybe we can have lunch." She liked the idea of that, and he seemed like a sweet guy. She smiled after he left. Maybe whether he called or not, she was ready after all. And maybe Faith was right, that the human spirit was stronger and more resilient than we thought. Faith said it a lot, and she believed it.

A week later, Violet called Faith in the office. She was back in the hospital. Labor had started again. She hadn't done anything to cause it. And this time her water had broken, so she had to deliver within twenty-four hours, or she could get a terrible infection. It was still early labor. The contractions were strong and she was worried about the babies. She was seven months now, so it was safe to deliver them, even though they were early. The doctor said they were small and they were going to try and let her deliver them vaginally, at least one of them, and then intervene with a C-section if they had to for the second twin. They had given her a shot of something to make the babies' lungs mature, since they were premature.

Faith called to check on her a few times throughout the day. Nothing had happened, but there was no turning back now. If she hadn't gone into strong labor within twenty-four hours of her water breaking, they would do a C-section. She was within a few hours of it the last time Faith called her, and then Phoebe called her one more time, and a nurse answered the phone and said she was in hard labor and had been moved to the delivery room in case they had to do a rapid C-section. She reported back to Faith and they were both concerned. It was showtime for Violet.

Jordan was with her, and they had just given her an epidural, which was supposed to ease the pain soon. It started to work, and a few minutes later, the doctor told her to start pushing. It was harder than anything she'd ever done in her entire life, and she was already exhausted from the contractions she'd had all day. She was tired and in pain and terrified for her babies. She felt guilty now for all the times she had complained about them and resented having to be in bed for the last month. What if one or both of them died? Maybe they knew she didn't want them, and they didn't want her either.

She was sobbing as they kept telling her to push. After a while, she just couldn't. They had told her the babies were small, but they still weren't coming out. One of the nurses shifted something inside her, which felt like tremendous pressure, and with the next pushes, the first baby started to come down. They put an oxygen mask on Violet and she felt dizzy, and then she heard a little wail in the room. The first twin had been born. There were two obstetricians and two pediatricians in the room and half a dozen nurses. They took the baby to the NICU in an incubator. She didn't even get to see her. She was already deep into pushing again, with everyone shouting at her to push harder. She felt like she was drowning between each contraction now as though she was going underwater and being held there. Then she heard them saying something about transverse, and someone told her they were going to do a C-section to get the second baby out. She wanted to ask if the baby was all right, if it was still alive, but they told her to count backward from nine, and at eight she was unconscious.

They had told Jordan to leave the room, and he was crying when he did. They brought the second baby out as quickly as they could, and they ran past him with the incubator to the NICU. He didn't know how either of his daughters was, or his wife, and there was no one to tell him. They were all busy. He wondered if Violet was going to die. They had given her a transfusion. It wasn't supposed to be like this. It was supposed to be easy and beautiful and very moving. Instead it was terrifying. What if he lost all three of them? He walked to the waiting room, and waited for someone to come and tell him what was going on. He finally went to the nurses' desk and asked the nurse on duty. He asked if his wife and daughters were alive and she felt sorry for him. They had forgotten all about him.

"Of course. Your wife is in the recovery room. She's still sedated. She'll sleep for a few hours and then we'll put her in a room. And your daughters are in the NICU for observation. They're in an incubator together because they're preemies, and we keep twins together. But they're a pretty good size. They're four pounds each. Would you like to see them?" He nodded, feeling drained, as though all the blood had left his body. He followed the nurse to the NICU. He was still wearing the scrubs, from the delivery room, and she put a gown over them and tied it in back, like a surgeon. They went inside and she handed him rubber gloves. Then he saw them. They were in one incubator just as she had said. They each wore a miniature diaper, like for a doll, and nothing else, and were under the warming lights. They were tiny, but they were perfectly formed, and they looked identical. They were both sleeping and one of them was sucking her thumb. They were alive, and so beautiful. He couldn't stop crying as he looked at them. He wanted to touch them, but he was afraid to. He wanted to see Vi and tell her how beautiful they were.

"Are they okay?" he asked the nurse, who had stayed with him, and she nodded.

"Small, but healthy. They have some catching up to do, they're eight weeks early, but they're doing well." She smiled at him. He looked like he'd been hit by a bus, and he felt it.

But the babies were alive. Now he wanted to see Violet to be sure she was too.

They brought her down to a room three hours later and she was still sleepy. He kissed her and she woke up halfway, and dozed between talking to him.

"Are they okay?"

"They're gorgeous, they look perfect." She nodded and smiled, and went back to sleep, as Jordan sat next to her and watched her. He didn't want to leave her. What if she died during the night, bled to death or choked? They were parents now, and he needed her. He couldn't do this without her. He had thought she was dying in the delivery room, and she thought so too.

He fell asleep in the chair next to her. It was all so much harder than they had told them it would be, than anyone had told them the day they got married and they said their vows to each other. It all seemed so easy then, but it wasn't. This was the next step. One of the big steps. Maybe the biggest, from people to parents. He could still see their little faces as he fell asleep. They looked like dolls. And he realized that he finally knew what love was, for his daughters and his wife. This was what he had meant when he promised to love her forever. Now he knew what love, honor, and cherish meant . . . it meant Violet and their babies.

Chapter 17

Christmas was a race against time this year, especially without Violet, whom Faith could always count on. But Phoebe was good too. And she had learned a lot since the summer.

Faith had been to see Violet in the hospital. She looked pretty badly beaten up. She'd had three transfusions, a normal delivery, and a C-section. But the babies were stable. Their lungs were responding, and they were a good size for preemies. They would be in the hospital for eight weeks, until their due date, and she could stay at the hospital with them all day to feed them. She was going to try and nurse them. She looked relieved, but not happy yet. The babies looked very frail, but her mother had told her that babies were hardier than they looked. Faith couldn't believe how tiny they were.

"Poor Vi looks awful. I don't know how women go through it. You're incredibly brave," Faith said when she talked to Hope.

"Sometimes it's not that bad. Vi's been through the wars. She'll bounce back. She's young, she'll be back on her feet in no time. And thank God the babies made it." Hope was close now too. She was due in ten days, on Christmas Day, and she said she felt fine. But she led a healthy life, and had an easy time with all her babies. Childbirth seemed to be easy for her, if there was such a thing. Faith wondered. She would rather have faced a rhinoceros charging straight at her than a baby coming out of her body. She couldn't imagine anything worse. And Violet looked it. Faith felt like a coward compared to her sister. And Hope would rather die or give birth ten times than plan a wedding. They each had their own kind of courage.

Faith hardly saw Edward at the moment, she was so busy with their big Russian wedding. They had identified the perfect artificial snow. It looked and felt like the real thing, except it wasn't cold to the touch, and it was so fine it crunched under their feet when they walked on it. They had tested it. It had been the one thing they'd been missing.

The wedding was to be on the twenty-third and everything was ready. The rehearsal dinner would be on the twenty-second. Faith would have Christmas with her family on

Christmas Eve. And maybe another day off, and then they had their other big wedding on New Year's Eve, the senator's daughter, and the boat wedding. After that she was taking two weeks off with Edward to go someplace warm.

He was organizing it, with no help from her. She told him to surprise her. Then all the bookings would start with new brides coming to the office in January to plan summer weddings. It was a never-ending cycle of manufactured joy to create everyone's dream wedding just the way they'd envisioned it as little girls, with pretty dresses and ball gowns with long trains, and lace veils, or sexy slip dresses slit up to the thigh, and a towering wedding cake, and a handsome prince waiting for them at the altar. They'd had one bride riding in on a white horse bareback like a medieval queen.

Faith was the keeper of dreams, the bestower of wishes, the magician who made it all happen. Some days, it was a heavy burden, but then, as they rode away with the dream complete, disappearing into the mists, for a moment she thought it was all worth it.

She wanted her own dreams now, and a taste of reality. She had waited a long time to have them. Edward was the closest she had ever come to the handsome prince in her own fantasies. He was the rescuer, the partner she had dreamed of, and a man, someone she could walk beside, and feel comfortable with in silence, or talk to in the dark of night. He came close enough to everything she had wanted and never found, until now. She didn't need to lock him in, or tie him down, or tether him. She knew he would always be beside her, because he wanted to be, just as she wanted to be with him. It was tether enough, with no need for more. The bonds that held them were strong.

The rehearsal dinner with the skating rink was as magical as she had hoped. People floated and glided on the ice with professional skaters to help them. The artificial snow was remarkable. They had ordered two truckloads. On the wedding night the czarina's palace was another fantasy with ice angels everywhere and ice stallions rearing. Ice lions and tigers, stands of Russian "vendors" ladling out caviar onto blinis and toast points. They had re-created the last days of grandeur of the czar and czarina for the wedding. It was worthy of a movie, and the father of the bride had one made. Every guest left with a tin of caviar instead of dream cake. Faith had outdone herself. Some people had babies. She had weddings. She gave fantasies to young women to cling to forever in memory in the hard times. She remembered them all. The girls who came to her in yoga clothes with tattoos and left like fairy princesses in the fairy tales of their own making. The last two big weddings of the year were going to be the most extraordinary so far. And the Albert wedding in July was almost as extravagant.

She slept until noon the day after. It was Christmas Eve, and Edward woke her gently, so she wouldn't sleep all day.

Her own caterer had arrived. They were hosting Christmas Eve dinner that night, for her mother and Jean-Pierre, Angus and Hope and the three boys, and Edward would be there. The next day would be Christmas dinner at Morgan and Alex's.

She wore a black velvet dress with matching high heels, simple diamond earrings, and her hair in a knot on Christmas Eve. She looked sleek and elegant when she was ready, and Edward smiled when he saw her. He was wearing a black velvet blazer and black slacks, and they made a handsome couple as they greeted her mother and Jean-Pierre and a waiter served them champagne. Angus wore his kilt, the one he had gotten married in, with his wonderful traditional jacket, and Hope wore an enormous red top and the only black maternity pants she could still get into. The three boys wore short black velvet pants and red sweaters. She had managed to get them all dressed and into the car in little red coats before they left Connecticut. They were a festive-looking group with the tree Edward had gotten and decorated and lit himself because Faith didn't have time, although they had had seventy-six decorated trees at the rehearsal dinner for her triumphant wedding. But Edward took care of the home front, which was what she needed and he understood. When he saw the photographs of the weddings she produced, he understood it all. She was a wizard, a wizardess for people with limitless imaginations and vast amounts of money or the reverse. What they wanted from her knew no bounds. She was the granter of wishes for their daughters. It was a kind of sacred trust for the most magical day of their lives. All their hopes rested on her, and she couldn't let them down. Other people gave birth to them, and she came into their lives for one special day, like the fairy godmother in Cinderella.

They spent a warm Christmas Eve together, and Hope got up and walked around the room a few times. She couldn't sit through a whole meal now without moving. The baby moved all the time, and got into awkward positions. They put the boys to sleep on Faith's guest-room king-sized bed, and covered them with a blanket, while the adults opened presents, drank wine, and laughed. Jean-Pierre seemed to be in glowing health, and they were going on another cruise in January. It had become a way of life now, to go to exotic places for a month or two, meet new people, enjoy being waited on, come home briefly, and leave again on another adventure. It had become their favorite thing to do. And between cruises, they went to Paris to see his mother.

Violet and Jordan were spending Christmas Eve with their babies. They had named them Lily and Rose. And Henrik had invited Phoebe out to dinner, since he had no family in

New York either, and they were going to midnight mass after dinner. Annabelle Albert was in Mexico with Jeremy, their baby, her sister and her baby, and their parents.

Edward smiled over at Faith from where he sat across the table admiring her, and she smiled at him. He looked very handsome in his velvet blazer. Hope left the table then for the fourth time, and Faith followed her out to the kitchen. The catering staff had just served the yule log and were cleaning up.

"Are you okay?" Faith asked her. She had an odd feeling about her. As though she felt her twin's body better than Hope did herself. It was part of being a twin.

"I think so. I have a backache, it's always like this at the end. You can't get comfortable anywhere."

"You were a good sport to come tonight," Faith said, and it was a long drive to the city and back. Her doctor had wanted her to stay in the city by then, but Hope wanted to be at home for Christmas with Angus and the boys on their farm. And they would drive to town when she went into labor.

Faith rubbed Hope's shoulders for a minute, and Hope smiled and then winced and doubled over, and then stood up and looked at Faith. "My back feels weird, and I have a huge feeling of pressure," she reported to Faith.

"Could you be in labor?"

"No, that's not like this. That's sharp, and it starts small and gets bigger, like a sword running through you."

"Sounds like fun," Faith said.

"This is like an elephant trying to back out of me, with its foot on my back."

"I don't like the sound of either one. Do you have contractions?"

"I have them all the time now. It just means you're getting ready. It'll be soon, maybe tomorrow or the day after."

"You should stay in town tonight," Faith said to her.

"The boys would be so disappointed. All their presents are at home. Let's go back to the table. I'm fine." She looked convincing, and they went back to the table. The men were enjoying the wine, Marianne was whispering something to Jean-Pierre, and the twins took their seats. Faith noticed that Hope wasn't talking and she winced a few times, and then it passed. She kept an eye on her, and she doubled over again when the others left the dining room.

"I think you're in labor," Faith said to her.

"I'm not, it's nothing like that."

"Maybe this time it's different."

"I've had three of them, I should know," she snapped at Faith. And then suddenly she looked panicked, rushed to the nearest bathroom, and threw up. Faith stayed with her. "I think it's something I ate," she said. "I'm sorry." And as she said it, a monumental pain tore through her and she couldn't stand up. Faith held on to her, put the lid down, and sat her on the toilet so she didn't fall. "I think the elephant just got loose."

"I think it's the baby," Faith said, and Hope nodded.

"I think you're right." Another pain ripped through her and she couldn't talk. Faith stuck her head out of the bathroom, and asked a waiter to get the man in the kilt. Angus appeared in the doorway a minute later and looked at his wife in surprise. She had seemed fine at dinner, and now she looked glazed and was clutching her sister's arm.

"What's up? Are you okay?"

"I don't know. I think it was something I ate, or maybe it's the baby." Two more pains pummeled her as they watched, and Angus and Faith exchanged a look.

"I think we should go," he said, and Faith ran to get her sister's coat. She had the feeling that whatever was happening was going to happen soon. Hope had slipped into a whole other state within minutes. She looked dazed and distracted. She didn't argue as they wrapped her in her coat, and she had to lean against Angus and he half carried her to the car parked outside. Faith ran into the living room to say they were going to make a quick run to the hospital. Edward asked if he should come.

"If you want to. They might send us home."

"Will you watch the children?" Hope asked her mother.

"Of course. She'll be fine," Faith reassured her sister.

"I'll watch the wine," Jean-Pierre offered, and they laughed, and Edward and Faith hurried out to the car. Hope was clutching the dashboard and grimacing in pain, as Angus started the car and sped off. The hospital was only a few blocks from Faith's house. And as they pulled into the driveway, Hope started to scream.

"Oh God . . . Angus . . . I don't know what's happening." She was being torn in half. Faith leapt out of the car and ran to get a nurse from the emergency room, who came back with her at a dead run.

"I think my sister's having a baby. It's her fourth one, and she says this is different. She's in terrible pain from enormous pressure."

"Thanks," the nurse said, and told a security guard to get a wheelchair fast. She turned back to Faith, who was standing outside the car, and Edward had gotten out too. Angus was with Hope, who was leaning forward with her head on the dashboard, moaning without stopping. "What's her name?" the nurse asked Faith.

"It's Hope." None of them knew if something terrible was wrong or if this was normal. But Angus had never seen it before, nor had Hope.

"Hi, Hope, let's get you out of here, shall we? You've got yourself pretty jammed in, and this doesn't look comfortable at all." Angus pressed the button to move the seat back and he and the nurse managed to pull Hope and get her in the wheelchair. Hope didn't seem able to cooperate at all.

"Oh my God, I can't sit, something is just pushing right through me." The nurse could guess what it was. She wheeled her into an exam room at full speed with Angus following in his red plaid kilt. Together, they got her on an exam table, as Hope screamed in pain, and the nurse pulled down her pants as fast as she could, covered her with a drape, and examined her.

While she did, she told Angus, "Can you get out to the desk fast, tell them I need a nurse now and an OB. I have a transverse past ten exiting now," she said, and he didn't ask her what it was. One of the nurses relayed the exact message, another nurse ran for the exam room, and the nurse at the desk called for an obstetrician "stat." Angus rushed back to the exam room, still in the dark about what was happening. The nurse who'd been with them since they arrived was explaining to Hope what she was feeling.

"I'm going to try to move the baby back up, Hope. It's lying sideways and trying to come out, we need to get the baby moved around, so we're head down here. That's the pressure you feel on your back." She looked at the other nurse and nodded, as the first nurse reached into Hope and with all her strength tried to move the baby. It didn't budge at first and Hope was screaming as they tried to apply enough pressure externally and internally to move it. The doctor rushed into the room then, saw what they were doing, and waited.

"Transverse presentation," the first nurse said.

"I can see that. Any movement?" the doctor asked. She started to say no, and suddenly Hope's whole belly changed shape, as though an elephant was shifting around. "We're almost there," she said to the doctor, and she told Hope not to push. They gave the baby an enormous push again both externally and internally, as Hope looked at Angus and screamed and he felt completely helpless as he watched. The first nurse stepped back and nodded to the doctor. He moved forward and spoke to Hope. He did an episiotomy with the instruments they handed him and told Hope to push. She was begging for relief and to get the baby out, she said it was killing her, and as she said it, the baby's head appeared, it gave a wail, and within seconds, the baby was out, looking outraged, and Hope was sobbing. It had been traumatic and quick. The baby was fine. The doctor cut the cord, and the baby stopped crying and looked around, as one of the nurses wrapped her in a blanket and handed her to Angus. She looked up at her father, and he was crying, and bent to show their daughter to Hope.

"What happened?" Hope asked, still shaken, and the doctor explained that the baby was lying sideways, and trying to push its way out sideways with the contractions. If Hope had pushed, she would have broken the baby's collarbone and shoulder and possibly her arm, and she still couldn't have gotten out, without the nurses turning her and the episiotomy. If that had failed, they would have done an emergency C-section. Her other deliveries had been easy, this one had been fast and terrifying, and excruciating. Faith had been right, she was in labor and didn't realize it.

They covered Hope with a drape and some blankets, took the baby to weigh her, and Angus bent over his wife to tell her how brave she was. Faith slipped in for a minute to make sure she was all right, and Hope was smiling.

"Ten pounds, two ounces," the nurse weighing her announced, and everyone laughed.

"You were right," the nurse said, "there was an elephant trying to get out. That's why she was so hard to move. We're going to take your wife and the baby upstairs in a few minutes and get them settled," she said to Angus. "You can come upstairs in a little while if you like." Angus nodded, still in shock. Faith stood next to her sister and kissed her.

"I'm glad you didn't have her at the house. We wouldn't have known what to do." Hope was smiling. The crisis was over, the drama had been brief, and they had the daughter they had hoped for. When they took Hope upstairs, Faith rejoined Edward and explained what had happened, and Angus joined them a minute later.

"My God, that was terrifying. Poor Hope. They had to turn the baby around while still inside to get her out. And she's huge. Poor Hope."

"I'm glad we came to the hospital. That would have been a nightmare at home," Faith said. Hope had had the baby twenty-two minutes after they left the house.

"I'll come home with you," Angus said. "I want to get out of my kilt. That's a bit much for here. Can I leave the boys with you? I want to change and come right back."

"Of course," Faith said. They drove home, still talking about what had happened. Angus changed. Marianne and Jean-Pierre left, relieved that all had turned out well in the end, and Angus went back to the hospital five minutes later, and Edward and Faith looked at each other.

"Exciting," he said.

"And scary as hell. No babies," she said to him, and he took her in his arms.

"No babies, I promise. Just us. I love you, Faith. I would die if anything happened to you." He sounded as though he meant it.

"No, you wouldn't, you'd find a better one, hopefully for you, a younger one."

"I love you, that's all I want."

"Me too," she said softly, as he held her, and she thought of her twin and what she'd just been through and was grateful it had turned out well, even if traumatic.

On Christmas night, Edward and Faith went to Morgan and Alex's home. Helen was there, holding Blake, who was a strapping five-month-old. The Christmas tree was lit and they were playing Christmas carols. It was a peaceful, happy scene. Edward and Faith told them what had happened to Hope the night before, and they were shaken by it too. Baby-making was not always as easy as people assumed.

Edward and Faith had visited Hope that afternoon, and she looked fine. They were giving her something for the pain, but she looked happy and relaxed. She said she was sore, but she was euphoric about her daughter. And she hardly mentioned the agony she'd been through the night before. It was almost as if she'd already forgotten. As though the baby's arrival canceled it out. Angus still looked shaken. She was going home in the morning, since the baby was healthy and a good size. Their nanny had come in from Connecticut to take the boys home that morning. And they were going to open their Christmas presents the next day when they were all home together. It was only one day late. Angus told them that Santa got caught in a snowstorm and would come that night.

"It was definitely exciting," Faith said, still shocked but relieved after the night before. Hope had come through it with courage and grace and was already bouncing back. She was born to have babies.

It was a quiet evening with Morgan and Alex and a delicious meal that night. Faith was part of the family now, and the mood in the house was warm and peaceful.

Their baby girl was due in a couple of months, and there was a sense of expectation. They had just bought a house in Purchase, New York, and were moving in April and giving up their city apartment. They were keeping the house in the Hamptons for the time being and were thinking of spending summers there. The house in Purchase was less than an hour out of the city, which would be convenient to commute. Morgan was excited about decorating it. They all had something to look forward to. New babies, new adventures, new homes. Edward and Faith had each other, which was all they needed and wanted. And she had a new year of weddings ahead, and brides she hadn't met yet.

There was so much to do and to say and to discover. Time they wanted to spend with the people they loved. They sat talking on the couch for a long time after dinner, basking in the warmth of their love and friendship. It was a perfect end to Christmas, with the baby born the day before, and another one coming soon into Alex and Morgan's life, a sister for Blake. They knew now that they had done the right thing when they adopted him. They loved him deeply.

They wished one another a merry Christmas when Edward and Faith left. Edward put an arm around her, and he hailed a cab. They went home to the house they shared. He was giving up his apartment. He never used it anymore.

They had everything they had ever wanted, for Christmas and every day of the year.

Chapter 18

On a perfect cameo blue, bright sunny day in May, Faith had brought them all together. They had so much to celebrate and were the people she loved most and cherished. Hope with her three boys and brand-new baby, Daphne, who was four months old, and Angus, best brother-in-law and proud dad, again. It was Jordan and Violet's first anniversary, which they were celebrating with four-and-a-half-month-old Lily and Rose. Violet was back in the office now and had been for two months. Phoebe had brought Henrik. She was still working for Faith, and not sure now if she wanted to stay or go back to nursing, and was in no hurry to decide. They had just come back from visiting Phoebe's mother and sister in San Diego.

Marianne and Jean-Pierre were just back from another cruise, and would be off on another one that summer.

Annabelle and Jeremy were there with their five-month-old son, Dylan. They had an anniversary coming up in two months. Morgan and Alex were still coasting on the memory of their wedding, due for an anniversary in three months, and Blake and Alexia were thriving at ten months and two months. Faith had met Wesley several times by then and he had joined them too. He was happy his father had finally found a woman he loved, and who was crazy about him.

So many people, so many dreams, so many children, so many love stories and weddings and births had happened in the last year. Old bonds had been broken and new ones formed. Faith wanted to celebrate them all. It seemed the perfect moment to do it. They would all be busy for the rest of the summer, and so would Faith with new brides.

"Do you have something to tell us?" Morgan asked. There was an aura of expectation in the air, of good things about to happen and good times ahead, acts of courage and lessons they would learn from them.

"Yes, we do." Faith smiled at Edward, as he stood there proudly. "You all want a wedding. Weddings are my job, not my dream. They are what I wish for others, not for myself. So are we getting married? No, we're not, and hopefully never will. I see brides every day. I don't need to be one. That wasn't my dream when I was a little girl. Edward was my dream." She looked tenderly at him. "So we've decided to skip to the fun part. Not the planning or the stress or the worry about whether the cake will look right, or the dress will fit, or the flowers will wilt if it's too hot. We don't need a tent or a band to celebrate with you. We are taking our honeymoon. Will we get married one day? Maybe we will. But not yet. And maybe never. We don't see why we have to. But we are taking our honeymoon. That's our dream. We're leaving for Paris, Portofino, and Venice next week. We'll be gone for three weeks. Violet and Phoebe can take care of everything while we're away. So happy anniversary, and happy birthday to all these little ones. We'll be back so I can do lots more weddings . . . just not mine yet. We love you." She beamed at them, assembled in their garden on a perfect day.

"We love each other, just as we are," she said, and kissed Edward, and he pulled her close, as she stood nestled under his wing, more radiant, happier, and more in love than any bride. It was more than enough for them. For now, and hopefully forever. Their real life had turned out to be better than any dream.

PALAZZO

After her parents perish in a tragic accident, Cosima Saverio assumes leadership of her family's haute couture Italian leather brand at just twenty-three. She must also care for her younger siblings: Allegra, who survived the tragedy that killed their parents, and Luca, who has a penchant for pretty women and poker tables.

Cosima copes with a wisdom beyond her years, but her needs are always secondary . . . until she meets Olivier Bayard, the founder of France's most successful ready-to-wear handbag company.

But Luca's gambling habit gets out of control and Cosima is forced to make an impossible choice to save him. Or is there another way to rescue everything she has fought for before it goes up in flames?

Read on for an extract . . .

Chapter 1

Cosima Saverio sat on the terrace of her penthouse apartment in Rome, looking out over the familiar monuments and rooftops of the city as the sun came up. In the distance, she could see Saint Peter's Basilica and Vatican City, the dome of the San Carlo al Corso Basilica, and to the north, the Villa Medici and the Borghese Gardens. It was a view she never tired of. It was her favorite time of day, before the city sprang to life. It was already warm and would be hot by midmorning. As she stood at the rail of the balcony a few minutes later, she could see below the Piazza di Spagna, the Spanish Steps, the Fontana della Barcaccia, and the Trinità dei Monti church.

The apartment was conveniently located on the top floor of the store, which was her family business. The Saverios made the finest leather goods in all of Italy, or all of Europe, rivaled only by Hermès, which was a worldwide enterprise. Saverio leathers were sold only in their two stores, one in Venice, the other in Rome.

Like all of her ancestors, Cosima had been born in Venice, to an illustrious family that traced its history back to the fifteenth century. The Palazzo Saverio in Venice still belonged to them, although her father had moved the family to Rome shortly after her younger sister, Allegra, was born, and Cosima had lived in the same apartment with her parents and brother and sister on the top floor over the store almost all her life. Her younger brother, Luca, had his own villa now on the Via Appia Antica, and her sister lived in a smaller apartment on the floor below her, with a design studio. It was more convenient for Allegra because it had an elevator, which didn't go to the top floor. Cosima lived in solitary splendor in the same apartment she had grown up in. She reached the penthouse apartment by a narrow staircase, and the terrace gave her a three-hundred-and-sixty-degree view of the city she considered her home. Venice was their history, but Rome was where she lived and worked, and ran the family business she had inherited fifteen years before, at twenty-three.

As a young girl, it had never been her plan to run the business or even work there. When they were children, her father intended to have her younger brother, Luca, run it one day, and step into his shoes. Luca had never shown any interest in it, even as a boy. His friends had been the spoiled, indulged sons of other Italian noblemen, and he had a passion for fast cars and beautiful women at an early age. He didn't have his father's interest in business, or his grandfather's talent for creating beauty as a remarkable artisan. Ottavio Saverio had designed each piece for his shop in Venice, whether a saddle or an alligator handbag or an exquisite pair of custom-made shoes. People who were familiar with the finest of everything could recognize a piece created by Saverio anywhere.

Ottavio Saverio had been the eighth child and only son of a respected banker in Venice. He had inherited the palazzo in Venice by default when each of his sisters married and moved away to Florence, Rome, and other cities in Europe. None of them wished to be burdened by the palazzo where they'd grown up. It was four centuries old and troublesome and expensive to maintain. Ottavio had used his inheritance to buy all of his sisters' shares of the palazzo. He had used what was left to establish the store in one of the narrow streets off the Piazza San Marco where he created his magnificent leather pieces, and gained a reputation throughout Italy, and eventually Europe, for the exquisite work he did. Each piece was a masterpiece of beauty and luxury, made of the finest leathers and exotic skins. Every creation was unique at first. He filled the orders quickly and the business grew into an astonishing success in less than a decade. For all the years that he ran it, he was the master craftsman and genius behind the name. Saverio products were sold only at the store in Venice. Women waited a year or even two for their orders to be filled and were never disappointed by the results. Ottavio's list of clients included royals, famous women, movie stars, and wealthy people from all over the world.

His son and only child, Alberto, never became a craftsman like his father, although Ottavio made him study as an apprentice for two years so he would understand the products they were selling and how they were made. But Alberto was more interested in the business side of the store. Once he inherited the company, Alberto maintained his father's tradition that Saverio products were sold only in their own store and nowhere else.

When his father died, Alberto kept the store in Venice, and moved his wife, Tizianna, and their three children to Rome. He bought the building that still housed their store, and built the apartment that had previously been home to their whole family and where Cosima lived alone now on the top floor. She had designed Allegra's apartment on the floor below, when she was old enough to live alone, so they each had privacy. Luca had already moved out by then, when he turned twenty-one and Allegra was still only seventeen.

Palazzo

When their father opened the store in Rome, it was spectacular and increased the business exponentially. Alberto had groomed his son to run the business ever since he was a little boy, but he had never succeeded in capturing Luca's interest. Luca neither understood nor cared about the magic of what they made.

What Alberto had wanted was to have their business grow without giving up any of his father's traditions. It was a fine line between the two, and Alberto had grandiose plans that were always just slightly more expensive to implement than he'd anticipated, so the business wasn't as profitable as it should have been. He had a flawless eye for quality and beauty and was an extremely elegant man himself. He and Tizianna were among the social leaders of both Venice and Rome and exuded an aura of elegance and style.

Cosima inherited some of that, but she had a more retiring nature than her parents and loved her studies. She'd always been relieved that she would never have to run the business. She worked at the store in Rome for a month every summer to please her father. She was a dutiful daughter. Luca managed to escape that because he was five years younger than Cosima, and Allegra was still a child.

In July and August the family went to their other home in Sardinia. They spent two months on the family's boats and entertaining the friends they invited to stay with them.

Invitations to their home were greatly sought after. Alberto and Tizianna were fabulous hosts, and were invited everywhere in return, or by new friends in the hopes of being invited to stay in their home. They were generous with their hospitality and lavish with their guests. Cosima still remembered the extravagant parties her parents gave, both in their apartment in Rome and at the palazzo in Venice, where they held grand balls.

After lengthy discussions with her father, Cosima had chosen a career in the law. She went to university in Rome and lived at home. She loved her years at university, her studies, and the friends she made. Her father teased her that she would be the attorney for the business one day. He never expected her to practice law, but he thought it would be useful for her in business, if she didn't marry first. Her mother had never worked, and he didn't expect his daughters to.

Allegra, the youngest of the three children, had inherited her grandfather's talent and had a passion for design. She was always sketching a dress or a bag or a shoe on a scrap of paper. She had a bright, happy nature and enjoyed living on the fringe of her parents' busy social life even when she was very young. They would let her stay at their parties for a short time, and she always wished she could stay for the entire evening. Cosima was less interested in their parties but always had a flock of suitors among the sons of their friends, even though Allegra was far more flirtatious than her older sister by nature. Cosima always had a more serious, studious side, much more so than her younger brother and sister.

Luca was five years younger than Cosima and Allegra was nine years younger than her older sister, four years younger than Luca, and hated being treated like a baby. She couldn't wait to grow up and discover a broader world. Luca hated spending time with his family and preferred to be with his own friends. He had a wild side in his teens. His parents struggled to curb it with little success.

At twenty-three, Cosima had one year of law school in Rome left to complete. She arrived at the family home in Sardinia after working at the store for a month during her school holiday, as she always did. She worked in the administrative offices, not with the customers, and won high praise every year for her efficiency. She had the precise mind of a future lawyer, and also her mother's blonde beauty. Allegra and Luca had their father's dark hair, and Cosima and Allegra both had their mother's deep blue eyes. Tizianna was from Florence, and Cosima had her typically Florentine fine-featured beauty. Luca and his father had classic aristocratic faces that belonged on a Roman coin.

The summer before Cosima's final year in law school, she

arrived in Sardinia just as her parents were about to leave for a weekend in Portofino with friends who had a home there and had just bought a new speedboat. Luca was supposed to go with them, but a party in Porto Rotondo given by friends of his changed his mind at the last minute and he decided to stay in Sardinia. Cosima stayed in Sardinia with him. She was tired after having worked six days a week at the store for the last month. So her parents left for the weekend and took fourteen-year-old Allegra with them, since their hosts had a daughter the same age. They had a son close to Luca's age too, but Luca found him dull and was happy to escape the weekend in Portofino. Even the lure of the new speedboat didn't sway him.

The house was quiet after they left. Luca disappeared immediately with his friends, and Cosima relaxed and lay in the sun and was happy to have some time alone. She knew they were expecting a house full of guests the following weekend and her parents would expect her to help entertain them, so she was happy to have time to read and take it easy before they came back.

The weekend in Portofino ended in disaster. The hosts allowed their exuberant, reckless nineteen-year-old son to drive them all in the new speedboat. He collided with another boat at full speed, going dangerously fast in the new boat he wasn't familiar with. The two boats crashed and exploded in midair. Both sets of parents were killed instantly, as were the hosts' son, who had been driving the boat, and daughter. The only survivor was Allegra, badly burned on much of her body and with a spinal cord injury so severe that she had to be airlifted to Rome for surgery.

Cosima got the call on Saturday afternoon. She came into the house from the pool to answer the phone. Twenty minutes later, she was dressed and waiting for a cab to take her to the airport to fly to Rome to be with Allegra. Her parents were dead, and she was in shock, unable to believe what had happened. She was torn between grief for her parents and terror for her sister after the accident. Everything rested on her now, and the responsibility for her brother too. She was suddenly faced with adult decisions. She couldn't reach Luca, who was on the family's boat in Porto Rotondo, before she left. She had to leave him a note with the terrible news. He called her crying when she got to Rome and they sobbed together about their parents and Allegra.

Cosima spent the next weeks at her sister's side as Allegra recovered from surgery and was kept in a medical coma while she healed from the burns. It gave Cosima much time to think and grieve for her parents. After the surgery, the doctors told Cosima that Allegra would never walk again. Her spinal cord had been severed. It was yet another terrible blow after losing their parents.

Cosima left Allegra only long enough to plan and attend her parents' funeral in Venice and returned to her sister at the hospital in Rome as quickly as she could. She let Luca return to Sardinia after the funeral, as he wished, since she had no time to spend with him while Allegra was in the hospital, and he didn't want to spend the rest of the summer in Rome.

Luca was greatly subdued and in deep grief over his parents at first. But as he began to feel better, he returned to his old ways and by the end of the summer was going wild with his friends, who came from all over Italy to visit him with no supervision. Cosima was in Rome, couldn't control her brother, and didn't want to leave her sister alone. Allegra was struggling with the loss of her parents too, and the use of her legs. Cosima left her only for very brief periods of time to go to her father's office and attempt to understand what she needed to know. Her father's assistant and the family attorney, Gian Battista di San Martino, were both very helpful, trying to impart as much information as they could in a short time. They brought papers to the hospital almost daily for Cosima to sign. And Gian Battista was a constant presence and strong support for Cosima to rely on. He took her out to dinner sometimes just so she would get a change of scene from the hospital.

It was two months later, in September, when she got Luca back into some semblance of control, and back to Rome. He refused to return to the university where he'd been studying, and insisted he needed time to "mourn" their parents, which in his case meant going to every party in the city, being out every night, and consuming large amounts of alcohol. But he was back at their apartment, and she got him to check in with her several times a day, so she at least knew where he was, although he often stayed out all night and came home in the morning. She suggested that he work at the store, which he refused to do, and with no set activity, he did whatever he wanted. He stayed out late, slept half the day. She didn't have time to force the issue with him. She was busy with Allegra. And Luca became harder and harder to control. He was enjoying having no parental supervision at eighteen, and paid little attention to Cosima and her rules.

Allegra's progress was slow but steady. She'd had several skin grafts and painful surgeries, but she was surprisingly brave, and philosophical about her injuries. She was quieter than before, after the loss of her parents. But unlike her older brother, she was back in school by Christmas, with a remarkably positive attitude. She would be in a wheelchair forever, but Cosima nursed her as lovingly as any mother, and without parents, the two sisters were even closer than before. Cosima had hired a man to carry Allegra up the staircase to their apartment. Luca was almost never there to help them.

Within six months, Cosima was more serious than ever,

still mourning their parents, and had been catapulted into full adulthood. She was running the business, learning as she went. It was the hardest year of her life, and once Allegra was out of the hospital, Cosima went to Venice as often as she could to oversee the store there. Sometimes Gian Battista went with her when he had the time. When he didn't, the palazzo in Venice, where they had spent holidays and family time, seemed achingly empty. It was painful to remember how vibrant it had been when her parents were alive, and how sad it seemed now. Cosima had no time to see her friends or do anything except work at the stores and take care of her sister. Gian Battista was the only source of support in her life.

Allegra was determined to be as independent as she could be once she came home from the hospital. She still talked about designing for the store one day, as though to confirm she had an active future ahead of her. Their longtime house-keeper, Flavia, helped Allegra when Cosima was at work. When she wasn't working or with Allegra, Cosima was chasing Luca down and trying to help him find a sense of direction. He took full advantage of the lack of parental control and fought Cosima on every point.

Their parents' estate was divided equally among them, and Cosima rapidly discovered that her father had spent more than the business had made, on their lifestyle, constant entertaining, several homes, luxurious boats and cars, and extravagant improvements to the store. She was constantly trying to rein in expenses, to pay the bills and her parents' debts, and fighting to keep the business afloat. She couldn't let it go under. She wanted to honor her father, which was a mammoth task for a girl then twenty-four. Her own studies fell by the wayside. She had more important tasks at hand while running the business, taking care of Allegra, and trying to keep Luca in control.

Her father had bought another, bigger building in Rome before he died, on the Via Condotti. He was hoping to enlarge the store into something even more grand. Cosima sold it as soon as she was able to, before construction was started. She sold it at a loss, but they needed the money, and she poured it back into the business. Their production was so meticulous and so slow that she wasn't able to increase their income immediately, and had to find money from other sources, just to keep the business going and meet their expenses and payroll.

They had a huge staff, particularly in Rome, of very fine and well-paid artisans, and a large sales staff with a limited amount to sell. Many of the long-term employees resented her ownership at her age, and the direction she was taking, with her constant concern about cutting costs. She kept a much more watchful eye on their cash flow than her father had. It didn't sit well with the employees, so she had a battle on her hands getting them to follow the new guidelines, directions, and boundaries she gave them. It was an intolerably hard time for her, with life-and-death struggles every day that made her miss her parents all the more, although she was aware now that some of their financial struggles were her father's fault.

A year after her parents' deaths, Cosima put the house in Sardinia on the market. Luca objected strenuously, but she told him point-blank that they were short of money, and since he had no solutions to offer and didn't want to work himself, he finally gave her his permission to sell their summer home. She was able to sell it at the end of August at a fair price, along with their boats, and the sale gave her much-needed cash to pay her parents' remaining debts and use for the business, and for the family personally. When she gave Luca his share, he spent it within months on new cars, and on the entourage of unsavory people he had collected around him, who preyed on him for money and what he could provide for them. She couldn't stop him, although she tried valiantly to convince him to be more prudent and more selective about his friends. He laughed at her.

She was forced to concentrate on the business, so she could pull it out of the slump her father had created and keep it running. It took another year of dedicated hard work and focus, but she finally increased their profits, and within another year, she could breathe again.

Five years after her parents' deaths, business was booming in both stores, Rome and Venice. Cosima had increased their production speed by adding more artisans and trimming off the fat elsewhere, despite grumbling from the old-timers, which she steadfastly ignored. Allegra was attending design school by then, and very efficient at leading her life from her wheelchair. Luca had taken a showy apartment in Milan and was dating models. He was twenty-three years old and had become a well-known playboy in Rome and Milan, and constantly asked Cosima for money. He had blown through most of his inheritance by then, and had developed a penchant for gambling, in Venice, San Remo, and Monte Carlo. Cosima had done nothing but work for the last five years, but it had borne fruit, and the business was safe for now.

It had now been fifteen years since her parents' deaths, as she watched the sun come up over Rome from her terrace. She no longer took two months of vacation in the summer, only a few weeks with Allegra, while remaining in frequent contact with her office. The days of extravagance and extreme luxury were over. She had worked hard for the last fifteen years and now Allegra did too. She took Allegra to more modestly priced beach resorts for their holidays, places where they could manage her wheelchair. Allegra was very independent and confident. She had finished design school and Cosima allowed her to introduce small leather items of her own design. Allegra dreamed of designing handbags for the store one day, with a more youthful look, but Cosima had stuck with their traditional models and didn't want to risk losing business with extreme innovations or excessively modern designs. They had their set, ultrareliable, loyal client base, and Cosima didn't want to lose that, so she kept Allegra on a very tight leash as to what she would allow her to design, none of which used her talent or challenged her, which was frustrating for Allegra. Cosima took no risks with the business and stuck with what had always worked.

Allegra rarely went to Venice now. The palazzo was too complicated for her in her wheelchair, and so was the city. Luca stayed at the palazzo occasionally and gave wild parties there, which Cosima scolded him for, and he always reminded her that he was part owner of the palazzo and the business, his share was equal to hers, and she couldn't tell him what to do. They had two old caretakers to watch over the palazzo. And all she could do now was coexist with Luca, knowing that she would wind up picking up the pieces of his messes later, and lending him money. He acted like the son of a rich man, with unlimited funds at his disposal, all of it provided by

Cosima to keep the peace and keep him out of trouble. She paid him a substantial allowance every month, which seemed like more than he deserved, since he always wasted it and gambled more than he admitted. He spent as little time as possible with her and told everyone that his older sister was a tyrant and a bore who didn't want him to have a good time and drove him crazy. Cosima felt as though she spent her life cleaning up after him and keeping him from spending as much as he wanted. As a result, he avoided her whenever possible, and tried to poison Allegra against her. He was painfully transparent in his manipulations, and called Cosima shamelessly for money, which she wouldn't give him. He even borrowed money from Allegra at times. She was far more careful with her money than he was, and always had some stashed away. He was totally without conscience or embarrassment about who he borrowed money from. He hadn't become someone Cosima was proud of. He was one of the burdens she managed and endured. She attempted to limit the damage as much as possible, which was all she could do. He couldn't be stopped, only reined in a little, like a wild young stallion.

But as the day dawned over Rome, for once she wasn't worrying about the business, or thinking about her brother, or even Allegra's future, which she worried about too. She was simply enjoying the view from her terrace of the elegant shops on the Via Condotti, the familiar area around the Piazza di Spagna, and the irresistible beauty and magic of Rome before she got swept up in the day and the decisions she would have to make all day at her desk.

She had recently rented out the Palazzo Saverio in Venice. She was determined never to sell it, and to preserve the family history. But renting it was one way to stop Luca from abusing the privilege of owning it. Renting it saved them money, since she hardly used it, and Allegra not at all now because it was on so many levels and had no elevator for her chair, which made it impossible for her without construction for accommodations. For the past six months, since renting the palazzo, Cosima had stayed in a small hotel when she was in Venice, which she was becoming accustomed to. She had rented the palazzo to an enormously wealthy American couple who owned a chain of department stores.

The Johnsons, Bill and Sally, were Texans, very pleasant people who would have loved to carry Saverio leather goods in their stores, but Cosima had explained it wasn't possible. It was against the family philosophy of keeping their goods exclusive to their own stores, a tradition she had upheld to honor her grandfather. Sally and Bill were gracious about it, and had brought in a decorator to transform the palazzo into Texan luxury. Cosima had agreed to it provided the Johnsons made no permanent structural alterations.

They were giving a housewarming party that weekend, which Cosima had agreed to attend, although she never went to big parties. She thought it would be rude not to accept the invitation, and she was curious to see what they'd done to the palazzo. But she was apprehensive too. She was sure it would be vulgar and nothing like the interior during her parents' lifetime, but she had to be practical now. She had rented the palazzo for an enormous amount, so she wouldn't have to sell it. And the Johnsons had agreed to the price without hesitating or complaining. They loved Venice, spent two months there every year, and were thrilled to have the palazzo. Sally had told Cosima that people would be flying in from all over the States and Europe for their party.

Despite how effusive the Johnsons were, and how larger than life, Cosima liked them. They had grown children she'd never met, and interesting taste, and it was always possible that they had done the palazzo beautifully, although the famous decorator they'd used had a reputation for over-the-top excess. He'd done a château in France, and Cosima had cringed when she saw the photographs. She hoped that the Johnsons hadn't gone too overboard in their décor at Palazzo Saverio, even though it was more than likely they had. But they hadn't bought it, and how far could they go in a rented house? She was about to find out.

She had important meetings that week before the party.

She had the entire new fall line of designs to approve, and she worked closely with the designers. They'd added a line of silk and cashmere clothes for men and women five years before. It was doing extremely well and had turned out to be a real moneymaker. They had also added a line of hunting clothes for men. They were very popular, along with their other equestrian items, which had been inspired by the saddles her grandfather had made.

Saverio's only real competition was Hermès, and even her grandfather had said that there was room in the world for both of them. Each house had its own distinctive style, and their clients were loyal. Both houses followed many of the same old-fashioned rules to protect their exclusivity and brand. Many of the Saverio customers loved having to come to Italy to buy from them.

Cosima entertained her biggest customers when they came to Rome, and invited them to dinner at her apartment, or their favorite restaurants, and even let them wander peacefully through the store after hours, noticing items they might not have seen otherwise, and she had her selling staff bring them some of the very latest items directly from their workrooms. Their signature handbag, the Tizianna, named after her mother, had been made famous by Sophia Loren. Grace Kelly had ordered three of them when they came out and wore them alternately with her Hermès Kellys. There was even a smaller one, for evening, named the Adria bag, which her grandfather had named for her grandmother when he created it. Cosima had the Tizianna in every color and wore them daily. It was a perfect work bag.

Luca objected vehemently to the signature bags, and said they were just one more old-fashioned element that kept them out of step with the modern world. He thought everything about Saverio was antiquated, and he had no respect for tradition. Allegra had designed a bag she named the Cosima, which she was dying to have made, but Cosima wouldn't let the workroom produce it. She thought it was too avant-garde and fashion-forward for their line. She insisted that Saverio wasn't dictated by passing fashion trends. It was about timeless elegance and style. Their products were classic. At twenty-nine, Allegra was hungry to move forward as a young designer, but Cosima kept her within the boundaries of their brand and history.

Luca was bored by all of it, except that their profits paid his bills. He was more interested in buying fast horses and gambling, or in almost anything for a quick profit. Whatever brought in fast, easy money, Luca liked. He considered their own products ancient history and predicted that one day Saverio would be viewed as the dinosaur of the industry. He dismissed his sister's success at keeping their stores relevant and alive as one of the most respected brands in the world, no matter how limited their distribution. That was part of the magic of Saverio products. Being hard to get created a high level of demand for them, none of which Luca understood or appreciated. History was of no interest to him, only easy money, which he was able to spend even faster than they could make it.

Cosima left the terrace to shower and dress, and she would stop for a cup of coffee with Allegra before she went to her office. She liked to be at her desk by eight o'clock. She would have a slew of emails to answer from suppliers and important customers, people who appreciated Saverio and couldn't get enough of them, many with famous names, and new customers begging to own one. The business was already far more successful than it had been in her father's day. It was still a struggle at times, but she had big dreams, and maybe one day she'd no longer have to worry about money. Until then, she was honoring the name, and carrying on the traditions, just as her grandfather and father would have wanted. It had been a long, hard climb for fifteen years to grow the business, selling only in the two cities her father and grandfather approved of, and she respected their wishes.

At thirty-eight, she felt as though she had only just started. They still had far to go, but she was sure that they would get there. She was thinking of opening a pop-up store for two weeks for Fashion Week in Milan, trying to keep the brand current and in full view in another city at a busy time, which would attract attention. She still had new ideas for the brand. Considering where she had started at twenty-three, unprepared to run the business, she had done a very good job. And there was always so much more to do. Every day there were new challenges for her to face. She could hardly wait to get to her desk each morning. She loved the business and all it represented. It was the epitome of elegance and style.

It was a new day, and a beautiful morning. She brushed her long blonde hair and twisted it into a knot without looking. Even after fifteen years of running the business, she was still excited about what lay ahead, as she stepped into the shower and began her day. She was grateful for how far they'd come. Her love of the business was the driving force in her life. She knew she had single-handedly kept it alive for the past fifteen years, and she had saved and improved the company she had inherited, with love and hard work.

Her family and their business were her life.

If you enjoyed

THE WEDDING PLANNER

you'll love these other titles by
Danielle Steel

WORTHY OPPONENTS

Family. Legacy. Trust.

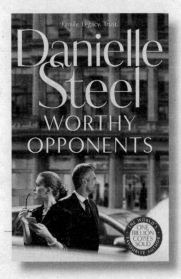

Spencer Brooke is the glamorous CEO of Brooke's,
one of New York's most respected luxury department
stores. A devoted single mother and wedded to her
career, Spencer has little time for a social life. But,
when successful entrepreneur Mike Weston enters her
life, offering investment at a time when the store most
needs it, she knows she must take his offer seriously.
Spencer faces a dilemma: can Mike Weston be who
or what she needs, and can she trust him? Or should
she remain independent, but risk the security
of her beloved company?

WITHOUT A TRACE

There are moments you will remember forever.

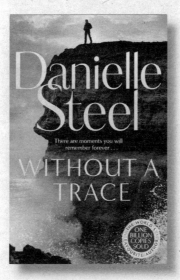

Charles Vincent feels trapped in his treadmill of a
life. He's wealthy and successful, doing a job he
doesn't enjoy, in a marriage where the romance died
years ago. One evening, Charlie leaves work, driving
towards his Normandy château. His car veers off the
road and into the sea. The accident should have
killed him but he escapes – and somehow finds the
strength to climb to safety. In the growing darkness,
he sees a light on in a cottage in the woods. He
knocks on the door and is greeted by Aude, an artist
escaping her own demons. This fateful meeting will
change Charlie's and Aude's lives forever . . .

THE WHITTIERS

Home is where the heart is . . .

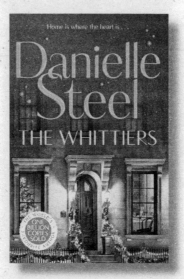

Connie and Preston Whittier raised their six children
in a once-grand Manhattan mansion. The children
are now adults, but the house remains the heart of
the family and somewhere they all love to return to.
But, on Connie and Preston's annual skiing holiday,
an avalanche hits their resort, resulting in tragedy.
Each of the Whittiers has their own personal
struggles, but now the future of the family – and
also their home – is in question. The house is a
refuge providing comfort . . . but each of them will
learn that to move forward and face their
challenges, they must be true to themselves and
come together to support one another.

THE HIGH NOTES

A star is born . . .

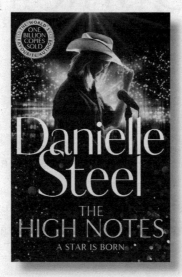

Iris Cooper grew up dirt-poor in Texas. Her mother
left when she was a baby, leaving her to be raised
by her rodeo cowboy dad who was too interested
in beer, whisky and women to be a good father.
Iris has a rare gift: the voice of an angel. After
singing in downtrodden bars, and many years on
the road, she finally gets a lucky break when she
meets Boy, another talented singer. Together they
travel to New York, where Iris's talent is recognized
by one of the top agents in the business. A star is
born and Iris finally gets the success she deserves.
But then tragedy strikes, and through it she
discovers another kind of love . . .

Danielle Steel

Have you liked Danielle Steel on Facebook?

Be the first to know about Danielle's latest books,
access exclusive competitions and stay in touch
with news about Danielle.

www.facebook.com/DanielleSteelOfficial